THE
FACTORY
GIRLS
of LARK LANE

ALSO BY PAM HOWES

Fast Movin' Train

THE MERSEY TRILOGY
The Lost Daughter of Liverpool
The Forgotten Family of Liverpool
The Liverpool Girl

THE ROCK N ROLL ROMANCE SERIES
Three Steps to Heaven
Til I Kissed You
Always on My Mind
That'll Be the Day
Not Fade Away

THE FAIRGROUND SERIES
Cathy's Clown

THE CHESHIRE SET SERIES
Hungry Eyes

SHORT STORIES
It's Only Words

THE
FACTORY
GIRLS
of LARK LANE

PAM HOWES

bookouture

Published by Bookouture in 2018

An imprint of StoryFire Ltd.

Carmelite House
50 Victoria Embankment
London EC4Y 0DZ

www.bookouture.com

ISBN: 978-1-78681-469-2
eBook ISBN: 978-1-78681-468-5

Dedicated to the memory of my big-boy cousin Brian Walton, 1943–2014, who left the UK for the wilds of the USA many decades past, and who we traced a few years ago, only to lose him a short time later. But we never forgot you, Brian, and now your delightful family are a big part of ours. xxx

Chapter One

Aigburth, Liverpool: December, 1940

Alice Turner rubbed at the steamed-up window with the corner of her hanky and peered out at the dark and gloomy night.

'Nearly there,' she said to her best pal and workmate, Millie Markham, who was sitting beside her on the crowded works' bus. 'Stand up now and ring the bell or he'll go whizzing past like he did last night.'

She gathered up several brown paper packages, her handbag and gas mask box. Millie did likewise and jumped to her feet.

'See youse two on Monday,' a large woman called out as they struggled down the aisle with their arms full. 'Enjoy your wedding day tomorrer, gel, and don't do anything I wouldn't do,' she added, winking slyly at Alice as they passed her.

Several passengers also shouted out congratulations.

'Thank you, Marlene,' Alice muttered through gritted teeth, her cheeks blushing bright pink as the bus lurched to a halt and she and Millie said goodbye to the driver and jumped down from the platform onto Aigburth Road. Trust Marlene to make a holy show of her in front of everyone. It was impossible to keep a secret at Rootes Munitions factory, where the occupants of the bus all worked. Nearly everyone knew everybody else's business, except

Alice, who tried to keep herself to herself most of the time – but today had been a bit special as the canteen had put on sarnies and buns along with pots of steaming tea for her team of colleagues, to help celebrate her forthcoming wedding day.

'Right, I'll come with you to yours and help you carry this lot,' Millie said, stamping her feet. 'Christ, it's freezing again tonight. Just what we need when I've only got a flimsy frock to wear for the wedding.' She sighed. 'Still, you've done well for pressies, Alice.' She indicated the brown-paper-wrapped packages. 'Lucky you. Some really nice stuff to put in your bottom drawer here for when you and Terry get your own place. Wish my fella would buck his ideas up and propose to *me*.' Millie rolled her eyes. 'Can't see that happening for years though, knowing him.'

Alice smiled as they hurried up the road and onto Lark Lane. 'Your turn will come, Millie. Alan will surprise you one of these days.'

They passed the bombed-out and boarded-up remains of the Princess Steam Laundry, where Alice's mam had worked for a while. She linked arms with her friend as they crossed over and made their way to a terraced house on Lucerne Street, home of Alice's family. Except there was hardly any family left there, apart from eighteen-year-old Alice and her mother who, now she was no longer employed, often took to her bed with a variety of nerve-related ailments. Her dad had passed away three years earlier following a heart attack while working down at the docks; he'd been gassed in the trenches during the First World War and had not been a strong man since. Her brother, Rodney, older than Alice by two years, was away with his regiment, currently stationed in France, as far as they knew. In spite of his promise to write each week, his letters home were infrequent and he wasn't allowed to say exactly where his placement was. They had to reply to him care of a BFPO address. Her younger brother Brian, who was just nine years old, had been evacuated late last year to North Wales and *his* letters indicated that he was really enjoying himself as he got a lot more to eat than he had at home and his new 'Auntie Jean' made smashing chocolate cakes. Alice had grinned as he'd ended his last letter with the afterthought, 'But I really am missing you and me mam, our Alice.' That one's stomach always came first, before anything else. Brian would be happy as Larry in his temporary home as long as he was being well fed.

Alice took a key from her coat pocket as they stood beside the shabby front door. The black paint was peeling and the doorknocker and letterbox looked dull and pitted and in need of a good rub with Brasso. Mam had lost heart in anything to do with the house since Dad had passed away and the war started in earnest. The step hadn't seen a donkey-stone in ages and neither had the windowsill. Alice felt a bit embarrassed. In spite of the windows being criss-crossed with tape to prevent any injuries from shards of flying glass in the event of an explosion, most houses on the street still had a well-cared-for look about them. Millie's home was always spotless as her mam was very house-proud, and she hated her friend seeing the mess in which she sometimes lived. To be fair to Millie, she'd never once turned her nose up at Alice's home, and today there was no choice other than to ask her in. There was no sign of life and the curtains were all closed, shutting out any light. That meant either her mam was still in bed from this morning and hadn't even bothered opening the curtains after Alice left for work, or she was up and organised with tea on the go. The day would depend on how she'd felt on waking up. The doctor had recently advised her to take a daily Yeast Vite to buck her up a bit, but they didn't seem to be working that well and Mam said you had to give them a chance to get into your blood system. She flatly refused to return to the surgery, even though they paid a weekly sum into Lloyd George's insurance scheme, saying, 'Doctors are for folks that are really poorly, and not for the likes of me, who's just got bad nerves and is at a funny age for a woman. And there might come a time when I really need the doctor, so I'll leave it until then.' There was no arguing with her mam so Alice didn't waste her breath.

She unlocked the door and pushed it open. There was a light coming from the scullery at the back of the house. Good, maybe Mam was up and the place would be tidy.

'Come on in,' she said to Millie. 'Mam, are you in the back?'

'Yes, love,' a voice answered.

Alice breathed a sigh of relief and invited Millie to follow her through to the back sitting room. The fire was lit and the table tidy, with that morning's breakfast pots cleared and a clean blue and white checked cloth covering the scratched wooden surface. Floral patterned china cups and saucers and a matching milk jug and sugar bowl waited alongside a covered tea pot, as though visitors were expected. The china was all they had in the decent pots department and even though the odd cup was chipped, Mam loved to use it. The faded floral curtains were drawn tightly across in line with the government blackout regulations. In spite of the shabby old furniture that they couldn't afford to replace right now, the room looked and felt cosy.

Alice's mam Edith popped her head around the sitting room door to greet the pair. Her eyes widened as she took in the packages that Alice and Millie had dropped onto the small sofa.

'Oh, looks like you've been spoiled, my love.' She gave Alice a kiss and smiled at Millie. She patted her hair into place and quickly glanced in the mirror on the chimney breast above the fireplace. Alice realised she'd had a trim and her hair had been styled into soft demi-waves that totally transformed her usually greasy light-brown mop.

'Mam, you look lovely,' she gasped and Millie nodded her approval too.

'It really suits you, Mrs Turner.'

'Well I couldn't let you down tomorrow, could I? Millie's mam sorted my hair out this afternoon. She's lent me a lovely navy and cream dress and jacket to wear as well, and I treated myself to a new pink lippy from Woolies.'

Alice felt herself filling up. She was relieved that her mam was making an effort. She knew how hard tomorrow would be as there was no Dad to give her away, but she was sure her mam would do her proud. It wasn't going to be a big fancy wedding anyway. Terry had only got a forty-eight-hour pass and then he had to go back to Fulwood Barracks in Preston with the worry of being sent overseas at a moment's notice on his shoulders. He'd so far been lucky but he'd told her it wouldn't be long now. When he'd asked her to marry him a month ago and her mam had given her permission to go ahead, saying, 'You don't know what's around the corner now with a war on,' Alice had been unable to focus on anything else for days. She had made the necessary arrangements almost in a daze. Marrying the love of her life who she'd met at school had always been a dream she'd kept close to her heart. A dream that she thought wouldn't happen for a few more years, until she was at least twenty-one.

Millie grinned at Edith. 'That outfit always looks nice on my mam. You'll look smashing in it, Mrs Turner. Right, I'll leave you two to have your tea in peace and I'll see you at my place first thing for your wedding hairdo, Alice. Hope you get a good night's beauty sleep.'

'Are you not stopping for a cuppa with us, love?' Edith asked.

'I'd better not. Mam has customers on a Friday night until eight and I usually have to get my dad's tea ready. I'll see you bright and early in the morning, Alice.'

Millie's mam ran a hairdressing salon from her front parlour and was always busy. As she told everyone who came in to have their hair done, 'There might be a war on, but we ladies still need to maintain standards.' Alice saw Millie out and shut the door on the cold night air with a thud. She hoped it would be a bit warmer by the morning, but the weather forecast was bad for all of December, with snow threatened for next week. Well, just as long as it didn't start snowing tonight. She'd no intention of arriving at the registry office with her wellies on. The wedding was booked for two thirty and that had been managed through pure luck and a cancellation. It seemed that many young couples had decided to take the plunge while they still could and most churches and registry offices were booked up well in advance this side of Christmas.

Alice shivered, wondering how many of the new husbands would make it back home in one piece when the war ended. Her Terry had better take care, or else his mother would have something to say to that Hitler fella and his cronies. Mrs Lomax, Terry's mother, had done more than a bit of grumbling when they'd told her they wanted to get wed as soon as possible. She'd looked Alice up and down, pursed her lips and said they were too young and what was the rush for. Terry had told her there was no ulterior motive other than wanting to make Alice his wife before he left for European shores, and at nineteen he didn't think he was too young. She'd begrudgingly given her consent after a few nerve-racking moments, and then asked where Alice would live after the wedding.

'I'll live with my mam, of course,' Alice had replied. 'I can't leave her alone while the boys are away. Besides, she needs my wages. It's the only money we have coming in, apart from the bit Rodney sends her when he can.'

Mrs Lomax had sighed. 'Well, it's not ideal. But then nothing is ideal right now, so we'll all have to make the best of the situation until Terry comes home for good and you can get a nice place of your own. I'll put on a little buffet here for you after the ceremony. You can ask your friends and your mother to come.'

Alice went back into the sitting room and joined her mam at the table. A plate of sarnies now stood in the middle and two currant buns sat side by side on another small plate.

'I'm sorry I haven't had time to cook anything hot for you with going out getting my hair done,' Edith apologised. 'But I managed to get some corned beef and a bit of cheese today.'

'Mam, don't worry. I had liver and onions for dinner, and we had a tea party in the canteen for me earlier, so I've had plenty today. You eat those sarnies. I'll just have a cuppa and a cake.'

'I did a silly thing today, Alice,' Edith confessed. 'I left my purse in the bakers. I must have put it down on the counter after I paid for the bread and came away without it. They sent the young girl who helps in there after me. She came running up Lark Lane, shouting my name.'

'Oh dear, Mam. Good job they're honest in there.'

'It is. I felt such a fool, I can tell you.'

Edith switched on the wireless in readiness for the Home Service's latest news. Not that they ever heard anything good, Alice thought. London was getting shelled on a regular basis and the threat to the port of Liverpool was always high. That blooming Hitler was a bad one. He'd get his comeuppance one day though, according to their foreman at work. The Halifax bombers that Rootes were building were going to be the planes that would win Britain the war and there was no doubt in anyone's mind that it would happen.

Edith poured the tea, and smiled. 'I can't believe my little girl is getting married tomorrow. It's such a shame your brothers are not here. But we'll celebrate when they come home. I don't think this war will last much longer. They were saying in the corner shop that it'll all be over next year.'

Alice sighed. The war had started shortly after Mr Chamberlain broadcast to the nation on the morning of Sunday September 3rd last year that Britain was at war with Germany. Everyone seemed confident then that it wouldn't last for long, but it was showing no signs of ending.

'The thought of my Terry and our Rodney away in another country and us not knowing where they are is scary. That's why

I'm glad I'm working on making the planes that will help us win this war. I feel like I'm doing something really important, although I still wish I'd chosen nursing at times.'

'I know you do, love. But you're doing a really tough job for a young girl. Your dad would have been very proud of you.' Edith's eyes filled and she brushed her tears away and took a sip of tea. 'Let's just make the best of things for now and hope what they say is true – that we'll all be back to normal by next year.'

'We can live in hope, Mam.'

Alice carried her mug of cocoa upstairs and drank it sitting on the narrow single bed. Her mam was already asleep in her own room. She'd told Alice not to sit up too long reading as they needed to be up early tomorrow. Alice hurried into the tiny bathroom and had a quick bath with the few regulation inches of water they were allowed. Not many terraced houses in Liverpool had bathrooms. Some of the girls she worked with, who lived down by the docks in the tenements, thought she was dead posh to have one. It made Alice thankful for her lot when they talked about the tin baths in front of the fire shared by at least six, and the lavatories out on the landings used by more than one family. Thank God her dad's parents had owned this little house and as an only child it had become his when they passed away. Alice and her brothers had been born here and once this war was over and Rodney came home they would start to look after it properly. At the moment most of Alice's wages went on buying food and putting money in the meters for gas and electricity, with a little bit left over to put towards clothes and the odd treat, like an occasional visit to the pictures. There was nothing left over for house maintenance and new furniture; it was all they could do to keep it clean, tidy and warm.

Back in her small bedroom, which was always freezing cold, Alice shivered and pulled a blanket around her shoulders as she looked at the wedding gifts from her workmates. She placed them in the bottom drawer of the tallboy cupboard that she stored her clothes in. She ran a hand over the beautiful hand-embroidered tray cloth and pillow cases and set them side by side with two soft pink hand-towels and matching flannel. A cutlery set, in a brown leather case, a gift from her foreman and his wife, went in next alongside a pair of ornamental black poodle dogs with long painted lashes and red collars. She smiled. The dogs would look lovely either end of a mantelpiece with a nice clock in between.

She smoothed the skirt of her new two-piece suit that was hanging from the picture rail. The blue wool tweed would pick out the colour of her bright blue eyes. A matching blue velvet pill-box hat with a small feather decoration sat on her dressing table. She wasn't a hat person, but both her mam and Millie had said she couldn't get married without one, it wasn't right. Even though Alice had grumbled that it was a waste of her precious clothing coupons, to keep them happy she'd got one – but she'd chosen the smallest and cheapest design she could find and planned to whip it off as soon as she could after the ceremony was over. She unpinned her dark brown hair and ran her fingers through the shoulder-length locks. If Millie's mam could just give it a bit of a trim tomorrow and style it into demi-waves that fanned her cheeks, she'd be happy. Terry loved to run his hands through her hair and she wanted to wear it loose and not all pinned up like a few brides' photos she'd seen recently. The French pleat seemed to be the favoured style for formal weddings, along with short finger-waves, but it wasn't to her liking. It was bad enough having to wear her hair trussed up and stuck under a turban all day for work, so it definitely wasn't going to happen on her wedding day. She might not have the long white lacy gown she'd always dreamed of, but she was still going to look as feminine as possible for Terry.

She slid in between the icy sheets, pulling the pink eiderdown up to her chin, and shivered with a mixture of cold and excitement, knowing that she'd never get to sleep if she didn't shut her mind to the thought of her handsome, dark-haired boyfriend and the one night they would spend together before he had to go back to his barracks before being sent away to God knows where. He'd been saving like mad and booked them a room at the very grand Adelphi Hotel in the city centre. It was the place where all the posh folk and politicians usually stayed when visiting Liverpool. After lecturing them about being extravagant and telling them they shouldn't be spending their savings like that when they could stay the night at the bungalow, Mrs Lomax had relented and kindly offered to stand half the costs as an extra wedding present for them. Alice was sure it was a night she'd remember all her life. She closed her eyes and willed sleep to come.

Chapter Two

Alice grabbed a towel and wrapped it around her head after Millie
had finished rinsing the suds from her hair over the bath, with a
large enamel jug. There were no sinks in the Bickerton Street front
parlour salon, and Millie's dad Harry had flatly
refused to go to the expense of having extra plumbing put in.
'Not with a war on,' he'd grumbled, so all hair-washing had to be
done in the bathroom. The fresh scent of Pears soap hung in the air.
Millie's mam melted down grated pieces of the soap in hot water
and it made a nice substitute for shampoo, which was hard to get
with all the shortages. The substance was a bit thick and gloopy
and took a while to rinse out, but the clients agreed it was better
than nothing and left their hair looking nice and shiny.

Downstairs, Millie's mam Marion, smartly dressed in her
brightly coloured cotton smock over a plain black fitted dress,
combs sticking out of every pocket, was waiting for the girls with
tea things and slices of angel cake at the ready on a trolley. Another
customer, who Alice recognised as Mrs Floyd from the Lark Lane
Post Office, was under a dryer by the bay window and she smiled
as Millie led Alice to a seat placed in front of a large wall mirror.
Alice took the cup of tea and slice of cake that Marion offered her.

'Now then,' Marion began. 'Our Millie tells me you'd like to
wear your hair loose and wavy, is that right?'

Alice, her mouth full of cake, nodded. She swallowed and took
a swig of tea to wash down the crumbs.

'Please, I don't want it fastening up. I'd like the same style as Millie.' Millie's dark blonde hair swung to her shoulders in bouncy curls with soft waves fanning her cheeks.

Marion nodded. 'I'll trim about an inch off the length, tidy up your fringe and fix it into pin curls with clips. Then you can pop under the dryer for a while and Millie will comb you out and set it. Finish your tea and then we'll make a start. Oh, get that, Millie love,' she said as the doorbell rang. 'It'll be Doris for her perm. She's always early. I'll swear that one can smell a pot of freshly brewed tea from Aigburth Road.'

Alice sat under the dryer watching Millie combing out Mrs Floyd's bleached, blonde hair after removing the metal curling pins. Millie smoothed each section down, arranging the ends under so that the effect was a rather glamorous style, and portly Mrs Floyd seemed delighted with the result.

She patted her waves and smiled, batting her lashes at her mirrored reflection. 'Well, old Floydy will think it's Lana Turner coming home to him,' she said with a throaty chuckle. 'I'll knock his socks off, swanning in looking like her.'

'You look lovely, Mrs Floyd,' Millie said, holding a mirror up so Mrs Floyd could see the back. 'Very glam indeed.'

'I think this hairdo calls for a night out at the Legion if we don't get any air raid warnings tonight.' Mrs Floyd got to her feet and Millie fetched her coat and gas mask box from the hall coat stand.

'Be with you in a minute,' she mouthed at Alice as she helped Mrs Floyd into her coat.

'Enjoy your wedding later, Alice,' Mrs Floyd shouted, bending down in front of the dryer. 'And let's hope the snow stays off until after the ceremony. All the very best to you and Terry, my love.'

'Thank you,' Alice said.

Millie switched off the dryer, and Doris, who was talking at the top of her voice as Marion combed perming solution through her hair, stopped suddenly. 'Thank God for that. I can hear meself speak now. What time's yer wedding, Alice?' she asked.

'Two thirty,' Alice replied, sitting in front of the big wall mirror again while Millie took the clips out of her hair. The heavy curls fell softly to her shoulders, soft, bouncy and shiny, just how she'd pictured they would look. Once Millie had worked her magic with the comb *she'd* also feel like a film star and Terry would love it.

'Well, if I'm done in time I've a packet of rice in my bag so I might just catch the pair of youse leaving the registry office. I can chuck a handful, but the rest is for puddin's.'

Alice laughed. 'That will be lovely,' she said.

'Are you 'aving an 'oneymoon, chuck?'

'Not really. Just one night in the Adelphi for a special treat. Terry has to go back to barracks on Sunday afternoon.'

'That's a shame. But I s'pose it's 'ard getting any time off now with this blooming war. You're lucky your Terry's still in England. Bloody 'itler's got a lot to answer for. All them little kiddies shipped miles away from 'ome an' all. Terrible. Still, a night at the Adelphi, eh? That's posh. Has he come up on Littlewoods treble chance, then?' She laughed at her own joke and continued. 'This war will all be over next year though, according to my old man. He'll soon be back safe and sound, you'll see.'

'Let's hope it is, and *all* our boys are back safe and sound,' Marion said, raising an eyebrow.

''Ere, doesn't your 'arry have any insider information, Marion? What with 'im working for the APS, like.'

'It's the ARP.' Marion laughed. 'No more than you or me, I'm afraid. Harry's an air raid warden, not the man in charge. You need to keep listening to the wireless for updates, that's what he'd tell you. It's the best help I can give you.'

'So 'e can't say how much longer we've got to lug them stinking rubber masks around with us then?'

'I'm afraid not, chuck.' Marion began to wind tiny sheets of white paper around strands of Doris's hair before rolling it onto perming rods, which didn't take long as her hair was quite short. 'There we go. All done. Under the dryer with you now and I'll fetch you a cuppa through.'

Millie finished smoothing down Alice's hair and held up a mirror to show her the back. Alice smiled as she moved her head and watched her hair swing smoothly from side to side. 'It's lovely. Just how I wanted it to look. You are clever. You'd make a great hairdresser, Millie.'

Millie laughed. 'Well, when we've won this war with the planes we're building, I might think about it. And you, Alice, you should think about taking up nurse training like you always wanted to do when we were at school.'

Alice sighed. 'One day, I might get the chance. Bit late when I'm married though, unless they change the rules about taking on married women some time.' She got to her feet and Millie brought her coat through. Alice had tucked a silky headscarf into her pocket to keep her hair nice until she got home and she placed it carefully over her waves and fastened it under her chin. She only lived one street away, but the air was cold and she didn't trust the snow not to start and ruin her hair before the celebrations began.

'I'll see you in an hour at yours,' Millie said. 'Mam's found a nice little silver fox-fur jacket that she'd forgotten she had, so I'm going to wear it over my frock to stop me freezing to death.'

She gave Alice a peck on the cheek and Marion and Doris waved goodbye and wished her luck as she left.

❁

Light snow was beginning to fall as Alice hurried up Lucerne Street, coating everywhere with a fine dusting of white, reminding her of icing sugar on mince pies. Not that they'd be having any this year as her mam had been unable to get any mincemeat and there was no dried fruit around to make their own. She dashed indoors, whipped off her scarf and shook the wet flakes off. In the back sitting room she examined her hair in the mirror and, satisfied it still looked fine, shouted up the stairs.

'You up there, Mam?'

'I'm here, chuck.' Edith popped her head around the bedroom door and stepped out onto the small landing. She was still wearing her dressing gown and slippers, and a hairnet to keep her newly set hair in place. 'Don't look so worried. I'm not poorly. I'm just not getting dressed until the last minute in case I spill something on Marion's nice frock. I was going to make us poached eggs on toast when you got back. You dashed out without your breakfast and you'll need something in your tummy or you'll be rumbling all through the service. Go and pop the kettle on and I'll be down in a few minutes. I'm just trying to match up a pair of stockings that haven't got ladders in them.'

Alice shook her head. She didn't have a pair she could lend her mam; the only good ones she had, she'd be wearing later. This bloody war. Life was fragile enough without the shortages and having no spare money, and it showed no signs of stopping. They missed Rodney's wages, although he sent a few pounds home when he had it to spare, but the last lot had gone on buying Christmas presents for Brian in Wales. He'd grown taller and needed new clothes. Mam had knitted him a navy blue jumper and matching warm socks from wool she'd bought at Paddy's Market. She'd managed to get him a pair of grey trousers and a white shirt that still looked like new, from a second-hand stall. Washed and pressed they'd made a nice outfit, so at least he'd look smart for the church service he'd told them he was going to on Christmas morning. The clothes would also do him for school, Mam said. They'd parcelled everything up along with a small bar of Cadbury's chocolate, the last one in the grocer's on Lark Lane, and a Meccano set that they'd saved up for. He'd been asking for one each birthday since

Dad died, but there had never been enough money to treat him. Alice smiled as she thought how excited her little brother would be with the unexpected surprise in his Christmas parcel. She felt a lump rise in her throat when she thought of how she wouldn't be able to share his joy. But at least he was safe for now and that was something to be thankful for.

In the kitchen she put the kettle on the gas hob and spooned tea leaves into the pot. The remains of a loaf stood on the bread board waiting to be sliced and Alice cut two pieces and put the remainder in the breadbin. She slid the slices under the grill and stood by the sink looking out of the window. The snow was coming down a bit faster now. She sighed and prayed it would stop soon. A taxi was booked to pick her, Mam and Millie up later to take them the couple of miles to the Mount Pleasant Registry Office. Terry had arranged it, and had also booked one for him and his mother and his best man, Jimmy, a fellow soldier who had managed to get a short leave at the same time. Their taxi would arrive a bit earlier than Alice's so that he'd be there waiting for her. But at this rate there'd be no photos taken on the registry office steps. They'd just have to be done inside. Mam appeared at her elbow as the kettle boiled. She shooed her away and Alice scurried off upstairs to recheck her outfit while Mam took over making them a bite to eat.

❀

At the very same moment the registrar instructed Terry to kiss his bride, the air raid warning siren wailed. There was a scuffling sound outside the front door, which was flung open by a member of the ARP with the instructions that they should get to the nearest shelter right away and make sure they took their gas masks with them.

Terry raised an eyebrow and smiled at Alice. 'Well that was well-timed, eh, gel? At least you've got my ring on your finger.'

Mrs Lomax shook her head so hard her hat wobbled. 'Is there to be no peace? Not even today?' She shook her fist towards the ceiling and the imaginary spectre of Hitler that lurked in every mind's eye. 'I'm sick and tired of this.'

'We all are, Madam,' the registrar said patiently, mopping his brow with a white hanky. 'But at least we got the ceremony conducted in peace and your son is now a married man. That's something to be grateful for, at least.'

'If you say so,' Mrs Lomax huffed as the wedding party made its way to the back of the building and filed into the shelter outside.

Alice clung onto her new husband's arm and Jimmy helped Edith and Millie to a seat inside the gloomy shelter. The snow had stopped but it was cold and Edith shivered in her thin dress and jacket. The registrar handed out some folded grey woollen blankets that were stored on a nearby shelf and Millie tucked one around Edith's shoulders and helped Mrs Lomax with hers.

The registrar smiled as everyone took a seat and, heads cocked to one side, they listened for the sound of enemy planes overhead.

'The three-thirty wedding may have to be put back,' he muttered to the assistant registrar, who reminded Alice of a sad dog with his long face and big brown eyes.

'I suspect you may be right,' the man said. 'Such a shame as the bridegroom only has today before he goes overseas.'

Alice chewed her lip as she listened to the exchange of words. She felt so sorry for the young couple whose wedding plans may be scuppered, never knowing if, or when, they would see each other again. She blinked away the tears that threatened. Thank God she and Terry had got the two-thirty slot. Any later and they wouldn't now be Mr and Mrs Lomax. She rested her head on his shoulder and he slid his arm around her and squeezed her tight. Within the hour the all-clear sirens sounded and thankfully there'd been no noise of bombs exploding nearby. That was the trouble; sometimes nothing happened, but they still had to dash into the closest air raid shelter. With loud cheers, the party made their way back indoors.

The registrar went into the office and came back out with Alice and Terry's marriage certificate. He shook their hands and wished them well as the front door burst open and an anxious-looking young couple in wedding finery almost fell in, followed by two other people who Alice assumed must be their witnesses, and an older man with a camera and stand.

'Come through, come through,' the registrar urged the young couple, who looked on the verge of tears. 'We've just time to marry you before we close, if we hurry.'

Alice saw the relief on the young bride-to-be's face as she thanked him, and she and the party followed him into the room.

'Are you here for us, mate?' Terry asked the photographer.

'Mr and Mrs Lomax?'

'We are.' Terry laughed. 'First time we've had our full title.'

'Then I'm here for you. I was hoping I wouldn't miss you. I had to go in the shelter two streets away. The snow has stopped, so shall we get a shot on the front steps while we can?' He took charge and arranged them into a group, and then took a couple of shots of Terry and Alice on their own and then one of them with their best man and bridesmaid. 'They'll be ready towards the end of next week,' he said, handing Terry a card. 'Give us a call a week on Monday and I'll let you know when to pick them up.'

'Will do. It'll be my wife here that picks them up as I'll be God knows where by then.'

'No problem,' the photographer said. 'I wish you all the best and you take care, young man. Go and sort Jerry out and win this war for us.'

Chapter Three

Alice held tight to Terry's hand as the taxi pulled up outside his mother's white-painted semi-detached bungalow on Linnet Lane. Terry thanked the driver, paid him and helped Alice out onto the snowy pavement. He supported her down the slippery garden path and fumbled in his pocket for a key.

'Looks like we're first back,' he said. He opened the door and swung her up into his arms. 'I know it's not our own threshold, but it's better than none,' he joked as he carried her inside and kicked the door closed with his foot. She wrapped her arms around his neck and he planted a lengthy kiss on her lips. 'Alone at last,' he whispered into her hair and kissed her again.

'Not for long,' Alice said as a car pulled up outside. 'Put me down. Here come the others.'

'Ah well, we've got tonight. And I can't wait.' He lowered her down and grinned as Alice blushed prettily.

The door opened and Mrs Lomax came inside followed by Edith and Millie, with Jimmy bringing up the rear.

'Why are you standing in the hall?' Mrs Lomax said. 'Go on into the sitting room. It should be nice and warm in there. I left the fire well banked up with nutty slack. Give it a good poke for me, Terry love, while I get the glasses out and we'll have a toast to the pair of you.'

She hurried off down the hall into the kitchen and Terry opened the sitting room door and led the way.

'Oh that's better,' Edith said, sinking down onto the sofa facing the fire. 'It's lovely and warm in here. I'm chilled right through with sitting in that shelter. I bet you are too, Millie love, with just that little frock on. That fur jacket won't keep the cold off your back; you'll get a chill on your kidneys. You need a long coat on in this weather.'

'I'm okay,' Millie said, holding her hands out to the fire that crackled and spat sparks as Terry thrust the poker into its middle. The flames roared up the chimney and the heat flowed into the cosy room.

'I'll take my jacket off,' Edith announced. 'Won't feel the benefit later if I leave it on now.'

Alice smiled. That was one of Mam's favourite sayings. 'You okay now, Mam?' she asked as Mrs Lomax came into the room with a silver tray and six small schooners of sherry.

'Now then, Jimmy,' she addressed the tall red-haired young soldier, who, like Terry, looked smart in military uniform. 'As Terry's best man, would you like to say a few words before we raise our glasses?' She handed out the drinks and took a seat beside Edith on the sofa. Milly sat on a chair under the window and Jimmy stood in front of the fireplace and looked at Alice and Terry, who were standing with their arms around each other, their relieved and happy smiles splitting their faces.

Jimmy coughed and cleared his throat. 'Well, I'm not used to making speeches in public, and I've only known Terry just over twelve months, so I can't tell you any funny stories or embarrassing anecdotes about his past, but during the time I *have* known him, we've become good pals and he's told me all about Alice and the life he hopes to make with her here in Liverpool when this blasted war is over. With the likes of Terry on our side, we've a good chance of winning this battle and I know he'll always have my back, as I will his. I'll look after him the best I can, Alice, I promise you. You've got a good one in Terry. So let's raise our glasses and wish the pair of them a long and loving marriage. I hope it won't be too long before they'll be back together and he's making her happy in that little home he's promised her.'

Alice smiled as the others toasted them and Terry pulled her closer, his brown eyes twinkling, and whispered, 'I'll be back before you know it.'

Mrs Lomax got to her feet and summoned Millie to follow her. Within minutes the pair had filled the dining table that was already covered with a white cloth. They'd brought in plates of sarnies, sausage rolls, fancy cakes and a trifle in a cut-glass bowl.

'You've been busy, Mrs Lomax,' Millie said, placing side plates in a pile next to some glass dishes and spoons. 'This is quite a feast.'

Mrs Lomax smiled and left the room but was back within seconds, carrying a single-tier wedding cake.

Alice's eyes grew round as her new mother-in-law laid the cake in the centre of the table and stood back with a proud smile.

'Did you make it?' Alice asked. 'It's beautiful.'

The cake was covered in white icing and decorated with tiny silver bells with a plaster of Paris bride and groom standing on the top.

'No dear. I couldn't get any dried fruit, and sugar is scarce as you know. But the bakery on Lark Lane had put a few Christmas cakes on display a couple of weeks ago. My friend Marjorie works in there and told me about them. So I paid them a visit and asked if they could perhaps alter one as my son was getting married and they agreed. They already had the bridal couple and the bells in stock. They removed the green marzipan tree that was decorating the top and replaced the red ruffle with a silver and white one. Like Marjorie said, the recipe is exactly the same, and we have to do our best in times of need.'

'Thanks, Mam, it's fabulous. We weren't expecting a wedding cake at all, so it makes it extra special,' Terry said and Alice nodded her agreement.

'Put the gramophone on, Terry,' his mother ordered. 'A nice bit of music will go down well while we all tuck in. Then you young ones can roll back the rug and have a dance. Might as well do what we can to give you a decent day. George next door will run you down to the Adelphi about half past six. He's offered, so I said yes on your behalf and I told him you'd need to go back to Alice's house to pick up her case. Then he'll run Millie and you home, Edith dear. Is that okay?'

'That's smashing, Mrs Lomax,' Millie said. 'What about you, Jimmy? Where are you staying tonight?'

'He's staying here in my old room,' Terry answered for Jimmy as he placed a record on the gramophone turntable and cranked it with the handle. Artie Shaw's melodic 'Begin the Beguine' filled the room as he continued. 'Then tomorrow we get the train back to Fulwood, unfortunately. Anyway, let's enjoy the afternoon, or what's left of it; put the war and the future out of our minds for now.'

Alice looked around the huge foyer of the Adelphi Hotel, her jaw dropping as she took in her elaborate surroundings. There were thick navy patterned carpets, stunning marble pillars and archways and sparkling chandeliers that hung from the glass-panelled ceiling. She wondered if Buckingham Palace in London where the King lived was as grand. She'd never seen anything like it. She stood back from the polished mahogany desk, beside the cases, while Terry gave the receptionist their details and signed the register. He was handed the keys to the room booked in the name of Mr and Mrs Lomax. A thrill ran through Alice as she heard the receptionist congratulating Terry, and she looked across and smiled and nodded a thank you to the smartly dressed woman. A uniformed porter was summoned and he carried their cases up the wide staircase to the room on the first floor. Terry gave the man a tip and closed the door behind him.

'It's all so posh, I'm frightened of touching anything,' Alice said as she gazed in awe around the attractive room whose windows overlooked Ranelagh Place. There were pipes and big radiators too and the room felt warm after the cold day outside.

'Best make the most of it, gel.' Terry grinned. 'It'll be the first and last time we spend a night in a room like this. It's costing an arm and a leg, but it's the only night we'll spend together for God knows how long, and I wanted it to be somewhere special, not in some grotty B&B, complete with a bed full of livestock.'

Alice laughed. She took off her jacket and laid it on the bed. 'They'd be bugs with knobs on though, if we caught any here.' She giggled. She sat down on the bed and sank into the comfort of the blue silk eiderdown that matched the curtains at the window. 'Oh my God, Terry, it's so soft and comfy.' She kicked off her shoes and swung her legs up, revelling in the luxury.

Terry kicked his shoes off, hung his jacket over the back of a chair and joined her. He traced a finger around her lips. 'We'll have a proper honeymoon when I'm home for good,' he promised.

Alice smiled and gave herself up to his passionate kisses.

❁

Alice snuggled down under the blankets and eiderdown as Terry climbed out of bed and pulled back the curtains to reveal more snow falling. A thick cover lay on the ground, and people were doing their best to hurry along the street while trying to stay upright.

'Bloody hell,' he muttered, 'let's hope we can get back to Aigburth in this. Come on, love, we need to get a move on or we'll miss the breakfast. They finish serving in half an hour.'

Alice reluctantly opened her eyes and stretched her arms above her head. 'Do we have to? I want to stay here with you forever. I don't want this to end.'

'Neither do I, gel, but they'll have me for desertion if I don't go back to barracks today. I'll jump in the shower first while you get your stuff together.'

'I've never used a shower before,' Alice said as she slid out of bed, naked. 'You'll have to show me what to do.'

Terry grinned and pulled her close. 'Better than that, you can share with me; it'll save us time for one thing.' He took her hand and led her into the bathroom.

Alice's sponge bag was on a shelf near the sink and Terry rooted inside until he found a bar of her favourite soap wrapped in a pink flannel.

'Camay, the soap for beautiful women,' he teased, quoting the manufacturer's slogan, and turned on the taps.

Alice giggled as the warm water showered down on the pair of them. Her hair would be like rats' tails when they'd finished, but as Terry lathered her with bubbles and kissed her long and hard, she didn't care and knew she would remember this precious time all her life.

After finishing her breakfast in the opulent dining room, and eating far more than she normally would – she probably wouldn't see bacon again for years, never mind a real egg – Alice sat back in her chair and stared at Terry as he popped the last morsel of sausage into his mouth, rolling his eyes in ecstasy. She loved him so much and their one night had been wonderful. He'd been tender but passionate with her and when they'd eventually fallen asleep in the early hours, wrapped in each other's arms, she'd felt complete and loved like never before. Then earlier, in the shower, his lovemaking had left her floating on clouds. How was she going to live without him, and for how long? All she'd have to keep her going were memories and his letters – when he got a chance to write them. What if he didn't come back? She didn't think she could bear it. Her chest felt tight and, as she took a deep breath, hot tears rolled down her cheeks. Terry smiled and took her hand. His own eyes looked moist.

'I don't want you to go,' she sobbed.

'I know, and I don't want to go, darling. But I've got no choice. I hate leaving you. I'll be back, I promise. Nothing will keep me away from you. Not even bloody Hitler and his cronies.'

He led her away from the dining table and back to the room to collect their belongings. They handed the key in at reception and left the warmth of the hotel for the cold and snowy street outside.

Lime Street station was busy and Alice looked around at the people bustling past as Terry checked the departures board. They weren't the only couple saying goodbye that day by the look of things. Sobbing women in the arms of uniformed men, not much older than she and Terry, dotted the station foyer, some holding young babies sandwiched between them. Well, at least that was one problem she didn't have, bringing up a child on her own while its father was stationed God knew where. And she had at least another hour with Terry on their journey home before he dropped her off at her mam's and made his way back to collect Jimmy.

❀

Terry held Alice close on the doorstep and kissed her long and hard.

'Write soon, please,' she begged, tears falling again as he picked up his case from the path. 'And take care of yourself.'

'I will, I promise. And you please look after yourself too, Alice. I love you more than life itself. Make sure you take shelter as soon as the warning sirens go off. And be careful at work with all the explosives lying around. Don't take any risks.'

She nodded through her tears. 'I'll be very careful. I don't go near the explosives. Millie and I are on a different floor, riveting the framework for the Halifax wings.'

'Right, well you and Millie get those planes built and help us lads to win this war. I'm relying on you, gel. Build the one with Hitler's name on it. Let's finish him off good and proper. Goodbye, my darling, I'll write as soon as I can. I love you.'

'And I love you.' Alice watched as he strode off down the road towards Lark Lane. At the corner he turned and waved one last time. Her heart broke as she closed the front door and made her way into the back sitting room. The fire was lit but there was no sign of her mam. She must have gone to church with Mona from up the road, but as it was now almost one o'clock she should be back soon. Alice flopped onto the sofa and sobbed her heart out.

Chapter Four

Alice tossed and turned for most of the night, alternating between sobbing into her pillow and telling herself not to be a mardy baby. Thousands of girls like her were parted from their loved ones and just had no choice but to get on with it. Her Terry would be fine. He'd miss her just as much as she'd miss him and there was nothing they could do about it. She decided to get up and get ready for work. Millie would be knocking on for her in an hour so at least she had time for tea and toast first. She rolled out of bed and dashed to the bathroom for a quick wash and to pin up her hair, ready to go under the dreaded turban that was waiting in her locker at Rootes.

As she made breakfast she thought back to what her mam had said over tea last night when she eventually arrived back from church and her usual cuppa afterwards at her pal Mona's. Mona had worked at the Princess Steam Laundry on Lark Lane with Mam and now it was closed because of serious bomb damage they were at a loose end. Mona had suggested they get together on a regular basis in the church hall and form a knitting group that would make socks for the soldiers. Mona thought it would be a good idea to get them both out of the house for a few hours a week. And also Mam said the newsagent's wife had asked her if she'd do a couple of mornings in the shop while her husband was doing his ARP duties. It would give her a bit of extra money so she'd said she'd love to help out.

Alice thought it was a great idea. It would do Mam good to have a bit of company again instead of sitting alone wallowing in aches and pains that would probably vanish once her mind was occupied. Most of the women she'd be spending time with were a similar age, so would all be going through the change, and Mam would realise it wasn't life-threatening and you could still live a normal life.

Alice finished her breakfast and poured a cup of tea for Mam and took it upstairs. If she woke her now it might spur her on to get up and go and talk to Mona some more. It would take a bit of pressure from Alice's shoulders if she wasn't the only breadwinner in the house again. She might even be able to save a bit of money for her and Terry's future home. She could have a nice little nest egg saved for when he got home that would give them a start at least.

❀

In spite of the cold morning and the snow still falling, Millie was smiling happily when Alice answered the door.

'I'm ready,' Alice said, shivering as she closed the front door behind her. She flicked the collar of her warm red coat up and pulled her knitted scarf, one of Mam's creations, tighter around her neck.

'Flipping heck, it's cold enough to take your breath away!' she exclaimed, linking Millie's arm as they slipped and slithered along Lucerne Street and onto Lark Lane. The snow wasn't as thick here and the pavements had been cleared a bit, ashes scattered on them by kindly shop owners to thaw the ice and snow so customers wouldn't slip and injure themselves. Alice made a mental note to do the same to their front path when she got home tonight.

They stood by the bus stop on Aigburth Road, stamping their feet, teeth chattering. Millie nudged Alice. 'So, how did it go?'

Alice smiled and felt her cheeks heating. 'We had a lovely time, thank you.'

'And the Adelphi? Is it as nice as they say it is?'

'Very posh,' Alice replied. 'Never seen anything like it. Shows you how the other half live.'

'I'll bet. You look very happy anyway. Sort of glowing.'

Alice smiled. 'Think that's down to the cold weather. And I've done nothing but cry all night, so I'm all blotchy. It was awful saying goodbye to him.'

Millie squeezed her arm. 'I'm sure.'

Alice blinked rapidly as the works' bus trundled slowly to the stop. 'I've just got to get on with it, haven't I? I'm not the only one. There were loads of girls saying goodbye to their husbands at Lime Street yesterday. Some even had little kiddies and babies with them. It's so sad.'

Millie nodded. 'Well at least you haven't got that problem and there's only you to think about.'

'True,' Alice said as they climbed aboard the bus and sat down, calling out hellos to the other passengers.

Millie rooted in her bag and pulled out a sheet of paper. She showed it to Alice. 'Jimmy gave me this,' she whispered. 'He wants me to write to him. Do you think I should?'

The paper had Jimmy's name and address at Fulwood Barracks written on it.

Alice's eyebrows shot up. 'But what about Alan? I thought you were madly in love with him? I mean, Jimmy's very nice, but, well, we don't know that much about him.'

Millie sighed. 'I am in love with Alan. But I felt sorry for Jimmy. And I like him. When he asked me if I'd got a boyfriend I lied and said no. Do you think that was really bad of me?'

Alice puffed out her cheeks. 'Crikey, I'm shocked. I wasn't expecting this.'

Millie shrugged, her blue eyes clouding. 'Alan hasn't written for ages, but his mother had a letter from him two weeks ago so nothing bad has happened to him. He could have spared the time to write to me too. I feel he doesn't really care that much about me. He was blowing hot and cold before he was sent abroad. Everyone else we know is either engaged or married. But Alan hasn't even suggested it for us. I don't want to be left on the shelf.'

'You're only eighteen, Millie, for goodness sake. But I suppose you've not got a lot to lose if he's being like that with you. And if you like Jimmy, it will be nice for him to have someone to keep in touch with back home. They all need to feel someone cares.'

'That's what I thought,' Millie said. 'No point in having all my eggs in the same basket, is there?'

Alice laughed as the bus picked up more passengers and the driver started to whistle Flanagan and Allen's 'Underneath the Arches' as loud as he could, with the passengers joining in and singing along to the chorus. He always gave them a tune on the journey in and by the time they pulled onto Speke Road and through the gates of the munitions factory, everybody was in a happy mood and bid the driver thank you and goodbye as they got off the bus.

'Nice to go into work feeling all jolly,' Millie said. 'Sod this war, let's get them planes built and the war won and then our boys can come home and we can have our lives back.'

'Hear, hear, Millie, gel,' said a large man, slapping her on the shoulder and nearly knocking her flying.

'Oi, Freddie, you watch it or else.' Millie put up two fists in a mock fighting gesture to their foreman.

'Oh aye,' Freddie said, a twinkle in his eye. 'You and whose army, queen?'

'Sod off.' Millie grinned and linked her arm through Alice's as they made their way inside and to the locker room where their khaki overalls, and the turbans Alice hated, were stored.

The noise was deafening on the factory floor as the girls took up their places on the benches. Parts of plane-wing framework awaited them along with the riveting guns that were used to drive the rivets into the frames. It was a tricky job and accuracy and concentration were all-important. There was no time for talking as they set to work. The only sound was the pop, pop, pop of the guns. Alice's wrist began to ache after a few hours and she put the gun down on the bench and flexed her fingers, before resuming her task. She glanced sideways at Millie, who looked miles away, in a trance and staring straight in front of her as she pressed the gun time and again.

A quick peek at the clock on the wall at the far end of the room showed ten more minutes to break time. Thank God. Big Freddie, the foreman, collected the completed frames and took them down to where the wings were being assembled and covered with skin, the last job on the current plane they were building. After a test flight down the runway and in the murky clouds above Liverpool, it would be handed over to RAF 611 Squadron, which was based in Speke. Their fleet of Halifaxes would soon be gracing the skies and doing the job they'd been commissioned to do.

Alice and the rest of the team cheered as the hooters sounded for break time. It was always good to catch up with everyone over a mug of hot tea and a mountain of toast – as long as the baker had delivered the bread order. Fingers crossed. They'd all want to know how the wedding went. She hoped they'd keep their bawdy comments about her wedding night to themselves as she didn't want her lovely memories tarnished by cheap jokes.

As the Halifax girls collected their tea and toast and found a table, Big Freddie wandered around the canteen with a sheet of paper on a clipboard and a pencil behind his ear. He stopped at each table to speak to the occupants and then scribbled something down on the paper.

'Wonder what Freddie's up to?' Alice mused, taking a sip of tea. 'Blimey, that's hotter than ever today. Watch you don't scald your lips, girls.'

'You moaning again, our Alice,' Freddie teased as he came to stand beside her.

'Cheeky,' she said, grinning up at him. 'I never moan.'

'Right,' Freddie began, 'with Christmas approaching and a lot of us separated from our loved ones, the management thought it would boost morale if we put on a show. We aim to do it on the last Friday before work finishes for Christmas, so that'll be the twentieth. The canteen will put on a bit of a spread and the idea is that anyone who fancies doing a spot, like singing or dancing, telling a few jokes or summat, can get up and entertain us. Me and the lads will put a makeshift stage together at the bottom end of the canteen, shift the tables out of the way and arrange the chairs so it feels like we're in a theatre. So, ladies, what can I put you down for? I've already got a Wilson, Keppel and Betty, and a Flanagan and Allen. I could do with some singers. Who's willing to give us a bit of Gracie Fields or Vera Lynn, then? Come on Millie, you know you can sing like an angel, I've heard you.'

Millie blushed furiously and almost choked on her toast. 'I can't bloody sing. Where'd you get that idea from?'

'You sing on the bus and your voice is better than anybody else's.'

'Yeah, come on, Millie,' Marlene yelled from down the other end of the table. 'You sing beautifully.'

'They're right,' Alice agreed. 'You could knock Gracie into a cocked hat if you put your mind to it.'

'Oh, I don't know,' Millie said, looking all flustered. 'Who'll play the music?'

'The works' band will,' Freddie said. 'They'll be playing a few Glenn Miller tunes so we can all have a dance, and sing some carols at the end of the night. I'll put you down for a couple of Gracie Fields songs then and perhaps you and Alice here can do a couple of other songs of your own choice. I'll leave you to think about it and let me know what you'll be singing by the end of the week.' He walked away as Alice stared after him, shaking her head.

'We could do the Boswell Sisters act,' Millie said, her enthusiasm growing. '"Alexander's Ragtime Band" and that "Cheek to Cheek" song from Fred Astaire's *Top Hat* film. You like that one, Alice. Come on, it'll be good fun.'

'Youse two will be great,' Marlene said. 'You'll bring the 'ouse down if Hitler don't do it first.' She laughed at her own joke and shoved half a slice of toast into her large mouth.

Alice sighed and chewed her lip. It couldn't do any harm after all. And it would stop her mooning around and moping after Terry. She and Millie could learn all the words and practise their dance steps.

'Okay then, let's do it.'

A group of girls from the shell assembly line were seated at the next table and cheered as Alice spoke.

Alice grinned. 'You won't be cheering when we get it all wrong on the night. You'll be chucking rotten eggs at us.'

'They'd have to be powdered ones then,' Josie, a slender girl with ginger hair, said, laughing. 'Not seen a real egg for weeks around here.'

Josie and her friends all had the tell-tale yellow-streaked hands and faces, as well as clothes, of the shell-making girls. No matter how hard they tried to wash it off during the day, the powder from the cordite used to pack the shells stayed put until they took showers after stripping off their working clothes in the locker rooms. Alice was so grateful that she'd been taken on as a riveter instead of a munitions girl. There were rumours going around that more women would be recruited to making shells and planes next year if the war continued. Some of the men on the production line would be conscripted and it would be down to the women left at home to carry on with the running of the factory in order to supply the troops. Alice hoped she might be offered a supervisory role in time, although there were still tales flying around from them who thought they were in the know that the war would be over in the next few months. Somehow, Alice couldn't see it happening.

She became aware that Marlene was shouting something across the table at her, and turned her attention back to the woman.

'Sorry, Marlene, I was miles away. What did you say?'

'Aw, were you thinking about that lovely 'ubby of yours? Bless him. I said, I 'ope it all went well on Saturday an' that the air raid didn't spoil things for the pair of youse.'

Alice smiled. 'We just made it in time. Spent the first couple of hours of our married life in a shelter, but it was okay.'

'An' the Adelphi? Is it as posh as they all say?'

'It's beautiful.' Alice hoped Marlene would leave it at that and breathed a sigh of relief as the end-of-break bell sounded. She jumped to her feet and pulled Millie up, leading the way back upstairs.

'I've been thinking,' Millie said. 'Mam plays the piano; she can play any tune at all by ear. I'll ask her if we can practise at ours while Dad's out doing his duties and we can sing and dance to our hearts' content. What do you think? We'll need costumes as well. Mrs Floyd at the post office is good with a needle and thread so she might help us out.'

'Sounds great,' Alice said as they took their places at the bench, new pieces of framework awaiting their attention. 'And it'll be something nice to do. Take our mind of our men-folk, all two of yours,' she said, lowering her voice and winking as Millie laughed and blushed.

Chapter Five

By the time the week before Christmas rolled around, the Rootes entertainments team were as word- and step-perfect as they were ever going to be. There'd been a couple of rehearsals on site with the bus coming back for the entertainers after dropping the rest of the workers off. 'Chesney Allen' and 'Bud Flanagan' had their costumes sorted, with Chesney wearing his Sunday-best suit and hat and Bud his rather large wife's fur coat and straw hat, with strict instructions not to ruin it, or he needn't bother coming home!

Kindly Mrs Floyd had knocked together costumes for 'Wilson, Keppel and Betty' from a couple of old white sheets and some tea towels, and Alice and Millie had a few different outfits fashioned from clothes out of their own wardrobes. Josie from the shell bench had agreed to make up the third sister in the Boswell Sisters act, and Big Freddie, whose wife had made him a suit from an old pair of floral curtains, was planning to do a few Max Miller songs and risqué jokes. He'd been heard singing 'Mary from the Dairy' on more than one occasion over the last few days, making them all laugh.

Alice was really looking forward to the show, which Freddie insisted on calling *The Rootes' Revue*. The last couple of weeks had flown by, and preparing for the show helped take her mind off the fact that Terry was now somewhere in Europe with the rest of the 42nd Lancashire Infantry Division. She'd had two letters from him since their wedding day and a Christmas card, but didn't have a clue when she would next hear from him. Her mam had started working her half days at the Lark Lane newsagent's and had been asked to do even more. So far so good. She seemed to be enjoying it and was so tired at night on her working days that she was sleeping better.

Even though young Brian wasn't around to make Christmas morning special with his excited squeals when he opened his stocking, they'd put up a tree and made an effort with some holly and ivy that Alice had fashioned into a garland and hung from the mantelpiece. They'd had a lovely Christmas card from Brian that he'd made himself, and a class photograph. He was seated on the front row, looking clean and tidy, hair neatly trimmed and smiling broadly. He'd put weight on, but looked happy enough and well-cared-for, which, although they both missed him badly, made Mam and Alice feel very lucky that he'd landed on his feet.

Mrs Lomax had invited Alice and her mother round for Christmas dinner and though Mam had pulled a face and said she'd think about it, Alice put her foot down.

'Terry's mam will be all on her own if we don't spend the day with her. It will be lovely to have dinner cooked for us as well and we can take something round for tea later to help out,' Alice said. 'You're missing our Rodney and Brian, but at least you've got me. Think how lonely she must feel with Terry God knows where. She's family now, Mam, so we're going.' She added slyly, 'And you know how lovely and warm it always is in her bungalow compared to here.' Mam had half-smiled and been forced to agree.

❦

Alice peered around the edge of the makeshift stage curtains draped across the front of the raised platform. Millie and Josie, standing behind her, giggled nervously as Freddie announced that the next act was 'The Boswell Sisters' and to give them a big hand. Two lads, on curtain duty, pulled back the drapes and the audience cheered and clapped as the threesome stepped forward. The works' band struck up with the opening chords of 'Alexander's Ragtime Band' and the girls' nerves flew out of the window as they began to sing and tapdance to the rhythm, the audience helping out with the chorus. Wearing blue dresses and white peep-toe shoes, their hair neatly styled by Millie's mam last night, Alice thought they cut quite a dash. So did the audience, if the amount of wolf-whistling from the men was anything to go by. Spurred on by the cheers and claps, they wiggled their hips and sang their hearts out, finishing the spot with 'Cheek to Cheek'.

Freddie came back on stage as the audience shouted for more. The girls trooped off and Freddie announced that Millie would be back later with a few Gracie and Vera numbers. Backstage, Alice felt elated and happy and hugged her co-singers, who hugged her back.

'I really enjoyed that,' she said, taking a deep breath. 'Have a quick drink to wet your whistle, Millie and then you'll be back on.' They could hear the audience laughing as Freddie introduced 'Flanagan and Allen' to uproarious cheers. 'This was a great idea of Freddie's. It's really cheered everyone up.' As she spoke, the loud wail of an air raid siren rent the air. 'Oh no! Typical. Just when we're having some fun. Bloody Hitler! I hate him for dictating our lives.'

The girls grabbed their coats and gas masks and followed the crowds leaving the building to hurry into the air raid shelters on site. Along with the docks, Rootes was always a possible target and the fear of a strike filled Alice with terror. With the amount of explosives in the factory for the shells, the whole place could go up and take them all with it. They squeezed alongside members of the audience and Freddie and a few other cast members and found seats on benches against the walls. After much cursing and complaining Freddie got to his feet.

'Sod this,' he shouted. 'Jerry's not ruining our night after all that rehearsing. Let's carry on with the show in here. Come on, Bud and Chesney, you were just about to begin. Give us a turn.'

The band members had a trumpet, clarinet and saxophone with them and they struck up with 'Underneath the Arches' and followed with 'Run Rabbit Run'. Everyone joined in and clapped along. And then Freddie asked Millie to do the best she could with what bit of accompaniment there was, and she gave them a rendition of 'We'll Meet Again' and Judy Garland's 'Over the Rainbow'.

The rest of the stay in the shelter was filled with carol singing and then the siren wailed again with the end of the warning.

'Thank God for that,' Freddie said. 'I'm starving and there's a buffet to be tackled. Come on, let's get back to it. A big thanks to all of you who managed to take our minds off what's going on out there.'

A big cheer went up and everyone clapped.

Alice linked her arms through Millie and Josie's as they made their way back indoors.

'Well, that was fun, if nothing else.' She sniffed the air. Something, not too far away, was burning and there'd been loud explosions towards the Mersey. 'I just hope no one was injured tonight, so close to Christmas Day. Hope our mams got to the shelter okay.'

❄

After several more air raid warnings and hours spent in shelters with strikes all over Liverpool by the Germans, Christmas morning dawned crisp and cold, but bright. Alice was up early as she and Mam planned to attend the carol service at St Michael's church before going to Mrs Lomax's. Mam had managed to get their bacon ration and two eggs, kept under the counter for favoured customers, and they enjoyed a cooked breakfast, the first Alice had eaten since her stay at the Adelphi. She dipped the last corner of toast in her egg yolk and savoured it; heaven only knew when she'd get another.

She and Mam exchanged presents. There was some fancy soap and matching talc for Mam, and a box of embroidered hankies.

Mam gave Alice a small blue bottle of Soir de Paris perfume, her favourite, and a silver picture frame to put her wedding photo in. Alice had collected the photos and put them in a little album. Now she could have the one of Terry and herself in pride of place. She hurried to get it from the album and slipped it into the frame.

'It looks lovely,' she said, popping the frame onto the mantelpiece and running the tip of her finger over Terry's smiling face. 'Thanks, Mam, it's perfect.'

'You're welcome, chuck. Nice to have it on display. We'd better get ready and make our way to church. I expect it'll be freezing in there, so wrap up warm. Now, where did we put Terry's mam's gifts? We need to leave them handy so we don't go without them later.'

Alice dashed into the front room that they never used much these days – there was never enough coal to spare to heat two rooms – and brought back a carrier bag.

'All wrapped and ready to go.' She placed the bag on the table and went out to the kitchen. 'We'll take a few of the mince pies that Freddie let me bring home from the buffet the other night as well,' she said, putting the tin on the table.

'Well, make sure you keep a couple back for our tea tomorrow.' Mam frowned. 'I'm not being mean but, well, Mrs Lomax has more money than us and I bet she's already got some mince pies in.'

Alice shook her head and took two mince pies back into the kitchen. She laughed to herself, thinking how those wouldn't last two seconds if Brian was here. She hoped he'd liked his present. They hadn't heard from Rodney for nearly three weeks now and she could only hope that he was well and that all the troops would at least get a decent hot dinner today, if nothing else. Millie had received a Christmas card and letter from Jimmy last week and she'd been oohing and aahing over it every spare minute. She'd not heard a word from Alan, although she'd sent him a letter and card in early December.

Alice linked her mam's arm on the walk to the church. It was still slippery underfoot, but once they'd crossed over Aigburth Road the pavements were clearer and Church Lane had been shovelled free of snow for the parishioners' comfort. St Michael's was packed and it wasn't half as cold inside as Mam had predicted. The pipes that ran along the floor in front of the pews were warm and Alice slipped her shoes off and placed her frozen feet on them, sighing blissfully and ignoring Mam's frown and her whispered, 'You'll get chilblains doing that.' Alice raised her eyebrows. If it wasn't one thing it was another with Mam. Cold in your kidneys if your back wasn't covered; brain damage if you took a bath or washed your hair when you were having your monthlies; and now chilblains.

The pew filled quickly and Alice shuffled along a bit further, dragging her discarded shoes with her. The vicar greeted everyone from his pulpit and the first carols were sung loud and clear. Two things struck Alice that morning. The congregation consisted mainly of women, and there was an absence of young voices in the choir, and only two male baritones.

She felt her eyes filling as the vicar said a prayer for all the children who were evacuated miles away from their families. And for the troops who were overseas fighting for their country. He prayed for the 365 people who had recently lost their lives during the recent direct hit air raids between the 20th and the 22nd in Birkenhead. He also prayed for peace and an end to the hostilities in the near future.

As they came out of church, following more rousing carols, Alice spotted Alan's mum and sister standing by the entrance porch. She hurried over to speak to them and asked if they'd heard from Alan recently. She was wondering if he might be stationed somewhere near Rodney and the post wasn't getting through to them, rather than that he was just ignoring Millie. Audrey, Alan's sister, greeted Alice with a big smile.

'Congratulations on your marriage, Alice. Such a shame the boys are away, isn't it? My Johnny is abroad now, but I've no idea where. I hate this war.'

'Me too,' Alice agreed.

'We heard from Alan last week,' Audrey said. 'He seems fine, but I think they all put on a brave face for us.'

'I'm sure you're right.' Alice turned as Mam came to stand beside her. If Alan could write to his family, he could surely find the time to write to Millie and let her down gently if he wasn't interested. It wasn't fair. Millie really loved him and she shouldn't have to feel guilty at keeping in touch with Jimmy. At least the lad took the time to put pen to paper. If Millie brought up the subject again, Alice might say something along the lines of letting Alan go and just enjoying writing to Jimmy.

Mrs Lomax brought through a tray of tea things into the cosy sitting room, where they'd all retired after eating mounds of roast dinner. A plate piled high with mince pies and Christmas cake, which was in fact the remains of Alice and Terry's wedding cake, waited on the coffee table. Alice felt a lump in her throat as she thought of her lovely new husband who should be here with them, celebrating their first Christmas together as a married couple. She could feel tears welling and blinked rapidly.

'I don't think I could eat another morsel, I'm that stuffed,' Mam said, relaxing back against the cushions on the sofa. 'It was a lovely dinner, best I've had for a long time. That goose was perfect. I could manage a cuppa, mind.'

'I'm glad you enjoyed it,' Mrs Lomax said. 'A friend of mine has a small farm and rears ducks and geese. I was lucky he reserved one for me as I believe the butcher on Lark Lane sold out of fowl very quickly this year. A lot of people who'd asked him to save them something had to settle for mince and sausages. Now then, I'll put the wireless on for the King's speech. We'll listen to it and then open our presents, shall we?'

Mrs Lomax nodded her head towards the small Christmas tree in the bay window under which she'd placed the parcels Alice had handed her, alongside some that were there already, waiting. She poured tea into three china cups and told them to help themselves to milk and sugar and proceeded to fiddle with the wireless set, which beeped and whistled until she'd set it to the correct station.

'He's speaking from Sandringham again today, I believe,' she announced, sitting down next to Mam. 'Are you okay, Edith? Please help yourself if you want a mince pie. We don't stand on ceremony in this house.'

❊

In the armchair near the bay window, Alice yawned and stretched her arms above her head. She was struggling to keep her eyes open in the warm and cosy room. She smiled at Mam and Mrs Lomax, who were flat out as King George brought his lengthy speech to an end.

Time and again during these last few months I have seen for myself the battered towns and cities of England, and I have seen the British people facing their ordeal. I can say to them that they may be justly proud of their race and nation. On every side I have seen a new and splendid spirit of good fellowship springing up in adversity, a real desire to share burdens and resources alike. Out of all this suffering there is a growing harmony which we must carry forward into the days to come when we have endured to the end and ours is the victory.

Then, when Christmas Days are happy again, and good will has come back to the world, we must hold fast to the spirit which binds us together now. We shall need this spirit in each of our own lives as men and women, and shall need it even more among the nations of the world. We must go on thinking less about ourselves and more for one another, for so, and so only, can we hope to make the world a better place and life a worthier thing.

And now I wish you all a happy Christmas and a happier New Year. We may look forward to it with sober confidence. We have surmounted a grave crisis. We do not underrate the dangers and difficulties which confront us still, but we take courage and comfort from the successes which our fighting men and their Allies have won at heavy odds by land and air and sea. The future will be hard, but our feet are planted on the path of victory, and with the help of God we shall make our way to justice and to peace.

Alice got to her feet, feeling slightly uplifted by the monarch's words, but a little uneasy all the same. She thought he might have finished with something along the lines of, 'Don't worry, soon your men-folk will be home safe and sound.' After all, surely he and Churchill had regular meetings and knew better than anyone what was going on? But if *they* didn't think it was going to be over soon, then all that talk from people about being back to normal in the next couple of months was just wishful thinking. She picked up the tray of tea things and took them into the back kitchen to wash. A fresh pot of tea was soon made and she carried everything back to the sitting room and gave Mam and Mrs Lomax a gentle shake each.

Mam's eyes flew open and she jumped. 'Ooh, I was just shutting my eyes for a minute. Has he started yet?'

'It's finished, Mam. Here, have another cuppa and a piece of cake.'

Mrs Lomax sat up, blinking. 'Oh dear, I must have dozed off.'

'You both did,' Alice said, laughing. She related what she could recall of the King's speech and they both nodded fondly.

'He's a lovely man,' Mrs Lomax began. 'I'm so glad he's managed to get that stammer under control. And Elizabeth is such a nice little girl; a credit to both her parents. Mind you, young Margaret always seems a handful, but you always get one, don't you? I mean, look at his brother and that flighty Wallis Simpson woman.' She shook her head disapprovingly and sipped her tea. 'Do you want to bring the presents over, Alice, love? Let's see what we've got.'

After unwrapping Mrs Lomax's gifts to her – a red knitted beret, a matching scarf and a copy of *Lark Rise* by Flora Thompson – Alice picked up the last parcel and her heart leapt to see the label was signed by Terry, with love. She tore off the wrapping paper and opened the small black box. Inside, nestling on white satin, was a heart-shaped gold locket.

'Open it up,' Mrs Lomax encouraged.

Alice did as she was told and gasped. Two small photographs of her and Terry sat in it, side by side. She turned the locket over. On the back their initials *T* and *A* were engraved, entwined together. Her eyes filled and she clasped the locket to her chest.

'How did…?' she sobbed, feeling completely overwhelmed and wanting nothing more than to be in Terry's arms right now.

'He brought it home with him the weekend you got married,' Mrs Lomax explained. 'He wrapped it ready and told me to give it to you on Christmas Day. That's why I invited you to come to me. And I'm glad I did because I've really enjoyed having your company. It's been a pleasure to cook for you both. It's lovely having a little family again. And maybe next year we'll all be together, us three, our boys and well, you never know,' she said, smiling at Alice. 'There might be a little one to put presents under the tree for some time in the future.'

Chapter Six

February 1941

As the last week of February approached and the war seemed no nearer ending than it ever had, Alice knew for certain that she was expecting a baby. She'd not seen sight nor sound of her monthlies since November, before her wedding day, and the overwhelming feeling of queasiness wouldn't go away. Plus there was her slightly expanding breasts and waistline to take into account. She'd already written to Terry two weeks ago when she first suspected something was going on, but had heard nothing back from him yet. From the minute Mrs Lomax had said on Christmas Day about a little one she'd felt almost jinxed. Both she and Terry had decided they would wait until the war ended and they were together in their own home before they'd start a family. The thought of being all alone with a new baby and bombs falling terrified her. Would the authorities make her go away? She knew that some pregnant mothers had been evacuated to Blackpool and were staying there until the war ended. But she couldn't leave her mam all alone. She'd never cope, so going away wasn't an option.

There would be no money coming in once she stopped working, except for Mam's small wages from the newsagent's. Alice didn't know how they would manage. Rodney would have to send a bit extra and Terry would too. He'd sent a few pounds with his last letter in January for her to put in the post office savings account towards their home. Now she'd need to draw it out again to buy baby things. It couldn't be worse timing, and after Terry had assured her he'd taken care. It must have happened the time in the shower when they'd been rushing to get ready, she thought as she hurried downstairs to answer the door to Millie.

'Oh, you look rough,' Millie said. 'You're so pale. Still feeling sickly?'

'Yes, but I haven't actually been sick. It's just this queasiness that lasts all day.'

'It'll perhaps ease off soon.' Apart from Alice's mam, there was only Millie party to her secret. No one at work had been told yet. She wanted to wait until after she'd heard from Terry in case her letter had gone astray. It wouldn't do for half of Liverpool to know before he did. But it was getting harder to stay smiling and not feel like curling up in bed all day.

'Are we ready then?' Millie said as Alice picked up her bag from the hall floor.

'As I'll ever be. Mam's already left for the newsagent's. She's on first shift today.'

❀

Alice struggled to hold on to her breakfast as the bus trundled along the roads towards Speke. They got off the bus, waving goodbye to the driver, who wasn't their usual man so there'd been no sing-song this morning, for which Alice was thankful as her head was banging too. She'd hardly slept, lying awake worrying what was going to happen to them all and crying into her pillow for Terry. She felt a wreck and knew she looked it too.

''Ere, are you all right, gel?' Marlene said, puffing as she hurried to catch up with Alice and Millie. 'You don't 'alf look wiped out, don't she, Millie?'

'I'm just tired,' Alice said. 'Not sleeping too well, listening out for air raids all the time, it's enough to keep anyone awake.'

'Ooh, not me, gel. I can sleep through anything.' Marlene bustled off, calling out to a young woman who was just going into the building. 'Florrie, 'ang on a minute.'

'Thank God for that,' Alice said as Millie linked arms with her. 'She'll guess soon enough, but not yet, I hope. I need to know that Terry knows first.'

'Of course you do,' Millie agreed. 'It's only right and proper. There might be something from him today when you get home.'

Alice took her place at the bench and concentrated on the job, her mind still working overtime. She looked around at her co-workers, heads bent in concentration as they popped rivets into the aircraft frames, and wondered what secrets they all held close. She looked across at the clock and felt it swimming in and out of focus. Next thing she knew, Millie was shaking her shoulders and then she was whisked from the floor where she had fallen and carried across the room in Big Freddie's strong arms with Millie on his heels.

He took her into a storeroom that doubled as a first aid room and laid her down on a small camp bed in the corner.

'Millie, get her some water, chuck,' he ordered. He patted Alice's cheeks as she came round a little. 'Did you bang your head as you fell?'

'I don't think so,' Alice mumbled. 'I seemed to just crumple, everything went blurry. I feel a bit sickly and dazed.'

She shuffled up the camp bed slightly as Millie came back in the room and closed the door. She handed Alice a glass of water and stood back with a worried expression.

Alice looked at Freddie's concerned face and smiled weakly. She took a sip of water as the buzzer rang for break time.

'I came out without any breakfast,' she fibbed, feeling her cheeks heating. 'I'll be fine when I've had my tea and toast.'

He was looking at her with a questioning expression. 'I'm not daft, Alice. My missus has had five of the little blighters, so I recognise a woman in the family way. But I'll keep my trap shut. I know you will tell us when you want to.'

'She's just waiting to hear back from Terry before she lets that lot out there know,' Millie explained. 'You know what Marlene's like.'

'I do.' Freddie nodded. 'You need to see a doctor soon to make sure it's all right for you to stay working here in your condition. There's a lot of dangerous stuff lying around in this factory. Not the best place for an expectant mother.'

Alice sighed and took another sip of water. 'I will. I won't be due for a good while. I'm not even three full months yet. It's a wedding-weekend baby and that was December seventh. I'll be twelve weeks at the weekend. Surely I'll be okay once this nauseous feeling goes away?'

'Tell you what,' Freddie said. 'Take it easy for the rest of today. I'll keep my eye on you, make sure you're okay. Go and get your toast and tea now and then take tomorrow off and get yourself to the doctor's. Just have him check you over. Tell him you work here, and see what he says.'

Millie helped Alice to her feet. 'Thank you, Freddie,' Alice said.

'You're welcome. Take an extra ten minutes when the others come back upstairs, seeing as you've missed half your break. You too, Millie. Go on now, before I change my mind.'

❖

First thing next morning, Alice smiled at Doctor Marshall as he greeted her and told her to take a seat. She sat down opposite him, placed her hands around her handbag and cleared her throat as he asked what he could do for her.

'I, er, I need to update my details, change my name,' Alice began. 'I'm a married lady now. My new name is Lomax.'

Doctor Marshall, who had been the family doctor all her life, smiled and nodded as he noted down Alice's name change.

'And your address? Is that still the same?'

'Oh, yes it is. Well, until my soldier husband comes home for good and we find a little place of our own. I'm staying at my mam's for now. Our Rodney and Brian are both away and she needs me.'

'Of course. I hope she's keeping well and busy. Best thing for her. Now is there anything else I can help you with, Alice?'

'Well, er, yes. I think I'm expecting a baby,' Alice blurted out and blushed as she told him her symptoms and the date she got married.

'Okay. Well, hop up onto the couch and I'll have a feel of your tummy, see what's going on in there.'

Alice slipped her shoes off and did as she was told. Doctor Marshall's hands were cold as he lifted her dress and touched her bare flesh. She flinched as he palpated her stomach.

'Sorry about the cold hands,' he said, helping her down from the couch, 'but I don't think there's any doubt. We'll get a urine sample test done to confirm.' He handed her a small labelled bottle and filled in a form with her details, to take to the nearest chemist. 'I'll have the results back early next week, if you want to pop back then, and I'll arrange for you to book in with one of our midwives. They will look after you for the next few months and then we'll arrange for you to have your baby as locally as we can. Unless of course you prefer to be delivered at home?'

Alice shook her head. 'I'd like the hospital if possible. It would be less for my mam to worry about.'

'Well that's fine. And congratulations, by the way. Where are you working at the moment, Alice?'

'Rootes Munitions,' she replied. 'I *was* told to ask if that's still okay. I'm on riveting duties on the aircraft wing frames.'

Doctor Marshall nodded. 'You're okay to continue as long as you are not near cordite or other explosives and the work doesn't involve any heavy lifting. You'll need to finish around the end of July. Give yourself some time to have a rest before the birth. The midwives will speak to you about all that nearer the delivery date.'

Alice got to her feet and thanked him. She made her way home and dashed upstairs to the bathroom. Her sample completed, she hurried up to the chemist's on Lark Lane and handed the bottle and form to the white-coated assistant. She popped her head into the newsagent's and spoke to her mam, telling her what Doctor Marshall had said.

'I'm going home for a cuppa now and then I might pop round to see Mrs Lomax. Shall I get us something nice for tea?'

Mam smiled. 'You'll be lucky, but you can try, chuck. Don't forget to take the ration books with you. They're in the top drawer in the kitchen. See if you can get a bit of meat and we'll make a pan of scouse. There's some veg wants using up, and we need a loaf as well. Don't go mad.' She laughed at her own joke.

'Chance would be a fine thing,' Alice said. 'See you later then.'

Alice strolled back up Lark Lane. The day was chilly but bright. It was lovely to have a bit of time off and just go at a slower pace. She let her thoughts turn to pushing her new baby around nearby Sefton Park in the summertime in a shiny new pram, Terry strolling proudly by her side. She blinked away tears as she spotted the postman on his bike turning into Lucerne Street, and quickened her pace. As she turned the corner she could see him pushing something through the letterbox. A joyous feeling rushed through her veins. Praying it was a letter from Terry, she ran down the street and let herself in. Sure enough, on the doormat were two blue envelopes with forces postmarks; one from her brother Rodney, addressed to her mam, and the other from her darling Terry.

Sitting on the sofa with a cup of tea, Alice cherished every word of Terry's letter for the third time. He was so sorry he couldn't be with her to share her unexpected good news, but he was thrilled to bits at the prospect of being a father, even if it was a bit sooner than they had planned. He pleaded with her to take the greatest care of herself and not to take any chances at work or anywhere else for that matter. He asked her to let his mam know and to be sure to write back as soon as she could with updates on what the doctor had said if she'd been to see him yet. He finished with how much he loved her and how doubly precious she was to him now that she was carrying his baby.

❀

Mrs Lomax almost dropped her tea as Alice imparted her news. Her face lit up with a joyous smile and she put down her cup and saucer and jumped to her feet, pulling Alice up with her.

'Isn't this the best news we could hope for?' she said, wonder in her voice. 'Something to look forward to.'

'Well yes,' Alice said, her voice wavering slightly. 'I would have preferred it if Terry were home though and we weren't in the middle of a war, but there you go. We'll just have to manage the best we can.'

Mrs Lomax nodded. 'And we will. Oh we will. We need to make sure you eat properly. I can get eggs from my friend at the farm, they're ducks' eggs, but they are good for you. And rabbits, he brings me rabbits, so stew and pies I can make to feed you up, and he lets me have fresh vegetables too from time to time.'

Alice grinned as she recalled Bud and Chesney in the air raid shelter at Christmas singing 'Run Rabbit Run'.

'I'll dig my knitting needles out and start making some clothes. We'll have the best-dressed baby in the Lark Lane area.'

Alice laughed. 'Between you and Mam, it'll have more clothes than we know what to do with.'

'We must order a pram, from Lewis's. Terry would want the best for his child if he were here. I know he would. It will be my treat. If you're not busy on Saturday morning we could take the tram into the city and go and have a look at the choices. How does that sound? They will of course keep it in the storeroom until we're ready to collect it nearer the time. It's bad luck to have prams hanging around for too long. But it's nice to go and choose one. Invite your mother to come along as well. We can have a bit of dinner in the Kardomah while we're out.'

'Thank you, I will do. We'll see you on Saturday then. We'll come here about eleven if that's okay.' She kissed her mother-in-law on the cheek and waved goodbye.

✾

Alice had a spring to her step as she walked back up Lark Lane, past the sorry site of the bombed-out Princess Laundry and into the butchers. She bought some best end of neck lamb pieces for the scouse and two rashers of bacon for tomorrow.

'I don't suppose you've got any real eggs?' she asked hopefully.

'For you, my queen, I can manage a couple,' the butcher said, reaching under the counter for a tray of brown eggs. 'One each for you and your mam, eh; will that do you?'

'Thank you very much.' Alice handed over the ration books and money and put her shopping into a bag. She said goodbye and called into the bakery for a standard white loaf.

'Best enjoy it while you can,' the baker's wife said. 'There's talk of cutting down on bread and giving us a recipe for a National Loaf made with wholemeal flour. There'll be no white bread available in time.'

Alice rolled her eyes. 'We'll starve to death at this rate. Hardly any meat, no real eggs to speak of and now taking away our bread! It's ridiculous.'

The baker's wife nodded and turned to the customer standing behind Alice, who was nodding her head in agreement.

'Mind how you go, chuck,' the baker's wife said, 'and say hello to your mam for me.'

'Will do.' Alice walked back to Lucerne Road, feeling a bit deflated after having felt so chirpy when she'd read Terry's letter.

Ah well, there were worse things happen at sea than brown bread. It would be better than nothing.

She made a start on the scouse for tea and when it was bubbling appetisingly in the pan on the gas hob she set to and cut two thick slices of bread, sticking them under the grill. Mam would be back for her dinner in a few minutes so cheese on toast would be a nice treat, before the small piece of cheese left over from Sunday's tea went mouldy. She crumbled the cheese into a basin, added a drop of milk, and salt and pepper, and mixed it all up together with a tiny bit of grated onion saved from the scouse. Alice realised at that point that the nausea she had been suffering for ages seemed to have eased off; last time Mam made the cheese mixture she'd shot upstairs to the bathroom when the smell had knocked her sick. Well not any more; all she felt today was starving. Mam let herself in at the front door as Alice rescued the bread before it burned, spread the mixture over the un-toasted side and popped it back under the grill to cook.

'Smells good in here,' Mam called out as she let herself in. 'But how come you're at home, love?'

Alice frowned. 'I've been to see the doctor, Mam, remember? I saw you in the shop earlier.'

Mam nodded, but looked a bit puzzled. 'Oh, of course you did. Dopey me. I'm getting a bit forgetful.'

Alice laughed. 'And that good smell is cheese on toast. Won't be a minute, sit yourself down.'

She handed her mam Rodney's letter and smiled as her face lit up and her eyes filled.

'Thank goodness for that,' Mam whispered. 'I know they say no news is good news, but it doesn't stop me fretting when we don't hear anything for weeks.'

Edith sat at the table and read her son's letter, tears streaming down her cheeks as she came to the end.

'What does he say?' Alice asked, placing a plate of cheese on toast in front of her and a cup of tea.

'Well not enough, as he can't say where they are of course. The food is rubbish; he's full of a cold through having permanently wet feet. Two of the platoon were killed in front of him the other week. It sounds awful. My poor boy. When will it all end? Why can't we all just get along and have peace? All this just because one foolish idiot wants his own way. If I could get my hands on Hitler I'd cut off more than his stupid moustache!'

Alice patted her hand. 'That makes two of us.'

She told her mam of Mrs Lomax's suggestion of pram-shopping and a treat in the Kardomah on Saturday. Mam's face lit up.

'That'll be lovely. Something nice for us to do as a family, what's left of us, that is.'

Chapter Seven

'What do you mean, there are no more prams under manufacture?' Mrs Lomax addressed the young woman on the nursery floor at Lewis's department store in the city centre. 'I've never heard anything so ridiculous. What is the country supposed to use to put babies in?'

'I'm sorry, Madam, but the Silver Cross factory in Leeds is now doing important war work and the metals that were used for pram chassis and wheels are now commissioned for shells and other ammunition. There is no metal to spare for anything else in the country at the moment.'

The poor girl looked close to tears and Alice stepped in between her furious mother-in-law and the assistant.

'The pram over there is rather nice, don't you think?' Alice steered Mrs Lomax towards a smart grey pram on a stand.

'Well, it's okay, but you can't beat a Silver Cross model. And the chrome is always lovely and shiny too. That looks a bit dull by comparison.'

The model, manufactured by Marmet, was perfectly adequate for pushing a baby in. The white interior was padded and comfortable to the touch and Alice liked the height of the handle. It was perfect for her. Terry might need to stoop a little when he pushed the pram, being at least six inches taller than her, but she would be the one doing most of that anyway. Okay, the metal was more of a painted finish rather than chrome, but it suited the style and colour of the pram just fine. Alice looked around. There was nothing else to choose from, just this one and a similar one with a hood at either end, for twins.

'I really don't think we have much choice,' Alice whispered. 'These look like the last two in the shop.'

The assistant moved towards them. 'It's the last of that model. We can store it for you, if you like. I can't say when we will have more in stock. It could be a long, long time.'

Mrs Lomax sighed and looked at Mam. 'What do you think, Edith dear?'

'It's very nice,' Edith replied. 'It's really kind of you to offer to buy it for Alice.'

'Very well. We'll take it. Not literally, you understand. If you'll store it for a few months that will be fine. I will pay you now.' She followed the girl over to the till.

'She's a bit of a bossy one,' Mam said. 'But you can't have what they no longer make. And we couldn't afford that. It'd have to be a second-hand pram if it was left to us, chuck.'

'I know, Mam,' Alice said. 'I'm very lucky. I'll be so proud to push the baby in that lovely pram, shiny wheels or not.'

Mrs Lomax came back over to them and smiled. 'We'll need to think about a cot soon as well. Although not as much metal goes into their manufacture, so hopefully there will be more choice.'

'I have some money in the post office that Terry sent me,' Alice said. 'I can buy a cot with that when the time comes. But we won't need a big cot right away, just a small cradle for the first few months, so we'll sort that out another time.'

They made their way downstairs and Mam stopped in haberdashery to buy some white wool and Mrs Lomax picked up some pale lemon. Alice chewed her lip as they pored over baby patterns for matinee jackets and booties. She could see her having a 'battle of the grannies' on her hands at some point, as each tried to outdo the other.

In the Kardomah café, just off Stanley Street, they ordered sandwiches, scones and pots of tea. The sandwiches were thinly cut and Alice thought the beef paste was tasty, with slices of tomato to add extra flavour. Mrs Lomax had referred to them as sandwiches and not sarnies as she'd placed the order. The scones, although light and fluffy, had hardly any fruit in them, victims of the shortages, and Mrs Lomax pulled a face as there was no jam on offer that day either. Alice was just glad to sit down and eat whatever they put in front of her. She was starving. This baby had certainly perked up her appetite now the queasiness had gone away. She was definitely eating for two. She'd be waddling like an elephant in no time. She'd never squeeze into the air raid shelters at work if she carried on like this.

'The clothes they make you wear at the factory, Alice, are they quite suitable for you now?' Mrs Lomax asked.

'They're very baggy,' Alice replied. 'And our foreman Freddie said if I need a bigger size he can get one for me. So work clothes are fine, it's just normal day-to-day wear that's getting a bit tight now. Mam's let a few seams out on a couple of my old dresses and I've got a skirt that we can alter too.'

'We'll get you a couple of nice maternity smocks while we're down this way then. My neighbour said Blacklers have some in. She got her daughter one last week.'

'Oh but there's no need—' Alice began.

'There's every need, my dear. If my Terry were here he'd be making sure you had everything you required. He's not here so I'm stepping in. I want to help as much as I can. When my husband died he left me well provided for and now I want to make sure his grandchild is as well looked after as Terry was. Please allow me the enjoyment of indulging myself.'

Alice smiled and patted her hand. 'Of course and it's a big help to us, as you know. Thank you.'

'My pleasure. I'm so very excited about this baby, as I'm sure Edith is.'

Mam nodded. 'I'm thrilled to bits. I just wish both granddads were still around to enjoy it too.'

❁

'Do you fancy it then?' Alice asked as she, Millie and Josie travelled to work the following Monday. She'd told them about the new pram, Josie now being in on her secret, and about being treated to two maternity tops from Blacklers; one of them, button-through, black and white gingham with a white Peter Pan collar, she was wearing now over a plain black skirt with an adjustable waistband, also a treat from her generous mother-in-law. And then she'd suggested they have a night out at the pictures.

'That's fine by me,' Josie said. 'Be nice to get out and relax a bit.'

'I'm up for that,' Millie said. 'But it will have to be Wednesday, because Mam's got customers tonight and tomorrow. She's really busy this week. Think they're all panicking in case we get bombed out and lose the house. What's on, do you know?'

'*Rebecca* is showing again. You know how much we loved it the first time as well as the book.'

Millie rolled her eyes. 'And Laurence Olivier,' she said, smiling dreamily. 'Well, in the absence of our own men, we need someone to drool over. You're on.'

Alice laughed. 'Smashing. Any word from Alan yet?'

Millie snorted. 'Not a bloody dickey bird. It really upsets me. Jimmy writes as often as he can. I'm getting to know him well. He's told me all about his family in Blackpool and his hobbies. He likes fishing, apparently. His dad has a boat at Fleetwood and that's what the family do for a living, catch fish and sell it. Well, they did, before the war. All three of his brothers are in the army now.'

'Has he got one going spare for me?' Josie said with a wink. 'I could do with someone to write to.'

'I'll ask him,' Millie said. 'Don't know if they've got girls, but there's no harm in writing, is there?'

'I wrote Terry a letter at the weekend and Mam's posting it for me today,' Alice said, a catch in her voice. 'He asked for one of our wedding photos, so I hope it doesn't go astray. God, I miss him so much. Oh, here we go,' she added as the bus driver began his morning whistling session. 'Appropriate, eh?' She smiled as everyone sang along to 'Wish Me Luck as You Wave Me Goodbye'.

❀

'Come on,' Big Freddie yelled as the girls came onto the factory floor. 'Everybody, over here by the windows.'

The workers crowded around him as he pointed proudly to the large four-engine plane that was lumbering slowly down the airport runway.

'The maiden flight of our very own plane, ladies, with a one-hundred-and-four-foot wingspan riveted by you lot.'

Alice watched in awe as the Halifax bomber took to the skies on its maiden test flight. The pride she felt swelling in her chest nearly choked her. Everyone cheered and a few of the girls burst into tears as it vanished into the clouds.

'What a magnificent sight,' Freddie said, overcome with emotion. 'Light as a feather, until it's loaded with bombs to take Hitler's lot out. That plane is something to be proud of, ladies. Right, come on then, let's get back to building another one before break time.'

'That was a wonderful experience,' Millie said. 'I wonder which wing was ours, Alice. Oooh, I feel all overcome. Can't wait to tell my dad.'

As the morning progressed and Alice was engrossed in her work, a loud noise from the floor above shook the ceiling and dust and debris fell onto the workbench.

'What the heck was that?' she exclaimed, putting her riveting gun to one side.

Freddie shook his head. 'Sounds like an explosion. Internally though, not outside. Tools down, ladies, but stay here a minute while I go and check. If the sirens go off, make your way to the shelters right away.'

He ran down the room and dashed out through the swing doors.

Freddie was gone a while. Marlene, who was standing by the windows, yelled, 'There's an ambulance pulling up outside. Oh my God, someone must be injured!'

They all watched as two attendants got out and carried a stretcher inside with them. Freddie appeared at the door, shaking his head. His face was ashen and his lips trembled as he called them all to his side.

'There's, er, there's been an accident upstairs in shells,' he began. He took a deep breath. 'One of the girls up there was wearing earrings and one fell off onto the belt carrying the open shells to the next stage. As you know, wearing anything metal is forbidden, and hiding them under a turban is just plain stupid. The resulting explosion has caused very serious injuries, not only to herself, but the young lady next to her has been killed.' He took a deep shuddering breath and continued. 'Next of kin are being informed immediately and names will be released later.'

Alice felt her legs giving way. She knew from the way Freddie had looked in her and Millie's direction that the girl who'd died was Josie, their lovely red-headed friend who they'd just planned a visit to the pictures with that morning and who'd sung and danced with them at the Christmas revue.

'Get Alice a chair before she falls down,' Freddie instructed Marlene, who was standing by his elbow shaking her head in disbelief.

Millie held Alice up and helped her to the chair. Freddie pushed her head gently down between her knees and held it there until Marlene appeared with a glass of water.

''Ere you are, gel,' Marlene said, putting her arm around Alice's shoulders and holding the glass to her lips. 'I know you've said nowt officially yet but I'm guessing youse are in the family way. You need to look after yourself Alice, an' that babby.'

Freddie sighed and looked around at his sobbing workforce. He'd get no more work out of them for the next few hours.

'Go down to the canteen, ladies. I'll come with you and tell the staff you're having an earlier break today and taking a bit longer over it. If they won't let you have extra sugar for shock, ask for some connie-onnie instead. This isn't a time for scrimping on stuff. Off you go. I'll join you in a minute. You too, Marlene, love. I'll see to Alice along with Millie here.'

Millie turned her tear-filled eyes to Freddie. 'Is it…?'

He put his arm around her shoulders. 'You know I'm not allowed to say anything just yet.'

'But if it wasn't Josie you would tell us, Freddie, so you don't need to say anything. We just know,' Alice said, tears streaming down her face. 'It's so unfair. She was a lovely friend, always happy and smiling. Her mam will be heartbroken. She was her only daughter. She's already lost one of her sons.'

'Someone is on the way to speak to both families,' Freddie said. 'The other girl, for all her stupidity, is in a bad way.' As he spoke the clanging bell of the ambulance leaving the premises sounded outside. 'That'll be her on her way to the hospital. The others up there will be sent home today now – they're too upset to carry on and none of them will be able to concentrate and that's dangerous. Management will send for the bus to take them home. Do you two want to leave with them? With Alice's condition, I don't want to take any chances. Might be best if you have a rest and come in tomorrow.'

Millie nodded. 'I'll come home with you and stay at yours until your mam finishes work, Alice.'

'Okay.' Alice smiled weakly. 'Thank you. What a dreadful thing to happen though. One minute we're all cheering at our lovely plane taking off, and now this. Talk about the highs and lows of this blooming war. And we haven't even left Liverpool like our boys have done.'

❀

Alice's mam was bursting with the news of how upset everyone was by the dreadful accident that had killed young Josie Roberts. By the time Alice and Millie had arrived home the news had started to circulate. Josie's mam's best friend worked in the bakery and she had been told and had let the rest of the Lark Lane shops know what had happened. A collection to help her mam had been put in place at the post office and people were chipping in with bits of spare change.

'We're a close community, Josie was one of ours,' Edith said, wrapping her hands around the cup of tea that Millie had poured her. 'You don't expect it when your girl goes off to work, that you won't see her again. There's always a chance that your lad might not come back home, but not your daughter when she's only working a few miles up the road. It's shocking. Thank goodness you two are not on the munitions floor. I'd have had to put my foot down, Alice. Especially now.' She shook her head sadly. 'I dread to think what's going to become of us all.' She stopped as someone knocked loudly on the front door. 'Go and see who it is, Millie love.'

A white-faced Mrs Lomax came bustling into the sitting room with Millie on her heels.

'Oh, Alice. Thank goodness,' she gasped. 'I heard that a young girl had been killed up at Rootes. No one could tell me her name so I ran all the way here as fast as I could. Oh dear, I don't mean that to sound as though I don't care about the poor young lady, it's just that…' She sank down next to Alice on the threadbare sofa and gave her a hug. 'I couldn't bear it.'

'It's okay, we understand,' Alice said, hugging her mother-in-law back. 'Thank you for caring. It was our lovely friend, Josie. Millie will pour you a cup of tea while you get your breath back, Mrs Lomax.'

Mrs Lomax blinked back tears. 'Thank you, my dear. And I'm so sorry to hear it was one of your friends.'

She squeezed Alice's hand as Alice took a deep shuddering breath and smiled sadly.

Chapter Eight

March 1941

Josie's funeral took place at St Michael's Church on the third Saturday of March, after an inquest had recorded her death as accidental. Her body was laid to rest in the family grave in the church grounds. The second victim of the explosion, a girl called Avril, was still in hospital. According to those who'd been to visit her she'd never be right again. Half of her face was missing and she'd lost both hands, and as Elsie, who'd worked closely with the girls, had said, 'Her head's not right; she's gone all mental over blaming herself for killing Josie. She'll end up in Newsham Park, you mark my words.'

Elsie's comments had struck a chill through Alice, and although she still felt angry that Josie had lost her life needlessly, she also felt a degree of pity for Avril. The earring that had caused the explosion was from a pair she'd received for Christmas from her boyfriend fighting overseas, and she couldn't bear not to wear them. Alice knew how that felt as she hated not wearing Terry's locket while at work and she wasn't even handling explosives, but rules were rules and were in place for the sake of everyone's safety. But the thought of Avril spending the rest of her life in a mental hospital with no hands to do anything for herself didn't even bear thinking about.

A buffet was held in the church hall after the funeral, with everyone bringing something along to help Josie's bereaved mother. In spite of rationing and shortages, the community had pulled their weight and a good spread was laid out on trestle tables covered with white cloths.

Alice sat down next to Millie, whose eyes were red from crying.

'I can't stop thinking about how happy she was at Christmas when we all sang together,' Millie wailed. 'It's just not right. She was too young and such a nice girl.'

'She was,' Alice agreed. 'Well, we owe it to Josie now to win this bloody war, one way or another.'

Easter weekend in April brought nice weather and, on Good Friday afternoon, Alice and Millie took a stroll around the boating lake at Sefton Park.

'This is lovely,' Alice said. 'Just to be outside without a coat and scarf is a treat. Summer dresses, cardies, peep-toe shoes and gas mask boxes though, what a combination, eh?'

They sat down by the side of the lake and ate the little picnic that Millie's mam had packed up for them. Jam sarnies, an apple each and a flask of tea.

'That'll be you soon.' Millie nodded in the direction of a young woman pushing a pram and pointing at the ducks on the lake, much to her baby's delight.

Alice's eyes were drawn to the young man trailing behind her, who was struggling along on crutches and had a patch over his right eye.

'I hope not. I want my Terry home, but I'd like him in one piece. Bless that poor fella. Bet he's from the convalescent home where they've taken a lot of injured soldiers who've been brought back from Europe, and they've let him out for a bit of time with his wife.'

'My dad's playing in the band soon if we don't get any air raid warnings,' Millie said. 'We'll go and watch him when we've finished our dinner.'

'That'll be nice. There's a few people out with babies and toddlers,' Alice said, looking around. 'Wonder why they haven't had the little ones evacuated, or even gone away with them.'

'Well have you thought about what *you* will do?'

'I'm not sure yet. I can't go away anywhere because of Mam and I'm not letting a new baby go to strangers, so I suppose I'll have to manage here and pray it doesn't get any worse before it's over.'

Millie packed up the flask and paper bags from their picnic and helped Alice up from the grass. They strolled over to the Palm House to use the toilet facilities and then sat down by the bandstand to listen to the ARP brass band. Millie's dad was playing trumpet and he waved to the girls in between tunes and took off his uniform cap to mop his sweaty head with a hanky. The ice-cream seller had stopped nearby, ringing his tricycle bell to attract attention. Alice looked longingly in his direction.

'Shall we?' She nodded at Millie. 'A cornet with raspberry syrup?'

'You've read my mind.' Millie laughed. 'I'll get them; you stay there and rest your legs and your bump.'

Alice laughed and ran her hands over her little mound. 'I'm not that big yet, getting there though. I'm sure it's started wriggling about. Either that or it's wind!'

Millie grinned and hurried over to join the queue for the ice-cream seller.

By Alice's reckoning, from her wedding date, and not the calendar months the midwife she'd seen recently insisted on working from, she was eighteen weeks this weekend, so she was almost halfway there. An article in *Woman's Weekly* magazine stated that a baby begins to move between sixteen and twenty-five weeks and the movements are called quickening and feel similar to bubbles popping, or butterflies. That was exactly what she likened the feeling to. She felt a little thrill of excitement and couldn't wait to tell Terry when she next wrote to him. She and Mam had been invited to tea on Easter Sunday at Mrs Lomax's, so she'd be able to tell her mother-in-law the good news.

❀

Alice's head had barely hit the pillow on Saturday night when the air raid warning wailed. Mam was banging on her door in seconds and the pair pulled on dressing gowns and slippers, grabbed their gas masks and a blanket each off their beds and hurried down the back yard to the Anderson shelter that served them and next door. They were quickly joined by the neighbours, who were clutching their two large cats. Mam wasn't that keen on cats but she didn't mind these two, who were treated like babies by Bert and Bessie Bradley. The elderly couple had no family and the cats were their life. Blackie and Ginger settled down on a blanket Bessie laid on the floor for them and were soon purring contentedly.

'Wouldn't you think they'd have some respect when you consider it's Easter weekend?' Bert complained. 'Bloody Luftwaffe, I'm sick and tired of this. I had enough last time.' Bert had never recovered from the previous war, when he'd suffered a back injury. He had been unable to work since. 'I thought we were winning last year over that three-month stretch when we took control of the skies.'

Alice nodded. Bert was referring to the Battle of Britain and thought what most Liverpudlians thought.

'We need to get more planes built, Alice. You tell 'em, gel.'

Alice smiled wearily. That was what everyone said and she sometimes wondered if the whole of Aigburth thought that she and Millie alone were responsible for the Halifax productions.

'We're going as fast as we can, Bert. We have a night shift on the go as well as us girls in the day.'

'Aye, well, best they get a move on.' Bert shifted his large backside to make more space for Bessie. He laid his head on her shoulder and within seconds was snoring.

Bessie rolled her eyes. 'He makes more bloody noise than them German planes,' she said. 'What I'd give for a good night's sleep.'

As the minutes ticked by, the sound of muffled explosions and Bert's snoring was more than Alice could stand – and besides that, she needed a wee and couldn't hold it much longer. The last few weeks she felt she'd never been off the lavvy. She jumped to her feet.

'Mam, I've got to go indoors,' she whispered.

'Oh no, chuck, you can't do that,' Mam said.

'Well I'll have to,' Alice muttered, jiggling from foot to foot. 'I need the lavvy and I need it right now.' She shot out of the shelter, shutting the door behind her, and ran back into the house. She flew upstairs and just made it in time as the siren wailed the end of the air raid. 'Oh, thank God for that, on both counts.' She breathed a sigh of relief and made her way downstairs as her mam came in at the back door. 'That was well-timed.'

Mam smiled. 'It was. There's a right stink of burning out there wafting up from the Mersey. Some poor buggers have copped it tonight. God help them. It's a rabbit warren down there with all those tenements and rows of terraces. I just hope there are enough shelters for them all. Right, chuck, let's try and get some sleep. I want to be up for the morning service tomorrow. We need to support the church while we can. The more prayers the better at the moment.'

❈

Alice put her hand over her mouth to stifle a yawn. She could hardly keep her eyes open as Mam and Mrs Lomax talked about last night and the awful news that had filtered through of direct hits in the centre of the city. Some of her workmates lived in the worst-affected areas and she just hoped they were safe. No deaths had been reported, but sometimes people's injuries were so horrific that death might just be a blessing.

'Do you want the last sandwich, Alice?' Mrs Lomax said, offering the plate towards her. 'Might as well, dear, it looks lonely on its own and I think your mother and I have had more than enough.'

'You're very lucky that you managed to get some salmon,' Mam said. 'We've not had a tin for nearly twelve months. I really enjoyed that.'

'Well truth be told, I had the tin in the pantry and have been hanging on to it for a special occasion. I've also got some pears and a tin of evaporated milk for dessert. We may as well use them up, because I won't open them just for me. It's nice to enjoy a proper Sunday tea once in a while. Alice looks tired. Maybe an early night's in order. At least you've got tomorrow off. Let's just hope there are no air raids tonight. I'll go and get the pears and milk dished up while Alice finishes her sandwich and then, before you go, I have a little surprise for you.'

Alice wolfed down the last sandwich, the pears and milk and a small piece of angel cake. She sat back with a contented sigh.

'I'm stuffed, but I really enjoyed all that. Thank you.'

'You're welcome.' Mrs Lomax smiled. 'Now shall we take a peep at my surprise? If you'd both like to follow me.'

Alice looked at her mam, who raised her eyebrows, and they both followed Mrs Lomax down the hall. She stopped outside the bedroom that had been Terry's and flung open the door, ushering them inside. Under the window, protected by a white sheet, stood the grey pram from Lewis's; and standing next to it, a little white cradle mounted on curved wooden rockers.

'With all the bombing going on around the city, I was concerned about getting them delivered safely, so my neighbour George took me to the store on Thursday and we arranged delivery for yesterday morning,' Mrs Lomax explained. 'And while I was there I saw the little cradle. I thought it might come in handy, either for you at home, or for me here if you ever leave the baby with me while you go out or go back to work.'

Alice flung her arms around the woman she'd thought was a bit too snobby for her own good when Terry had first introduced them. But now she was beginning to appreciate what a kindly mother-in-law she had.

'Thank you so much. It's beautiful. And I agree that the pram is safer here than in the city at the moment. Are you sure it's not in your way?'

'Not at all. This is Terry's room, and he certainly won't need it for a while, if ever again. You'll be looking for your own place once he gets back. I just hope he'll be able to finish his training to become an engineer when the war is over.'

'I'm sure he will,' Mam chipped in. 'My Rodney was training to be an engine driver before he joined up. They'll pick up many skills while they're overseas, I shouldn't wonder.'

Alice chewed her lip. Staying alive and one step ahead of the enemy was the best skill those boys could learn right now. But she kept her mouth shut. Both mothers needed to think about a future in which their sons came back to a country with jobs waiting for them.

Chapter Nine

Following the accident at Rootes, Alice and Millie had postponed their planned trip to the pictures. But they knew that fun-loving Josie wouldn't have wanted them to mourn forever. She'd have been the first to declare that Hitler shouldn't stand in the way of them going out and enjoying themselves. They decided on an Easter Monday visit, which would round off the four-day holiday nicely. They made their way to the Mayfair picture house in Aigburth and stood outside looking up at the poster. Neither had any idea which film was currently showing and Millie squealed with delight when she saw that Cary Grant's film, *His Girl Friday*, was advertised.

'One of your heart-throbs,' Alice said, laughing. 'That's lucky. We could have been stuck with something dead boring.' She looked up at the façade of the lovely building, which was lit up by neon lights running up both sides and along the three large arched windows above the entrance foyer, illuminating the Mayfair's name. 'Doesn't it always look grand,' she said.

Millie nodded and linked her arm through Alice's as they queued for seats.

'Two nine-pennies in the stalls please,' Alice said, handing over a two-bob bit to the blonde girl in the kiosk. 'Do you want some sweets?' she asked Millie.

'We haven't a lot of choice, love,' the girl said. 'No chocolate at the moment, but we've got wine gums and bags of boiled sweets. The ladies will be round with ice-cream later.'

'Oh, wine gums,' Millie said, handing over a shilling. 'We'll share a bag. That okay with you, Alice?'

'Yes, I love 'em. Except the green ones,' she said as they walked towards the entrance doors. 'And I know you don't either, so they can go home to your dad.'

They laughed as the usherette showed them to their seats on the front row. Millie's dad always got the left-over green sweets of any variety. The organist was playing the Compton organ that had risen from the orchestra pit and the atmosphere was relaxing. Last night had been undisturbed and Alice had slept like a log. Mam had left her to have a lie-in this morning while she attempted a bit of housework. On the way back from Mrs Lomax's, Mam had confessed that she'd been mortified when she had turned up out of the blue the day of the factory explosion. After yesterday's visit for tea, she said she was going to get to grips with sorting out the house the best she could before the baby arrived. There wasn't much she could do about replacing the furniture, she'd said, but she could at least make a few new cushion covers and a rag rug for in front of the hearth. After all, they had enough old clothes she could cut up and use. By the time Alice got up for breakfast the steps and windowsill had been freshly donkey-stoned and the brass letterbox and knocker were gleaming. The downstairs windows were as sparkling as they could be with all the tape on them, and the patch of front garden, now cleared of weeds, revealed a few sprouting bulbs that had been hidden: late daffodils that would brighten the garden up a bit.

Another thing Alice had noticed was that since Mam had been told about the baby she hadn't complained of feeling off-colour as much and seemed to have a new spring in her step. Alice was also surprised, but happy, by how well Mam and her mother-in-law got along. It was a good thing for them all as she would need help from the pair when she had the baby and was ready to go back to work. And that was another thing on her mind. Would Rootes allow her to remain in their employ? They seemed to prefer women who didn't have the responsibility of children at home. Most of the mothers who worked there either had sons in the forces or younger children who were evacuated out of danger, and could work extra hours as and when they were needed.

There was a possibility she would have to look for another job. But there was ages to go before she needed to think about that anyway. She settled into her seat as the organist stopped playing and he and the Compton sank from view. The lights dimmed and the Pathé news came on.

It wasn't the best news and there was nothing much to cheer them up. Film clips of planes and the destruction in and around London and other cities, including their own; but then a clip of several Halifax bombers above the skies of Liverpool made them smile and Alice and Millie gave a little cheer.

The munitions team were a subdued bunch of workers since the accident and there was now a morning jewellery inspection for each girl. Not that anyone would dare since witnessing first-hand the serious consequences of flouting the rules. The Halifax girls were also checked and even the wearing of a wedding ring was now forbidden, just in case anyone had to go up to the munitions floor with a message. Alice kept her ring in her purse and stored it away in her handbag in the locker while she was working. She hated not wearing it; it hadn't left her hand since Terry had slipped it on, but there wasn't a choice, and after losing Josie, it was a small price to pay. Avril was still in hospital and likely to remain there for many months. Elsie visited her each Friday evening, but said there was little response from her and she just spent the hour chatting to Avril's mother to pass the time.

The team were turning out planes at a great speed and as fast as one was handed over to the RAF another was nearing completion, following a similar pattern in factories up and down the country. There was hardly a minute to breathe in each busy day, and apart from breaks and the regular air raid warnings, the time flew by. Alice's mam greeted her each night with a newspaper full of reports about how many tons of bombs had been dropped on the major cities. Places with ports seemed to be the worst hit and Liverpool's dockside was always under threat.

Terry's latest letter had worried Alice when he'd told her not to be too upset if she didn't hear from him for a while as letters were taking ages to get through and the replies home took even longer, waiting to be picked up from the camps for posting. All letters were vetted and no locations of platoons were to be given away in case they fell into enemy hands. Alice was aware of the slogan 'Loose Lips Sink Ships'. Terry reassured her that she was in his thoughts every waking minute and he couldn't wait to hold her in his arms again. She slept with the letter under her pillow at night to comfort her.

❀

The first week of May brought the worst attacks Liverpool had experienced and night after night the air raid sirens wailed almost continuously. Alice felt weary from spending more time in the shelters than out of them. Work was halted at Rootes on numerous occasions as the workforce downed tools and hurried into their shelters.

Mam arrived home from work following her afternoon shift, most of which had been spent sheltering with Teresa, the newsagent's wife, while her husband was out on ARP duties, and threw a copy of *The Times* on the table.

'Just read that. It's getting more ridiculous by the day. I don't know what's to become of us all. There were no copies of the *Echo* left today. They all went first thing. Everybody wants the latest to see exactly which areas of the city have suffered the most.'

The Times's front page carried the following report: 'The Germans stated that Saturday night's attack on Liverpool was one of the heaviest ever made by their air force on Britain. Several hundred bombers had been used, visibility was good and docks and industrial works, storehouses and business centres had been hit. In addition to many smaller fires, one conflagration, it was claimed, was greater than any hitherto observed during a night attack.'

'I don't know what they mean by that last bit,' Mam said, frowning. 'Them toffs in London don't speak proper English like what we do up here, but it sounds bad, doesn't it? They're right about Saturday night though, it was shocking. We must have been in that shelter for hours listening to them planes flying low overhead. We're lucky we've still got a house to call home. An ARP warden told us today that loads of streets down by the docks are flattened and many of the tenements as well. It's a damn good job all those kiddies are out of the way. There have been a lot of people killed but they don't seem able to put a number on it just yet. I suppose as they clear the rubble they'll find more bodies. It's terrible. The cathedral's been hit and a lot of the stained glass windows and parts of the roof are damaged. A big ship down the docks full of munitions and ready to go to the lads abroad got hit too and exploded all over the show. And it's a good job Terry's mam got the baby's pram when she did. That woman must have second sight. There's not much left of Lewis's, and Blacklers got hit as well. The buggers have nearly wiped Liverpool off the map. I hope they rot in hell.'

'What about the Three Graces?' Alice asked. 'I hope to God they are okay. Those lovely buildings are the first thing people see when the ships are approaching Liverpool. They're special to us all.'

'As far as I know they're safe. Teresa's hubby gives us all the news first-hand about what's gone on when he comes off his watch and he didn't say anything about the Graces.'

Alice shook her head. 'It's never-ending. I hope Mrs Lomax is okay. Have you seen her this week, Mam? I feel I should go round but I'm that tired when I get home from work, and this little devil wriggles all day and night and keeps me awake, never mind the air raids.' She patted her bump gently.

'She hasn't been in for her magazine this week yet, but I'm sure she'll be okay, chuck. I'd ask the paperboy to give her a knock but his mother sent him away to his auntie's in the country once the bombing got really bad and we've no one to replace him.'

Alice nodded. 'I'll pop over at the weekend if I can. Let's have something to eat now before the sirens go off again, as no doubt they will do. I'm going to make a flask of tea as well, just in case they do, so we've got something to drink at least.'

❦

One Saturday morning, at the end of May, a telegram was delivered with the news that no household wanted to hear. Alice's brother Rodney was missing in action. Alice held her mam while she sobbed against her shoulder.

'Mam, he might be okay. Missing isn't the same as, well, you know, is it? Maybe he's been taken prisoner, or he's in a hospital and they're not sure who he is, or something. You hear it all the time on the news and see it in the papers.' She waited for Mam's sobs to subside, tears rolling down her own cheeks. 'He'll come home one day, I'm sure he will.'

Mam looked up and shook her head. 'How can you be so positive?'

'Because we have no choice, Mam. We have to keep going, believing he's all right.'

'I want our Brian back.' Mam got to her feet. 'I can't bear this. I need him here with me.'

Alice shook her head. 'No, Mam, you can't do that. Leave him where we know he's safe. People are getting killed all the time here. Brian is being well looked after and he's away from the dangers he'd face in Liverpool. You wouldn't want him to get injured. You'd never forgive yourself. Why don't you go and see him? His evacuee family invited you to go at any time.'

Mam stared out of the window, her lips pursed in a straight line. 'I can't go away. I can't leave you in your condition. What if something happened? And what if they bring another telegram about Rodney?'

'I'll be all right, Mam. I daresay I can always go and stay with Terry's mam if I feel I need to. If you want to go and see Brian, I'll be fine. And if another telegram arrives I can phone the post office in the village where Brian's staying and get a message to you somehow. Please have a think about it. It will do you good to spend some time with him. I bet he's really missing you, even though he makes out he's okay. He's only a little boy and sometimes I bet he really needs his mam.'

Chapter Ten

August 1941

Alice's mam's eventual stay for a couple of weeks with Brian's evacuee family had extended to over two months due to Brian being taken ill with scarlet fever and anyone in contact with him being quarantined for several weeks. Alice had moved into Terry's old bedroom in her mother-in-law's bungalow. She was enjoying being looked after and looking forward to finishing work for a few months. She'd carried on for a few extra weeks but was ready to put her feet up now. All the stuff she needed for her baby was in place at the bungalow. Mrs Lomax and her neighbour had knitted enough little jackets to last a lifetime, along with booties and hats. Her family home had been locked up until her mam was allowed home. There'd been panic in Mam's voice when they'd spoken on a very crackly phone line about leaving her alone to cope, but Alice had assured her that she was just fine.

As she set out to meet Millie at the bus stop for her last day at work, she popped a letter in the post-box for her mam, along with a birthday card for her youngest brother. She'd put a ten-shilling note in with the card and told him to treat himself to anything he liked when he was well enough to go out again. He'd love that, spending his own money. It would go a long way, knowing how thrifty her little brother was when he had any pocket money.

Millie was already at the bus stop, sitting on a nearby garden wall, as Alice arrived.

'Was there any news on your Rodney yesterday?' she asked.

Alice had popped in to her home each day before walking back to Terry's mam's to check for post.

'Nothing. No news is good news on that score though. Haven't heard from Terry for over a week either.'

'I've had nothing from Jimmy lately. Think it's just hard for them to get anything out of Europe at the moment.'

Alice sighed. 'I'm terrified every time we listen to the news. Terry's mam insists we have it on every night after tea. The Germans have taken Soviet prisoners of war to a gas chamber in a place called Auschwitz and killed them all, according to last night's news, and they're said to be rounding up Jewish people too. What if they're holding our Rodney and other British soldiers? How would we know until it's too late? I don't think I can stand any more of this. So much for the war being over soon. It just gets worse with each passing day. At least my mam and our Brian are safe enough for now.'

Millie squeezed her arm. 'Here's the bus. Let's get your last day out of the way and hope we can get through it without too many incidents.'

When the first break bell rang, Alice put down her riveting gun on the bench and placed her hands each side of her aching back. She took a deep breath as her baby took a hefty kick at her ribs.

'Ouch! Little bugger,' she muttered, getting to her feet. 'I suppose you want your toast, do you?'

'Talking to yourself again, Alice,' Freddie teased. 'Have you got a minute? You go on down, Millie. Save Alice some toast.'

Millie smiled as Freddie gave her a wink that Alice missed.

Alice followed Freddie to the window. He pulled out a chair for her to sit on.

'I just wanted to let you know that if you plan on returning to work after you've had the nipper, we'd be more than happy to see you back here with us,' Freddie said. 'Now I know it won't be for a few months, but if it helps you out and you can get your own and Terry's mam to help with baby-minding then the job is still yours.'

'Oh, well that's good to know. Thank you. I'm sure they will pull their weight. We need my wages. Mam can still do her bit at the newsagent's when it's Mrs Lomax's turn to mind the baby. They can fight it out between them. I won't get a sniff in until Terry is home and we're back to normal, whatever that is these days. Thank you, Freddie. You've taken a weight off my mind.'

'Good. Let's hope you get some more news about Rodney soon, eh?' He gave Alice a hug. 'Let's go and get that tea and toast before they scoff the lot.'

As Alice and Freddie walked into the canteen a cheer went up and everyone began to clap. Alice looked around in amazement. The staff had decorated the place with balloons and bright-coloured crepe paper streamers. In the centre of the room a table was laid with a white cloth, and a stack of gaily wrapped parcels sat on it.

'For me?' Alice clapped a hand to her mouth. 'Oh my goodness, so that's why you kept me talking, Freddie.'

'Well you didn't think you'd get away without some sort of celebration, did you?' Freddie laughed and gave her a hug.

Millie came and took her hand and led her to the table, where a mug of tea waited along with a plate of toast.

'And look.' She pointed to a small jar. 'We've even managed to get a pot of WI jam for the occasion. Get stuck in and then you can open your pressies.'

※

By the end of the afternoon shift Alice was in agony. Her back was killing her and had been all afternoon. All she wanted to do was get home to Mrs Lomax's and lie in a hot bath, all regulation six inches of it. But it was better than nothing. Along with Millie she changed out of her work clothes and pulled on her skirt and smock-top. As she bent to slip on her shoes the wail of an air raid siren sounded.

'Oh for crying out loud,' Alice moaned. 'I don't bloody believe it.' She grabbed her cardigan, handbag, gas mask and Millie's arm and followed the other women out of the building. The bus was already waiting to take them home but Freddie ushered the driver into the shelter along with everyone else.

'Here, sit down,' Millie said, helping her onto a bench. 'Take the weight off your feet. You look weary.'

'I am.' Alice felt like crying. 'My back is aching so badly.' She stopped as a pain gripped her around the middle. 'Ouch.' She bent forward and groaned. 'Oh no, no, no!'

'What?' Millie asked. 'Oh God, Alice, not here.' She looked around, wild-eyed as Alice doubled over again. 'Help, someone. I think Alice's baby is coming.'

'Bloody hell!' Freddie exclaimed, running to their side. 'Now don't panic, it takes ages, Alice. The raid'll be over before you get started properly. Marlene, get yourself over here, gel.'

Marlene puffed her way across the shelter as all eyes turned to Alice. 'Right, Freddie, you take the men away over there an', girls,' she addressed their fellow workers, 'make yourselves into a wall to keep 'er private. Now, Alice, we've all 'ad babies other than you and Millie. First ones take ages so I'm sure you'll be tucked up safe in 'ospital by the time this little 'un shows its face, but let's get you comfortable for now.'

She pointed to the blankets on another bench. Millie spread them out and she and Marlene helped Alice to lie down, using another couple of folded blankets to support her head.

Alice let out another groan and gripped Millie by the hand. 'Oh God, it hurts.'

'Take a couple of deep breaths an' try and relax,' Marlene advised. 'Next time you get a pain, pant along with it like the midwives showed you at the clinic an' grip mine an' Millie's 'ands. That's it,' she encouraged. 'That's the way.'

Alice cried out as another pain racked her body. She turned fear-filled eyes towards Marlene.

'It's too early. I'm not due for another month according to the midwife.'

'What do they know,' Marlene scoffed. 'All them charts an' calendars they go off. This is an 'oneymoon baby so it'll come when it's ready, not when they say it should.' Marlene's brow furrowed as she did a quick count on her fingers and nodded. 'See, most of last December to now is eight months give or take a week or two. It's not far off full-term, Alice. It'll be fine, chuck, you mark my words. We could do with some 'ot water and clean towels though. I think we're going to need them,' she said as Alice cried out again. 'The contractions are coming in fast now. Fred,' she yelled over her shoulder. 'Any chance of nipping back inside to get some water an' towels, this little 'un will need them, an' a pair of scissors, just in case. I can't 'ear any planes or bombs going off just yet. If you was quick, like.'

'Leave it with me,' Freddie called back. 'Nobody else move,' he instructed and dashed away. He was back within minutes with a kettle that had boiled just as the warning went off and a handful of clean tea towels from the kitchen. He'd also grabbed a mixing bowl, and a pair of scissors that he'd shoved in his pocket.

Millie took them from him. 'Thanks Fred.'

'Do you think it's gonna happen soon?' he asked, a worried frown on his face.

Millie shrugged. 'I don't know. I thought these things took ages, but Marlene seems to know what she's doing.'

'Right,' he said, backing away. 'I'll leave it with you good ladies. Shout if you need anything,' he said as the drone of enemy aircraft sounded overhead.

'I think some prayers wouldn't go amiss,' Millie said as a loud explosion sounded nearby. 'I hope that's missed the factory building. All those explosives in there.'

Marlene poured the hot water into the mixing bowl and dropped the scissors in. 'That'll sterilise them a bit,' she muttered as Alice looked horrified. 'Don't worry, chuck, they're not for cutting you. They're to cut the cord if the baby arrives soon. Does anybody 'ave a ribbon, or anything really thin that I can use to be going on with?' she asked.

'I've got shoelaces,' one woman called. 'They're quite new so if you drop one in the water it will help sterilise it.'

'Perfect,' Marlene said as the woman handed over a brown shoelace. 'Right, let's get on with it then.'

She spread a couple of the tea towels under Alice. As Alice had lifted her bottom her waters had broken and gushed all over the blanket. Marlene had whipped it away along with Alice's wet knickers and made her comfortable.

'We're in business,' she said as Alice let out a yell and grabbed Millie's hand again. 'Just go with the flow, gel, an' tell me when you get a feeling like you need the lavvy, number twos, I mean. That feeling means the baby is getting ready to be pushed out. Do that panting thing in between your contractions. An' think on this, you'll 'ave something nice to tell your Terry in your next letter. 'Ave you thought of any names?'

Alice grimaced and shook her head. 'Not really, but I told Terry I like Catherine for a girl's name, Cathy for short, and maybe James after my late dad, Jimmy.'

'Oh, I love Cathy,' Millie said. 'It's such a pretty name. And Jimmy is Terry's best friend, so that would please him too.'

Alice looked up. 'Then Cathy it will be, and maybe Millicent and Marlene as extra names.'

'Oh, chuck.' Marlene's eyes filled. 'Thank you. I've never 'ad anyone named after me before. But you just watch; it's bound to be a James!'

She knelt between Alice's legs and encouraged her to bear down with each contraction and then pant in between.

With one final push, Catherine Millicent Marlene Lomax arrived just after eight o'clock, the same time as the end-of-air-raid warning siren sounded. As she took her first breath in Marlene's arms and let out a loud wail, a cheer went up and people started crying and hugging each other. Congratulations were called out to Alice, who was still surrounded by her wall of co-workers to protect her privacy.

Tears tumbled down Marlene's chubby cheeks as she wrapped the baby in a clean tea towel and laid her on Alice's chest. She deftly cut the cord and tied the end with the shoelace, breathing a sigh of relief. Millie stood by her side in stunned silence, her hands over her mouth.

Freddie shouted from the shelter doorway that he was going inside to call for an ambulance.

'As soon as they can, Fred. I'm trying to see to the afterbirth but we might need a bit of 'elp,' Marlene shouted, looking worriedly up at Millie. 'Take the baby while I get Alice propped up a bit more. One of you ladies can go out an' tell that bus driver not to go anywhere without me. Millie, you go with Alice and I'll nip in to your place on me way 'ome an' tell your mam so that she won't be worrying about where you are. I'll tell 'er to go round an' let Terry's mam know. They'll probably both make their way to the 'ospital.'

A clanging bell outside the shelter door heralded the arrival of an ambulance.

'Thank God for that,' Marlene said, wiping her sweaty brow. 'They can take over now. Well done, gel.' She gave a pale-faced Alice a peck on the cheek. 'We'll look after your presents, don't worry about anything. Just go an' finish the job in the 'ospital.'

Alice blew her a kiss as she and Cathy were lifted onto a stretcher. 'Thank you so much. I couldn't have done it without you.'

'My pleasure, chuck.'

Chapter Eleven

October 1941

Alice smiled proudly at her tiny daughter nestled in Millie's arms. Dressed in a white lace gown and pretty matching bonnet, Cathy had looked suitably unimpressed, frowning as the vicar sprinkled holy water on her forehead and made the sign of a cross before handing her back to her waiting godmother. Millie, Marlene and Freddie had done their god-daughter proud today. After Cathy's traumatic entrance into the world in the shelter at Rootes they'd all visited the hospital regularly to check up on the new arrival and her mother, who had been rushed to theatre on admission with a retained placenta that had required a surgical procedure.

Alice had no hesitation in asking them to be Cathy's godparents after all the support they'd given her, and Terry had agreed she'd made good choices in his reply to her wonderful news. Mrs Lomax had arranged the christening and invited everyone back to the bungalow for a celebration buffet afterwards. She'd produced a parcel she'd brought down from the loft when Alice arrived home with Cathy. Alice opened the tissue-wrapped gown and lacy cap and looked enquiringly at her mother-in-law.

'It was Terry's,' his mother said. 'I kept it, just in case. But you can have a new one if you like,' she continued as Alice's eyes filled with tears.

'Oh no, this will be just fine. It's beautiful and it will be lovely and very special for Cathy to be christened wearing her daddy's gown. Maybe we can get her a girlie bonnet to wear instead of the little cap.'

'We will indeed.' Granny Lomax looked adoringly at the dark-haired, blue-eyed baby she cradled in her arms. 'I think she's the most beautiful little girl I've ever seen.'

'Me too,' Alice said, smiling, 'but I think we might be biased.'

When Alice's mam had arrived back from Wales soon after Cathy's birth, she had a surprise in tow. Young Brian had insisted on coming back to Liverpool with her. He'd told them all that now he was nearly ten he should be home to look after them. His new niece needed her uncle, he said. Mam and Brian had moved back into the house and Alice had stayed on at Granny Lomax's, as Terry's mam insisted they all call her now.

Alice felt worried about Brian being brought back home to Liverpool, but was enjoying having her little brother dropping in each day. He'd grown, so wasn't so little any more. He was nut brown from the sunshine and fresh air and playing outdoors all summer and he'd gained a fair bit of weight, but that would drop off now he was back on Liverpool rations. Mam had got him a place in school again close by and he'd also been offered a short newspaper round as soon as Mam was back in work at the newsagent's. He loved it and enjoyed earning his own pocket money. He'd saved up from his wages and had bought Cathy a little pink rattle that she loved, and he spent ages singing nursery rhymes and talking to her. It made Alice's heart swell to see the way her daughter never took her eyes off Uncle Brian.

Mam had written to Rodney at his usual forces address to let him know he had a niece, but there had been no response. None had been expected, but she still insisted that it was only right and proper in case he'd been found alive and well and letters from home would be good for him. Alice had nodded and let her get on with it. If it made her mam feel better to think there was hope, then who was she to dash that hope away? After all, hope was the only thing they had to cling onto until they heard otherwise.

In spite of the regular air raids, the partly demolished state of the city and the tragic loss of so many lives, the people of Liverpool did their best to try to carry on with life. Nothing dented their renowned sense of humour. When Alice took a tram over to Speke with Cathy to pop into work to see her friends one dinnertime, Freddie rushed towards her and whisked his god-daughter away to the other side of the canteen, where she was fussed over and passed around like a parcel. When she was handed back she was dressed in a tiny blue overall like the Halifax girls wore, with a red spotted hanky fashioned into a turban on her head.

'Our latest recruit,' he said as Alice laughed at her daughter, who stuck her fingers into her mouth and chomped on them. Not in the least bit bothered by all the adulation she was receiving, Cathy wanted her feed and let out an impatient wail.

'Any idea when you'll be coming back to work?' Marlene asked as she stuck the feeding bottle into Cathy's searching mouth.

'Not until after Christmas,' Alice replied. 'I don't really want to leave her just yet. But I can't survive on peanuts so I'll get myself sorted out as soon as I can. She's still waking up in the night and I'm so tired during the day, I'd fall asleep on the bench.'

Alice sighed; she received the statutory army wife's payment of twenty-one shillings a week. Terry sent what he could when he could, but there was always the danger of paper money going missing in transit. If it hadn't been for Granny Lomax's generous hospitality, she and Cathy would have starved as they'd never be able to eat as well at her mam's with Brian there as well now. Granny Lomax excelled herself at providing hot meals for them all, and her mam and Brian came round for tea several nights a week. Granny's friend with the farm kept her well supplied with rabbits and vegetables and the occasional chicken; although he liked to keep them for egg-laying, he had promised her one for Christmas this year. In return for her feeding them like kings, Brian helped with a few jobs around the house and garden. One day he came running inside from the garage, excited because he'd found Terry's Harley-Davidson motorcycle stored under an old blanket.

'I can't wait for our Terry to get home,' he said. 'He can give me a ride on the back of his bike.'

Granny Lomax pulled a face. 'Dangerous, those things. I hated him going out on it. I'm glad Alice stopped him riding it.'

'Oh, I didn't really stop him,' Alice said. 'But I wouldn't get on it when we were going out, so we always used the tram or bus. But I know he rode it if I wasn't with him.'

'Yes, well.' Mrs Lomax pursed her lips. 'Let's hope he gets rid of it when he comes home. He's got responsibilities now.'

❁

As Christmas approached, Granny Lomax suggested they take a trip into the city one afternoon to see what was happening with the clearance of the lovely buildings that had been damaged and to do a bit of Christmas shopping. They dropped Cathy off at Alice's mam's and made their way to the station. The trains from Aigburth were still running regularly to Lime Street and as they came out onto the street Alice was pleased to see that the Adelphi in the distance had suffered nothing more than a few broken windows that were currently boarded up. It was a different matter with Lewis's store though, where only a few months ago they'd chosen Cathy's pram. It was practically demolished by the shelling and workmen were in the throes of pulling down dangerous parts and boarding up the rest. They called into the Kardomah café for a cup of tea before starting their shopping. A middle-aged couple were saying that the German air assaults were diminishing now that Hitler had lately turned his attention towards attacking the Soviet Union.

'I wouldn't trust him as far as I could throw him,' Granny Lomax said to the thick-set man on the table behind them, after listening to the man pontificating that he knew exactly what Hitler's tactics would be next. It was unusual to see a man out with his wife these days as most were away fighting or doing other war-related work. 'He's leading us into a false sense of security. He'll be back with a vengeance, you mark my words.'

'I think he's had enough,' the man said. 'He knows he can't beat us now. Anyway, what do you women know about these things? You should all bugger off back into the kitchen where you belong and leave this war to us men to sort out.'

Alice suppressed a giggle as Granny Lomax got to her feet, her face flushing an angry shade of red. She pointed a finger at the man and poked him in the chest.

'I'll tell you what we women know,' she began, drawing herself up to her full five-foot-four. 'If it wasn't for the women of this world we'd have lost everything. Women have kept this whole country going. My daughter-in-law here has been building the Halifax bombers that are fighting our battles. What job have you been doing while she's been hard at work in Rootes factory?'

'He hurt his back before the war started,' the man's wife said. 'Didn't you, Arthur? He can't lift anything so the forces wouldn't have him.'

'He could do ARP work, a lot of men do that who can't be signed up. Some were even injured in the last war but they're still doing their bit for King and country. My poor boy is on the front line, God knows where, helping to keep the likes of you alive. You should be ashamed of yourself.'

Alice chewed her lip. Her mother-in-law really had the bit between her teeth today.

The woman got to her feet. 'Well I hope your boy comes back safe and sound, Missus, but my Arthur here can't do nowt about it. It's not his fault. Come on you,' she said, yanking his sleeve as he slurped the last of his tea.

He followed his wife, putting on a limp as he passed Granny Lomax, who shouted after him.

'Bad back, huh! It's all my eye and Betty Martin. You're just lazy.'

As the shop door closed behind the couple, a ripple of applause sounded and smiles lit up faces.

'Well said, Missus.' A woman with a red headscarf nodded in Granny Lomax's direction. 'Armchair bleeding politician, he is. Nowt wrong with him that a rifle up the backside won't cure. Always been a lazy bugger, has Arthur Fairfax.'

'Yes, well.' Granny Lomax sat back down, her lips twitching. She started to laugh.

Alice joined in. 'What are you like?' She grinned. 'He could have floored you then.'

'I don't think he'd have dared, do you?'

'I suppose not. But still…'

'That was for Terry, and all the lads who are doing their best for us all.' She picked up her cup and took a sip of tea as Alice shook her head. 'Now if I could just get my hands on that bloody Hitler…'

Chapter Twelve

February 1942

Alice groaned and sat up, rubbing her eyes. Cathy was crying again. She glanced at the alarm clock on the bedside table. Three thirty, middle of the flipping night, well, Saturday morning. She crawled out of bed and went over to the cot in the corner of the room. Her daughter was rosy-cheeked and snot from her runny nose had been rubbed across her cheeks by her chubby fists. At nearly six months Cathy was cutting her back teeth, and didn't they all know about it. There'd been a few sleepless nights when her front teeth came through, but this latest lot had been going on for the past few weeks and showed no signs of finishing any time soon. Alice scooped Cathy up and sighed. She was wet through too and would no doubt assume it was breakfast time. But as her baby shot her a winning smile Alice's heart melted and she cuddled her close.

'Little monkey, aren't you?' She wiped Cathy's nose, changed her nappy and carried her into the sitting room. 'Now sit still for a minute,' she ordered, putting her down on the rug, 'and I'll warm you some milk.' She gave Cathy her pink rattle from Brian to play with and some coloured wooden building bricks.

In the kitchen Alice leant against the sink, yawning, while the milk heated in a small saucepan. This just wouldn't do. She was hoping to go back to work next week. Already she'd had more time off than she'd planned to. But Cathy's teething and the subsequent sleepless nights had put that plan on hold. There was no way Alice could concentrate on her job without a full night's sleep. And not only that; Millie had told her a few of the Halifax girls had recently been moved upstairs to munitions. She really didn't want to do that. She had her daughter to think about and with one parent already putting his life on the line daily, she couldn't run the risk of making her an orphan in the event of another explosion.

She poured the warmed milk into a bottle and took it through to Cathy. While she fed her baby, Alice went over the recent conversation she'd had with Millie.

'I'm thinking of leaving Rootes,' Millie had announced out of the blue.

'What? Why? Where will you go?'

'I thought about joining the Land Army. I'm sick of being stuck indoors and of being in the city. I fancy some country air and not spending as much time rammed together in flipping air raid shelters with flatulent old men and moaning women.'

'Erm, well I get the old men thing, but I think most of their wives have got cause to moan at the moment, Millie.' Alice stared at her friend, whose look of determination shocked her. 'And you hate cows; they always used to scare you as a kid. What if you're asked to milk them?'

The idea of neat and tidy Millie grappling in the mud with a cow was beyond anything she could imagine. She'd always thought that Millie would finish the war out at Rootes and then start a proper hairdressing course at a smart city centre salon when it was all over.

'If you leave Rootes, I don't fancy going back.'

'Come with me, Alice. Join the Land Army. It'll be fun.'

'For one thing I can't leave Cathy. And it's not really my idea of fun.'

'Terry's mam would look after Cathy, surely.'

'Not on a full-time basis with me miles away, and unable to come home at night. I just can't do it.'

'Well I'm going to apply,' Millie said. 'I just want to do something different. I feel a bit down at the moment. There's hardly ever a word from Alan and even when there is it's almost like he finds it's a chore to write to me.'

Alice nodded. 'I understand and I don't blame you on that score, but have you talked it over with your mam and dad?'

'Not yet. I will do this weekend, though.'

'I might have come with you if I didn't have the baby. I'm going to have to look for a job if you go away. I'm not going back to Rootes without you there.'

'Tell you what we need to cheer us up,' Millie said. 'A good night out. There's a dance on at Aigburth Legion on Saturday night. We should go. A few of the girls from work are going and it's to raise money for wounded soldiers. There's a buffet and a raffle and they've got a band on that plays Glenn Miller stuff.'

'How much is it?' Alice chewed her lip. She was a bit skint as usual but really fancied a nice night out. She hadn't had one in ages.

'Let me treat you,' Millie said generously. 'An early birthday pressie.'

'Okay.' Alice nodded. 'It's not my birthday for ages yet, but you're on, thank you. I'll look forward to being human again for a while and wearing clothes that are not covered in baby puke and dribble.'

As she leant Cathy forward to wind her, Alice couldn't wait for tonight to come round. With a bit of luck she might get forty winks when Cathy took her afternoon nap and before she got ready to go out. Granny Lomax had told her it would do her good to get out with young people and that she'd be more than happy to look after Cathy, who'd be in bed anyway. The Legion, on Ullet Road, was only a short distance, so they could easily walk it. Millie would knock on for her at seven.

Alice checked her appearance in the full-length mirror in Granny Lomax's bedroom. She smoothed down the skirt of her blue floral button-through dress and slipped on the smart jacket that was half of the suit she'd worn on her wedding day. The blue was a perfect match for the flowers in the dress as well as her eyes. Granny Lomax had made her go and see Millie's mam this morning to get her hair washed and trimmed and it looked so much fresher than when she'd got up in the middle of the night. Millie's mam had worked her usual magic and the gentle waves fanned her cheeks, while the back swung gently. With a dusting of face powder, a touch of rouge and a slick of Tangee lipstick, Alice felt almost human again for the first time in weeks. She crept into the bedroom she shared with Cathy and collected her handbag. Cathy was asleep, flat on her back with her arms flung either side of her head. She'd kicked off the sheet and blankets and Alice pulled them back again, holding her breath as her daughter mumbled and quietly cried out. She settled again and Alice left the room, not even daring to stroke her sweaty little head, closing the door behind her. She went to join her mother-in-law, who was knitting a pink cardigan for Cathy and listening to the evening news on the wireless.

'You look lovely, Alice. Did you manage to pair up some stockings from the few we have left between us?'

'I did.' Alice held out a slender leg for inspection. 'And thank you for baby-sitting. She's flat out so hopefully she won't be any bother.'

'My pleasure. I love looking after her, you know that. You can go out any time you like. A break will do you good.'

The sound of the gate opening had Alice rushing to the door before Millie rattled the letterbox.

'Were you nosying out the window?' Millie asked as Alice flung open the door.

'We heard the gate squeaking. Just don't want Madam to wake up before I get out. Come on in for a minute.'

'Evening, Mrs Lomax,' Millie greeted her, following Alice into the sitting room. 'Oh, that's a pretty shade of pink.'

'Thank you, dear, and good evening to you too.' She held up her knitting for Millie's inspection. 'It's a little cardigan for Cathy, for springtime. I shall make her a nice bonnet to go with it.'

'Lovely.' Millie smiled politely and looked at Alice. 'Are we ready for off then?'

'We are. We'll be back around eleven thirty, I would think,' Alice said. 'Is that okay?'

'Might be a bit too early for the dance to finish,' Granny Lomax said. 'Just come home when you're ready. I'll be in bed anyway, as long as Madam stays asleep, so creep in quietly. Now off you go and enjoy yourselves.'

Alice bagged a table in the Legion and Millie sidled self-consciously over to the bar. Neither was used to getting their own drinks, but times were changing and the place was filling up with women who would all soon be queuing for their drinks too. So far there was just one man in the place and he was busy at the other end of the room, moving tables around to suit a party that wanted to sit together. Alice noticed that he had a limp and she wondered if he was one of the soldiers the dance was being held for. He turned and caught her staring at him. He winked, blue eyes twinkling, and raised his hand as she blushed furiously and pushed her gloves into her coat pocket. Cheeky devil; she was a married woman. But then again, he wouldn't know that, she told herself. He grinned, ran his hands through his dark hair and carried on moving furniture as she took another quick peep from under her fringe.

Millie arrived back with two tall schooners of sherry and put them on the table. She took off her coat, draped it over the back of a chair and sat down.

'Cheers.' She picked up her drink and held it out towards Alice, who did likewise, and they clinked glasses. 'You look a bit flushed, what's up?'

Alice nodded her head in the direction of the man who'd winked. 'Him over there. He waved, and winked at me.'

'Probably just being friendly,' Millie said, watching the man limp across to a group of soldiers who were just coming into the room; some of them were on crutches and others in wheelchairs with bandages covering various body parts, including heads and hands. 'Oh, it's Jack Dawson, he's a local lad. Alan knows him. He's a soldier, or he *was*. He got injured before his platoon even left the country. He was accidentally shot in the foot on a training exercise. I see he's still limping quite badly. It's okay to be friendly with other men, Alice, especially in circumstances like now. Some of those poor boys will be miles away from home and may need a friendly face to chat to.'

Alice nodded as she and Millie were joined by several girls from their team at Rootes. Another schooner of sherry and they were all up on the dance floor, taking turns to be the male or female lead. A couple of the young soldiers, arms in slings, joined them and did the best they could to partner first one girl and then another, but the majority, in wheelchairs or on crutches, cheered on their comrades who'd ventured up to dance.

'They're a good band,' Millie puffed, stopping to take a breath from attempting a jitterbug with a smiling young man who had one arm in a sling.

'Very good,' Alice said, laughing at Millie's red face. 'I'm sitting down for a minute. I'm out of breath.'

She made her way back to her seat, fanning her warm face with her hand.

'You okay?' the man called Jack Dawson asked as he collected empty glasses from the table.

'Oh, yes, I'm fine, thank you. Just a bit tired. I've got a teething baby at home who doesn't seem to know day from night at the moment.'

He laughed. 'Rather you than me. You married then?'

'Yes. I'm married to Terry Lomax. He's a soldier stationed abroad, unfortunately.'

'Think I know him. Mate of a mate of mine. Alan. In fact, that's Alan's girl on the floor with one of our lads. Maureen, Molly?'

'Millie. Yes, she's Alan's girlfriend,' Alice replied, thinking, *Not that you'd know it.*

'How is Al? Not heard from him for ages.'

'Fine, as far as we know.'

'And your Terry? Is he okay? He used to have a motorbike if I remember rightly. A Harley-Davidson.'

'He's as okay as he can be, under the circumstances. He still has the bike; it's in his mother's garage.'

'Remember me to him next time you write. Dawson's the name, Jack. I lost half my right foot before we even got sent abroad, so I'm out of it for now. I do my bit, helping with the lads at the nursing home to keep their spirits up and giving a hand to the manager here at the Legion. Keeps me out of mischief.'

Alice nodded and smiled politely as he made his way back to the bar with the empty glasses. She'd noticed a long scar on Jack's right cheek and wondered if that was something to do with him being injured as well, but hadn't liked to ask.

Millie flopped down beside her. 'Phew. He might have his arm in a sling but Charlie can certainly move.'

'I noticed.' Alice laughed. 'Seems a nice lad.'

'He is. Got a girl at home in Wales though. And he's going back there as soon as his arm and shoulder are recovered.'

'Well you've got Alan and Jimmy in tow! That Jack fella just asked after Alan. Seems he knows Terry too.'

'Ah, well there you go. He's harmless enough, I think.'

'How did he get that scar on his face?'

Millie frowned. 'I seem to remember there was a fight among a few of Alan's mates a year or so ago, before the war started anyway.

Jack was trying to get off with one of the lads' girls and he got his face slashed. Why they can't just fight with fists is beyond me. It was wrong of him to flirt with the girl, but *she* was leading him on, and he's the one who ends up with the injury.'

'Bit of a ladies' man then, is he?'

Millie laughed. 'So they say. I don't really know that much about him, to be honest, but he seems nice enough.'

They were joined by the other girls and pooled together what bit of money they had for another round of drinks.

Millie and one of the others went across to the bar and the tray of drinks was carried over to the table by Jack, who winked at Alice as he placed the tray down.

'Couldn't trust these two not to spill the lot,' he teased. 'Bit too tiddly for their own good, if you ask me. I'll be doing the raffle draw in a few minutes. Hope you've all got your tickets, ladies.'

Alice rooted in her bag for the raffle tickets she'd bought at the door as they came in. She watched as Jack went up on stage and called out the winning numbers as they were picked from a wooden drum that he turned with a handle. To her delight, one of her numbers came out and she was presented with a box of scented bath cubes and a handshake from Jack, and cheers from the girls at her table.

As she walked back from the stage she spotted a postcard pinned to one of the pillars that supported the bar. The Legion was advertising for bar staff and occasional help with functions, including wedding buffets and christening teas. Interested parties were to enquire with the steward for further details. Alice chewed her lip. If Millie left Rootes she didn't want to return, but she needed to work. The Legion was so handy in that it was less than five minutes' walk away, and most of the work would be in the evenings when Cathy was sleeping, or in the afternoons at weekends for weddings and christenings. The shifts certainly wouldn't be anywhere near as long as those at Rootes. It was worth thinking about, at least. She'd have a chat with Millie on the way home, see what she thought. Maybe she could do part-time at Rootes and the Legion job as well. The money would come in handy and she could get some savings in the bank for when Terry arrived home, ready for their own little place.

Chapter Thirteen

April 1942

Alice held back tears as she joined Millie's parents on the platform at Aigburth station. It was the Saturday morning following Easter and Millie was off to a farm in Cumbria in the Lake District. It was a long journey and her mam had done her a pack-up and a flask to take with her. Two other young girls who Alice knew vaguely were also going to the same farm, so Millie wouldn't be entirely alone with strangers. She was going to miss her terribly; they'd been best friends since primary school. Damn this bloody war, robbing her of most of the people she loved.

'Write to me as soon as you get there,' Alice begged. 'And if it's really horrible, you must come home. Be careful around the cows.'

Millie smiled. 'I'll be fine. I'll miss you and my little god-daughter.' She kissed a wriggling Cathy in Alice's arms and gave them a group hug.

'Please look after yourself.' Alice choked on her words.

'Come on, gel, you'd best get on,' Millie's dad said, picking up her suitcase from the platform and placing it in the nearest doorway on the train. 'Give your mam a hug now. Write as soon as you can.'

'Don't forget to forward any letters from Jimmy or Alan to that address I've given you,' Millie said, giving her mam a big hug.

'I promise. Now come on, that guard's looking a bit anxious. You're last to get on. He'll be waving his flag and you'll miss it.'

Millie jumped on board, retrieving her case and waving frantically as the guard blew his whistle and waved his flag and the train puffed out of the station. Alice burst into tears. Millie's mam took Cathy from her and carried her out to the waiting car. Millie's dad took Alice's arm and they walked slowly out onto the station approach.

'We'll all miss her, chuck. But she'll be back before you know it,' he said, patting Alice's hand. 'There was no talking her out of it, but I can't see her lasting five minutes in all that muck and mud, and we all know how much she hates cows; she's not that keen on sheep or horses either. Don't know what she was thinking of. Our Millie was never one for getting her hands dirty. She was told they've got evacuees at the farm, so maybe she'll take a turn at looking after them. We'll see. Come on now; let's get you and that little 'un back to your ma-in-law's.'

Alice pushed the pram with her sleeping daughter round to her mam's house. After parking Cathy in the small front garden she let herself in and called out that it was only her. No reply. She frowned. Mam was usually in on a Saturday afternoon and there was no sign of Brian either. She went through to the back sitting room. The place was clean and tidy, in spite of her brother's shoes and school satchel on the floor and a pile of comics and exercise books on the table. Damn, she needed to check with Mam which mornings she could have Cathy next week as she was starting back on the early shift at Rootes. She made a mug of tea and carried it through to sit on the sofa.

She didn't have too long to wait as Mam arrived home a few minutes later armed with a string bag of potatoes, a swede, carrots and a single onion. She carried another bag from which wool poked out of the top, black and navy wool – for soldiers' socks, no doubt.

Alice poured her mam a cuppa and Mam produced a packet of Arrowroot biscuits from the depths of the wool bag.

'Are you okay, Mam?'

'Not bad, love. Just been to pick up my supplies from the church hall for sock-making. One of the ladies had the bright idea of unpicking old jumpers and winding the wool into hanks around the back of a dining chair. Then she washes them and lets them drip on the line. Goes nice and straight then so we can roll it into balls. Finish your tea and I'll use your hands, then I can make a start on a pair of socks tonight. Our Brian always seems to get the wool in a tangle when I ask him to help.'

Alice swigged the rest of her tea and held her arms out. Mam looped a hank of wool around each hand and proceeded to make a ball.

'Might as well as get as much as we can done before Cathy wakes up for a feed.'

'Where *is* our Brian?' Alice asked, flexing her fingers as Mam wound the wool.

'He's at the church hall. I left him there and he'll come home with his mate Alfie who's coming for his tea. That's what the veg is for, a pan of blind scouse for them. They've started a bit of a lads' club. Brian wants to learn to box. I've given him your dad's old gloves. I've had them lying around doing nothing all this time, so he might as well get some use from them. They're a bit big but the trainer said once his hands are bandaged they'll fit better. They'll have to do for now, because I can't afford to buy any new ones. It'll give him something to do and it's a bit of exercise too. He's lost some of the weight he gained in Wales, but he's still a bit too chubby for my liking.'

Alice smiled. 'It's only puppy fat, he'll lose it eventually. Anyway, Mam, are you okay to have Cathy on Monday for me going back to work?'

'Yes, of course. I can do Wednesday as well but I'm working the rest of the week.'

'That's fine, Mam. Terry's mam will do any days you can't do. I'll be here about half seven with her though. I know it's ridiculously early, but eight till one is the only shift they could give me.'

'And are you going to still do the Legion shifts at the weekend? It'll be a lot for you love, you'll be shattered.'

Alice nodded. She'd taken the bull by the horns and had approached the steward of the Legion the day after the soldiers' dance and asked about the job vacancy. He'd taken her on immediately and she'd done two weekends now and was working tonight. So far there had been no weddings or christenings but she had made it clear that she was available to work the extra time if any bookings came in.

She'd enjoyed herself, and Jack Dawson had seemed pleased to see her. He'd taken her under his wing, and had shown her how to pull a pint in the correct way to avoid a large head, and how to do an accurate measure of spirits. He'd also walked her to the gate of the bungalow on Linnet Lane when their shifts had finished. She'd been secretly dreading walking home alone in the blackout, although it was only a very short walk, as there was not a chink of light to be seen anywhere, so she felt safer with Jack limping along beside her. Less likelihood of a lurking German spy waiting to jump out at her if she was accompanied. Although she hadn't actually heard of that happening to anyone yet, there was always a first time. Alice knew she had an overactive imagination but, then again, enemy planes had been shot down in the area. For all they knew, Germans could have parachuted to safety and be hiding anywhere. Jack had lodgings in a house on Parkfield Road, nor far from Lark Lane, so it was on his way home.

'I'm keeping the bar job on, Mam. It's better for me to do two jobs like this and then I get to spend the afternoons and weekday evenings with Cathy. Sunday isn't a late night so I'm okay for getting up early on Monday. I need the money to save up. I'd like to find a little house or flat and have it all ready for when Terry comes home. Living with his mam is lovely, just the two of us and Cathy, but it'll be too crowded with Terry there as well. We'll have no privacy.' She blushed as she realised what she was implying.

But her mam seemed to understand and smiled as she finished winding the hank of wool and freed Alice's hands.

Alice got to her feet. 'I'd better get back and then I can see to Cathy's tea and bath and get ready for tonight's shift. I'll see you on Monday morning. Say hello to our Brian and tell him I'm sorry I missed him.'

She gave her mam a hug and set off back to Linnet Lane with a still-slumbering Cathy. As she rounded the corner someone called her name and she whipped around, frowning. Millie was running behind her, dragging a case and waving frantically.

Alice stared open-mouthed as her friend dropped the case on the pavement.

'I couldn't do it, Alice,' she gasped, red-faced and out of breath. 'I got off the train at the next station, which was miles away, and made my way back here. I don't even know what I was thinking of, for goodness sake. The Land Army! Me and cows, I mean. Who was I kidding?'

Alice flung her arms around Millie and gave her a hug. 'Thank goodness for that. I didn't think you'd last long, I have to admit, but I thought it'd be longer than this.'

They both laughed hysterically, close to tears with relief and happiness. 'Let's go to Granny's and have a brew,' Alice suggested. 'She made a nice cake earlier. Come on, you daft thing. Then you can go home and shock your mam and dad, although I bet *they* won't be that surprised either.'

❀

Alice brushed a speck of fluff from her new black skirt and tucked her white blouse into the waistband. She felt quite smart in her waitressing uniform, C&A's best, and although she didn't have a single unladdered stocking left she'd compromised like so many other women had to and managed to draw a fine line up the backs of her legs with an eyebrow pencil. Satisfied that they looked equal and like seamed stockings, as she twisted this way and that in front of the mirror, Alice picked up her jacket and handbag from the bed. Cathy was sound asleep, thank God. She closed the door quietly behind her and went into the sitting room to say goodnight to her mother-in-law.

'See you later,' she said. 'She's flat out.'

Granny Lomax looked up from her *Woman's Weekly* magazine and smiled. 'I'll no doubt be in bed when you get back, so I"ll see you in the morning. Be careful walking home in the dark.'

'I will.' Alice hurried out into the hall before her flushed cheeks aroused any suspicions. She hadn't told her mother-in-law that she was escorted home to the gate by Terry's pal. Not that there was anything wrong in a colleague seeing another home safely, but she just had a feeling it would be frowned upon. In fact, she hadn't said anything to anyone. She didn't know why. It just didn't seem right. Jack was nothing if not a gentleman, but something made her keep it to herself. She'd written to Terry only this week, telling him about her new job and that she was going back to Rootes part-time soon, but she didn't tell him that his old friend also worked at the Legion. Next time she would, just in case anyone saw her walking down the road with Jack and told her mother-in-law.

The Legion was filling up as Alice took her place behind the bar. She looped her hair back behind her ears and smiled at the girl waiting to be served.

'Two large gin and oranges, chuck,' the girl said, flashing a gap-toothed smile at Alice.

'Small is all you can have, I'm afraid, Maisie,' Jack said, coming up behind Alice. 'We're nearly out of gin and we've not much sherry left either. Not had a delivery this week. That budget last week was a killer. Putting the taxes up on our fags and booze, the only pleasures some of us men have left.'

'Oh, poor Jack,' Maisie teased. 'But tell me about it. Woodbines are up to nine-pence for ten. And income tax is now ten bob in the pound. Hardly worth working. Still, I suppose somebody has to pay for this bloody war. But it's always the ones with the least who have to suffer.' She handed Alice half a crown and waited for her change. 'Are we having a sing-song tonight? Will old Frankie be playing the piano?'

'He is. About nine,' Jack replied. 'And we've got a game of lotto coming up just before that.'

'Look forward to it, but we call it bingo now, Jack.' She winked at him and clip-clopped away on her regulation two-inch high heels, wiggling her backside in a skirt that skimmed her shapely hips.

Alice observed Jack staring longingly after Maisie. She shook her head as she began to wash the glasses that he'd collected earlier; it seemed Millie was right, she thought, Jack was a ladies' man all right. She sighed and wished her Terry was here, looking at her with that same longing in his eyes that made her stomach flip. She missed him so much. Her thoughts turned back to their lovely wedding day. It seemed so long ago now. She longed to feel his arms around her, holding her tight, and to taste his kisses once more.

Alice dried the glasses and had no time to wallow further in her memories as the club filled and Jack left the bar to call the bingo numbers, with Maisie's delighted pal winning a five-bob full-house prize.

At the end of the evening, as everyone joined in with 'White Cliffs of Dover', and Alice was tidying away the last of the glasses collected by Jack and wondering how Millie had got on once she arrived back at her own house, the wailing of the air raid siren rent the air. She shook her head, wiped her hands and hung up the tea towel. Just as she was wondering whether she'd have time to run home and make sure Granny Lomax and Cathy were safely in a shelter, Jack grabbed her elbow and thrust her handbag and jacket at her.

'Out the back, now,' he ordered and ushered the customers along with her. Maisie and her pal had old Frankie by the arms and helped him inside the Anderson shelter in the grounds at the back of the club. Jack joined them after switching off all the lights, plunging everywhere into darkness.

'You okay?' he said to Alice, who blew out her cheeks and nodded. The smell of the mix of alcohol, cigarette smoke and cheap perfume in a confined space was so overpowering, it made her eyes water.

'Yes, apart from being dead on my legs. Those bloody Germans don't half pick their moments.'

'Never mind, gel,' Maisie shouted across from the bench where she was sandwiched in between old Frankie and her friend. 'Worse things happen at sea.'

And they did. Alice thought about all the little evacuee children who had died after the SS *City of Benares* was torpedoed in 1940 on its way to Canada from Liverpool, causing Winston Churchill to cancel the Children's Overseas Reception Board plan to relocate British children abroad. Thank God her mam had put her foot down about Brian going with them. As dangerous a place as Liverpool was for her precious little brother, and though she half-wished he'd stayed in Wales, at least they still had him.

By the time the all-clear sounded, Alice was almost asleep. She prayed that Cathy wouldn't still be awake when she got home, but no doubt she would be after being woken up by the racket of the sirens. She got up to leave the shelter as Jack pulled on her arm to slow her down. He limped along beside her, said goodnight to their customers and checked to make sure all the club doors were locked.

'Ready?' he said to Alice.

'Er, yes, but just leave me at the corner,' she said. 'My mother-in-law will be up no doubt and she might be a bit funny if I'm seen walking home with a strange man. Oh, I'm sorry, that sounds awful.' She blushed and chewed her lip.

Jack laughed. 'Don't worry. I won't get you into bother from Terry's mam. Come on. It's been a long night.'

Chapter Fourteen

On Monday morning Alice gave Mam feeding and changing instructions with regards to looking after Cathy, and dashed off to catch the works' bus, leaving her daughter waving her little arms after her at the gate in her mam's arms.

Her eyes filled as she hurried around the corner and she blinked her tears away. Leaving Cathy for almost six hours was a wrench. She was looking forward to catching up with Marlene and her other workmates again, but she'd give her right arm to be able to stay at home and be a full-time mum to her baby. But the need to earn enough money to help her mam out with Brian and get her and Terry a place of their own was driving her on. It was for all of them and was something she had to do. Everyone had to make sacrifices these days. At least her child was still here with family, unlike thousands of others. But going to Rootes today without Millie felt strange. Hopefully she would be able to get her old job back when she applied again.

The bus trundled into view and she climbed on board.

Marlene shouted out to her. 'Alice! I've saved you a seat. Good to 'ave you back, gel.'

Alice sat down and gave Marlene a hug. 'Nice to be back. How's things at the factory?'

'As 'ectic as always,' Marlene said, rolling her eyes. ''Ey up, 'ere's Freddie,' she added as they pulled up further along Aigburth Road and their foreman jumped on, waving to them as he stayed up front to stand beside the driver and chat to him. 'They've taken some of our girls off wings an' put them upstairs on munitions. We've a lot of new ones joined us since you finished. We'll miss Millie though.'

'Ah well,' Alice said, smiling. 'She, er, she hasn't gone away. Well she did, on Saturday morning, but she came back in the afternoon. She decided the Land Army wasn't really for her.'

Marlene burst out laughing. 'What's she like? I knew she wouldn't stick it out for long, but 'alf a day, she's a one is our Millie. Oh well, let's hope she comes back then. And 'ow's your Terry doing, chuck?'

'I wish I knew.' Alice sighed. It was over three weeks since Terry's last letter. She'd sent him two photos of Cathy and one of her and Cathy sitting on the back lawn at the bungalow. She hoped he'd got them. 'Letters are taking ages to come through.'

'I know. It's the same for me. Not 'eard from my Stan for over two weeks now. Any news on your brother that went missing?'

'Sadly, not a word, but my younger brother is still home with Mam. He won't go back to Wales, even though we've told him it's safer if he does.'

Marlene nodded. 'I expect your mam is out of 'er mind with worry about Rodney an' glad to have the young one back.'

Alice shrugged. 'She doesn't say much, other than "No news is good news."'

'Best she keeps on thinking that way then. Oh, 'ere we go; time for a sing-song,' Marlene finished as the driver started to whistle 'I've Got a Gal in Kalamazoo', with everyone joining in.

Alice smiled and felt her spirits lift. She had a lot to be thankful for. A nice roof over her head, two kind grannies to care for Cathy, a husband who loved her, a couple of jobs, and she would soon have a bit more money coming in to save for their future. And her best friend was back where she belonged. She was one of the lucky ones.

❁

Freddie welcomed Alice back with a hug and handed over her new overalls and a turban. She got changed, and put her clothes and handbag in the locker. Freddie led her over to sit beside Marlene. He handed her a riveting gun and she got to work right away, feeling like she'd never been away, the pop, pop, pop of the guns the only noise on the floor as each girl concentrated on her job. By the time the first break bell rang out, Alice's right wrist was killing her. She flexed her fingers and grimaced.

Marlene smiled and scratched her greasy brown hair under the front of her turban.

'It'll take a while to build up your strength again, chuck. Let's go get a cuppa an' 'ave a rest. You can meet the new shell ladies. They're all curious to meet the gel who gave birth in the shelter. You're famous.' She laughed.

'Oh God!' Alice grinned. 'That was a day and a half, wasn't it?'

'I'll say, an' not one to be repeated again in an 'urry.'

As Marlene and Alice carried their tea and toast to a table near the window a voice called out Alice's name, screeched it, in fact. She whipped around, frowning.

Maisie, the girl who'd been in the Legion on Saturday night, came hurrying over, the tell-tale yellow from cordite coating the hair that had fallen out of the front of her turban.

'Alice, I didn't realise you were the Alice that was coming back to work today. They all talk about you up there.' She raised her eyes to the ceiling, indicating the floor above.

Alice laughed. 'Nice to see you again, Maisie, I had no idea you worked here now.'

'For my sins.' Maisie grinned. 'I'd rather be back in Lewis's, but there's no store left to work in right now until they rebuild it. Hey, can I ask you summat? That fella you work with at the Legion, Jack, is he okay? He's asked me to go to the pictures with him tomorrow night. They're showing *Babes On Broadway* with Judy Garland and Mickey Rooney at the Mayfair.'

'Grab your brew an' come and sit with us, Maisie,' Marlene suggested. 'I didn't know you worked at the Legion, Alice,' she continued as Maisie went to grab her mug of tea from a nearby table and joined them.

'Er, yes, just Saturday and Sunday nights while Terry's mam looks after Cathy. I started the other week. I needed to earn a bit of money.'

'An' will you give it up now you're back with us?'

'No, I can fit both jobs in as long as the mams can help me. Might as well work while I'm able. Doing two part-time jobs fits in better for me and Cathy.'

'Don't blame you, chuck.'

Alice turned to Maisie. 'I don't really know Jack that well, but he seems nice enough. I'm sure you'll be okay with him.'

Maisie nodded. 'Ah right. I thought you knew him well with him walking you home after work, like. Why does he limp? I didn't like to ask him. Was he injured?'

'He was a soldier and got accidentally shot on a training exercise,' Alice replied. Marlene's eyebrows had shot up her forehead at the mention of Jack walking her home. Damn it. 'He lost half his foot so the army let him go. He helps out with the injured soldiers at the nursing home and does a few nights at the Legion.'

Maisie smiled as Marlene frowned. 'What's this Jack fella's surname?'

'Dawson,' Alice replied as Marlene pursed her lips and nodded slowly. 'Why, do you know him?'

Marlene frowned again. 'If it's the same one, I know of 'im. There can't be that many Jacks in Aigburth who blew 'alf their foot off. This Jack used to go out with a friend of a friend. She broke it off when 'e started knocking 'er about after he'd been drinking. You just be careful, both of you – he's a boozer, a one for the ladies an' a bit too handy with 'is fists. They say 'e shot 'imself on purpose to get out of going abroad.'

'But why would he do that?' Alice asked. 'He limps really badly. He might not even have got injured if he'd gone abroad. He always seems very nice to me. Not nasty or anything. He doesn't drink much either when he's at work, just the odd pint. Mind you, there's not much *to* drink at the moment. The steward said they'd have to close this weekend if they don't get a delivery mid-week. I'm sure you'll be fine with him, Maisie. And I'd rather be safe with Jack walking home with me on the way to his own place than get accosted by a German.'

Marlene slurped her tea and rolled her eyes. 'Well, forewarned is forearmed. Don't say I didn't warn you. It might just be rumours, but they 'ave to start somewhere.'

Alice caught a tram home after her shift was over. The works' bus only ran in the morning and evening, and again for the night shift. She stared out of the window, glad to see signs of spring in the air. A blue sky and green leaves bursting through on the trees made her feel good. It was still a bit nippy but getting warmer by the day. If it didn't rain she might take Cathy a walk around Sefton Park later.

The pram was on the front garden and her daughter fast asleep as Alice let herself into her mam's house.

'Only me, Mam,' she called out. The back door stood open and she could hear Mam talking to Bessie next door. Alice popped her head out. Both were pegging washing on the line and gossiping at the same time over the wall between the gardens. Bessie's cats, Blackie and Ginger, were stretched out on top of the wall, enjoying the rays of the sun.

'Oh, Alice love,' Mam said, looking puzzled. 'I wasn't expecting you home until teatime. How did it go?'

Alice frowned. 'I was only working until one, Mam, I told you this morning. But it was fine thanks. Feel a bit tired now, but at least I've got a few hours to spend with Cathy before bedtime.'

Mam nodded, but still looked puzzled. 'Oh well, not to worry. That's me getting mixed up. I thought you were working a full day. I bet you're hungry. There's some soup in that pan on the stove. It's not much, just pea soup left over from last night's tea. Put a light under it and I'll butter you a slice of bread.'

As the soup heated and filled the kitchen with a tasty aroma, Alice realised just how hungry she was. All she'd had today was porridge first thing and a slice of toast at ten on her break. She wolfed down the soup and wiped around the bowl with the bread Mam gave her.

'I was ready for that,' she said, sitting back with a contented sigh. 'Thanks, Mam.'

'You're welcome, chuck.' Mam took the empty bowl to the kitchen and brought in a pot of tea and two slices of yellow cake. 'Not very appetising-looking, is it? But one of the ladies at the sock-knitting club devised the recipe from rations so it's better than nothing. If you eat it while it's still warm with a bit of stewed apple and custard it makes a nice enough pudding too. I gave Cathy some mashed potato for her dinner, with a bit of the soup mixed in it to make it mushy. She seemed to enjoy it. The bowl was empty anyway! And she's had a bottle of National Dried milk, so that's why she's flat out. Full tummy. She's been as good as gold, sat on the rug and played with her bricks for a bit before we went down to the shops, then I fed and changed her and I was going to take her out for another walk. But you can do that now.'

'You've done well, Mam, thanks so much. Hopefully she'll sleep for a bit longer now while I get the washing out of the way at Granny's place.'

'Bet she's done it for you.'

'Probably, knowing her.' Alice laughed and got to her feet. 'She spoils us. Right, I'll get off. Thanks again, Mam. See you soon.'

Alice walked home to Linnet Lane pushing the pram, deep in thought. Her mam's forgetfulness seemed to be getting worse. Maybe it was just her age and it happened to most people as they got older; although Granny Lomax, who was a similar age to Mam, didn't seem to forget anything. She was always on the ball.

She wasn't at home when Alice arrived back, and the baby was still sleeping, so Alice parked the pram on the back lawn and went indoors. Two lines of washing were blowing in the slight breeze; a job less to do. There was a letter from Terry on the dining table and Alice hurried to the sofa and sat down to read it. Her hands shook as she ripped open the envelope. She devoured his words and then went back to the beginning to read them again at a more leisurely pace. He loved the photos she'd sent and thought Cathy was the most beautiful baby in the world. He told her little of his whereabouts other than that he was doing his best to keep safe along with Jimmy. He congratulated her on getting her little job at the Legion and told her to make sure she kept a lookout over her shoulder on the short walk home in the dark. He said it worried him, but he knew she was a sensible girl and would hurry along and not dawdle.

She got a pad and pen from the bureau and started to write back to him immediately. She gave him all the latest news about herself and Cathy and his mam, the air raids and the struggles to get stuff at the shops. She told him about Millie's brief adventure with the Land Army. She assured him that she was perfectly safe on her walk home from the Legion and that the barman who accompanied her to the corner of the lane, to make sure she got back safely, was an acquaintance of his who was no longer a soldier due to his injuries. She gave him Jack's name; after all, she had nothing to hide and would rather hear from Terry that Jack was a bad lot than from Marlene, who had always been prone to exaggeration. If Terry said to keep away from him then she would. But for now Jack was keeping her safe and they should all be thankful for that.

She finished her letter and pushed Cathy, who had now woken up, along to Lark Lane to catch the last post and then headed over to Millie's mam's house to see what her friend's plans were for the future.

❀

Millie was sweeping hair into a dustpan as Alice popped her head into the front room salon.

'Alice, come on in,' she said. 'I've almost finished here. Mam said I could take the rest of the afternoon off as we're shutting up shop early while she takes a break.'

'Oh well in that case, do you fancy a stroll around Sefton Park with me and little Madam? It's quite a pleasant afternoon.'

'I'd love to. I was going to pop round to Terry's mam's to see if you were back from work. I'll just let Mam know I'm going out.'

As they strolled through the park and sat down on a seat near the boating lake, Alice said, 'Have you decided what you are going to do yet?'

Millie shrugged. 'I'll help Mam for a few weeks as she's not feeling too good with her bad chest, but I'll go to Rootes and speak to Freddie when she's feeling more up to managing on her own. See if I can get my old job back.'

'I'm sure he'll welcome you back with open arms.'

Millie smiled. 'One day, Alice, when this is all over and we're doing something we really want to do, hairdressing in a posh salon in the city for me, nursing for you, we'll look back on this time and wonder how we got through it all.'

Alice laughed. 'I think I can kiss goodbye to my nursing dreams. I'm sure Terry will want more children, and *you* might be married by then too.'

Millie laughed and rolled her eyes. 'And pigs might fly,' she said wistfully.

Chapter Fifteen

August 1942

Two weeks before Cathy's first birthday the news the family had been dreading was delivered by telegram. Alice arrived back from work following a phone call from Mr Floyd at the Lark Lane Post Office, requesting that she be allowed to leave for home immediately.

Freddie had put her in a taxi, his face grave. 'Take your time, gel. Your mam will need you right now.'

Everyone knew Alice's older brother was missing in action and a phone call to work usually only meant bad news.

Mam was huddled in a corner of the sofa clutching the telegram. She was rocking back and forth and crying, loud wailing sobs that struck Alice through the heart. Her eyes went to the framed photograph on the mantelpiece of her tall, good-looking brother, smart in his army uniform. To think she'd never see him again, never have him ribbing her and pulling her leg, was just unbelievable. Deep down she'd known, but had blocked the possibility, because while there was no news, there was always the chance he'd be found alive and well.

The newsagent's wife, Teresa Thomas, greeted Alice from the kitchen and brought a tray of tea things through.

'Do you think we should get Brian home from school, Alice love? I thought I'd better wait for you to arrive before I did anything.'

Alice poured a cup of tea and put two spoons of sugar in it. She sat beside her mam.

'Here, Mam,' she coaxed, 'drink a bit of this. It's got extra sugar in it. Come on. It will do you good.'

She held it to her mam's lips as she took a couple of sips.

'He's not coming home,' Mam wailed, pushing Alice's arm away. 'My Rodney, he's not coming home.'

Alice chewed her lip. All she wanted to do was curl up in a ball and howl, but she had to stay strong for Mam and Brian. She was all they had.

'I think we'll leave it until Brian's home at four,' she whispered to Teresa, holding her mam close. 'Let Mam have a bit of time to get her head around the news. I don't want to leave her to go up to the school.'

Teresa nodded. 'I understand, chuck. It's terrible; we were doing a window display when your next-door neighbour came to the shop to tell us the telegram boy was at the house. So we hurried back here. I don't know what to say to Edith. I really don't.'

Alice shrugged. 'I don't think there's anything anyone can say that will make it any easier. I don't even know what to do now. I expect Rodney's regiment will be in touch with us soon.'

'Perhaps the vicar could come and offer a few words of comfort to your mam. She may appreciate something like that; a little prayer or two.'

'That's a lovely idea.'

'Shall I pop up to the vicarage on my way home?'

'Oh please, if you would. Could you also do me a big favour and let Terry's mam know? She's got the baby today and she'll be expecting me back within the hour. Just tell her I'll be home later, after our Brian is in from school.'

'I will, chuck. I'll leave you both in peace for now, and I'll pop back tonight.'

❀

Alice helped her mam up to bed and tucked her in. Sleep was the best thing for her. She couldn't stop shaking and said she felt cold.

'You try and shut your eyes for a while before our Brian gets home.'

Mam clutched Alice's hand. 'I think I knew, you know. I think I always knew. I couldn't admit it to myself, but I knew deep down we'd never see him again.'

Alice swallowed the huge lump that threatened to choke her. She squeezed Mam's hand and went to draw the curtains across.

'Will *you* tell Brian, chuck? I don't think I can do it.'

Alice nodded. 'I'm going back downstairs now, Mam, to tidy up. Shout me if you need anything.'

Downstairs Alice stared at the telegram; just a few short, clipped lines that had tipped their world upside down. She wondered how many similar telegrams had been delivered to families like theirs today. She dreaded the thought that one day something similar might be delivered to Granny Lomax's house. There were no guarantees.

She felt like a zombie as she washed that morning's breakfast dishes and tidied the kitchen and sitting room. Jobs Mam usually did when she finished work at dinnertime. She'd just sat down to while away the hour until Brian arrived home when the door-knocker rattled lightly. She ran to open it. Granny Lomax had parked the pram on the scrap of lawn and she came inside carrying a basket covered with a tea towel.

'She's just shut her eyes,' she announced as Alice stepped back to let her in. 'Now I know you won't have given any thought to tonight's meal, so I've brought a rabbit pie and rice pudding. I'll put them in the oven to keep hot and I'll peel the spuds and carrots here. Brian will still need feeding even if you and your mother don't want any.' She put the basket down on the table and took Alice into her arms. 'I'm so sorry, my love. I really am. How *is* your mother?'

'She's lying down,' Alice said. 'I just feel numb. There was always hope, until now.' The tears she'd tried to hold onto tumbled down her cheeks, soaking Granny Lomax's shoulder.

'Is Brian not here?'

'Not yet. I didn't want to leave Mam on her own.' Alice sobbed.

'I understand. But I think you should meet him from school and take him somewhere quiet to tell him, before someone else does. You know how quickly news spreads around here. If you hurry now they'll let him out before finishing time and then he doesn't have to face all those questions his pals will throw at him. I'll sit here and listen out for your mam and Cathy.'

Alice wiped her eyes. 'Thank you. I'll go right away. And thank you so much for the food.'

She wasn't hungry at all right now, but she knew her brother would be.

❦

Alice took Brian to St Michael's churchyard and led him to their father's grave. The headmaster had given his permission for Brian to leave with her as soon as she'd explained why she was there, telling her to keep him at home for the rest of the week.

There was a bench close by and they sat side by side. She held his hand as he looked at her from underneath his dark fringe. He was so much a younger version of Rodney and their dad that it quite took her breath away. He spoke first.

'What's up, our Alice? Why have you been crying? Is me mam all right? Why have you come to get me early? Where's our Cathy?' His questions tumbled over each other and Alice saw the fear of the unknown in his blue eyes.

'Mam and Cathy are at home with Granny Lomax,' she began. She took his sweaty hand in hers. 'I'm crying because I'm feeling very sad. We've had some bad news, Brian. Now you have to be a brave boy for Mam. She's going to need lots of love and looking after.'

She swallowed hard and continued. 'We had another telegram today from the army. I'm afraid Rodney won't be coming home when the war finishes. He died somewhere out in France. It's taken them a long time to be sure it was him. That's why they told us he was missing at first.'

Brian's eyes brimmed with tears, but he swiped them away with the back of his hand. He nodded. 'Don't you worry; I'm the man of the house now. I'll look after me mam and you and our Cathy. I'll get a proper job as soon as I can leave school. Where *is* me mam?'

'She's at home with Granny Lomax, like I told you. Come on, let's set off and see how she's doing.'

Alice took his arm as they walked slowly back to Lucerne Street. Her poor little brother. What a mucked-up last few years he'd had. Losing his dad so young, being shipped off to Wales, and now dealing with the loss of his big brother. She made a decision to move back in with Mam and Brian right away. They needed her. She had a feeling this shock was going to set her mam right back to how she had been after Dad had passed away. The next few months were going to be a struggle, of that she was certain.

There would be no funeral in Liverpool for Rodney as his body would be buried in France, but the vicar held a service for him and two other soldiers from the parish who had also died abroad while on duty. Alice held Mam up in the pew and supported her while the congregation stood to sing a hymn. She felt worried to death about Mam's wellbeing. She'd retreated into herself, spending the last few days up in her bedroom, crying and not eating. Last night

Alice had practically forced her to take a bath and wash her hair in readiness to get her to church this morning.

'Come on, Mam, we can't let him down,' Alice cajoled. 'Think how it would look if you didn't put in an appearance, and the mothers of the other young men do. It's the last thing we can do for him. We have to be there, united as a family.'

Alice had taken the week off work to get as organised as she could. Brian had been very quiet all week, just helping when she'd asked him to, running errands for her. Granny Lomax had looked after Cathy each afternoon and had brought them ready-prepared meals round. Alice had been touched and grateful at how kind their neighbours had been this last week. There wasn't a day went by that one or another didn't knock on the door with a little gift of food to help them out.

Considering times were hard and money and goods in short supply, the community pulled together as it always did. Maisie had called round with Jack Dawson in tow and had handed over an envelope containing a few pounds that they'd collected from the Legion customers. Jack gave her a bouquet of summer flowers and said, 'For you and your mam from us all at the Legion.' Alice had been overwhelmed and Jack had given her an awkward hug. He and Maisie had taken their leave with the words, 'Let us know if there's anything we can do.' Marlene and Freddie had called in too and again a collection had been made at Rootes and given to Alice with their condolences.

Alice didn't know how she was going to manage to go back to work. She needed to as there was no money coming in and she didn't want to spend any of the collection money. What she planned to do with that was have Rodney's name put on Dad's headstone at the grave. His body would never be buried in Liverpool, but his name would live on alongside their dad's. Mam was in no fit state to look after Cathy or even to be left alone at the moment. Granny Lomax had made a suggestion yesterday that Alice said she'd talk to Mam about.

'When you go back to work and bring Cathy round to me in the morning, bring your mother as well, dear. She can keep me company and I can keep my eye on her. We'll be able to go for walks to Sefton Park or catch the tram for a bit of a ride out. See what she thinks of the idea.'

Alice thought it sounded ideal. But she hadn't broached the plan with Mam yet. She'd need to pick her moment.

Over breakfast the next morning, Alice told Mam of Granny Lomax's suggestion.

'It'll be good for you both and Cathy will have her grannies under one roof to play with her. What do you think, Mam? I really do have to go back to work, we need the money.'

'Oh I don't know, chuck. It will mean getting up really early to be ready and I'm not at my best first thing, as you know.'

'Well, think about it. Maybe you could see our Brian off to school, walk with him halfway and then go on to Linnet Lane. I'll take Cathy first thing, then you can join them.'

'I'll see.'

Alice shrugged and finished her toast. Cathy's first birthday had gone by in a blur and although Granny Lomax had thrown a little party for her, it had only been attended by Alice and Brian and Millie. On her birthday itself Cathy had delighted them all by walking across the bungalow's sitting room before flopping down on the rug, giggling. There'd been no stopping her since and now she was into everything. All the ornaments had been moved to higher shelves and the cloth on the dining table was tucked under at the edges so that she couldn't pull on it and cause the pots to fall off. She was a work and a half, and two grannies to keep up with her antics was a good idea.

Alice was halfway through her morning chores when the doorknocker rattled.

'Mam, can you see who it is?' Alice popped her head around the sitting room door. Her mam was staring into space on the sofa, appearing not to have heard, so Alice hurried to answer, wiping her hands down the front of Mam's old cross-over pinny that she'd slipped on over her summer dress, before opening the door a fraction and peering out. She breathed a sigh of relief that it wasn't the telegram boy, her one dread, and smiled as the woman on the path turned around.

'Millie! What are you doing here?' Alice flung her arms around her friend and nearly knocked her flying. She hadn't seen Millie since Rodney's service as she hadn't had a minute to herself and her friend was still helping out at her mam's salon.

'I've got a day off,' Millie said. 'I broke a tooth and have been in agony so Mam made me go to the dentist to get it sorted. I thought you might need some help here.'

'Come on in. Mam,' she yelled, 'look who's here.' She grabbed Millie by the arm and propelled her down the narrow hall into the sitting room.

Mam looked up briefly and smiled. 'Nice to see you, Millie.'

'You too, Mrs Turner. I hope things are getting a bit easier.' Mam nodded and went back to staring into space.

'Come through to the kitchen and I'll put the kettle on,' Alice said. She shook her head as Millie followed her.

'She's not right again, is she?' Millie whispered. 'The light's gone out of her eyes.'

'That's one way of putting it.' Alice filled the kettle. 'Think I need to make her see the doctor. I've been concerned about her for a while, even before Rodney. She's been forgetful for a good few months, you know, muddled up with things. It takes me all my time at the moment to get her up and dressed, never mind anything else; and she's eating just enough to keep a mouse alive. Thank God our Brian's home, at least he keeps talking to her, even though half the time she doesn't even seem to know he's there.'

Millie shook her head. 'It must be so hard for her.' She glanced around the room. 'Where's my little god-daughter then?'

'Granny Lomax has got her. She takes her out to give me a chance to get on with things here.' Alice brewed a pot of tea, took a cup through to her mam and invited Millie to sit in the garden on a bench that her dad had made years ago. 'Might as well enjoy the sun while we can.'

'Now my mam's feeling a bit better I'm going to pop into Rootes soon to see if Freddie will give me a job again,' Millie said.

'I'm sure he will. I'm in next Monday again, so why don't you go down and see Freddie and we might be able to start back on the same day.'

'I'll do it tomorrow,' Millie said. 'And I'll call in on the way home; let you know what they say.'

Chapter Sixteen

True to her word, Millie arrived next morning and reached the door at the same time as the postman. He had a letter for Brian from his evacuee family. Alice thanked him as she let Millie in. Cathy was playing on the rug with her bricks and Mam was still in bed; there was no rousing her, although Alice had tried three times.

'Nothing from Terry?' Millie asked, slipping her lightweight jacket off and hanging it over the back of a chair. 'Oh, just look at her.'

She knelt beside Cathy and tickled her under the chin. Cathy stared, and then smiled and held her arms out to Millie.

'Oh, she's a little love,' Millie said, scooping Cathy up for a cuddle.

'She's a monkey.' Alice laughed. 'And since she started walking you need eyes in your backside once she's off. My letters from Terry go to his mam's,' she added, placing Brian's letter next to the clock on the mantelpiece. 'I've been expecting one soon as I wrote to tell him about Rodney and I sent another a few days before that. It just takes forever.' Alice went to put a light under the kettle and then stood waiting in the doorway for it to boil. 'What about you, what's happening with Alan?'

Millie shrugged and chewed her lip. 'I don't know. I have a gut feeling he's going to tell me it's over soon. His letters are so infrequent and so vague, like he's playing for time. I'm still writing to Terry's friend Jimmy and we seem to be getting quite friendly. He says he can't wait to come home to see me again.'

Alice gave Millie a hug; she didn't quite know what to say. 'Alan needs a kick up the backside. Jimmy seems to be a very nice man.'

'I think so. Where's your mam?' Millie looked around.

'She won't get up. I took her some tea and toast up earlier, but she's not even touched it. I'll do a fresh brew in a minute. Anyway, did you go to Rootes?'

'Yes, and I'm back in full-time on Monday. On riveting the wing frames again with you. Thank God, I was praying like mad that they wouldn't say I had to do munitions. The thought terrifies me.'

'Yeah, and me too after what happened to Josie. It breaks my heart thinking about her and how she should still be with us and enjoying her life,' Alice said. 'But it's great that you're joining us again. I'll have to meet you at the bus stop as I take Cathy to Terry's mam's first thing. And of course I finish at one. But at least we get to spend some time together. I'm so happy that you're back, I really am.'

'Let *me* take your mam's cuppa up,' Millie said. 'She might rouse for me, a different face and all that.'

She put Cathy back down on the rug and Alice gave her half a Farley's Rusk to chew on while she brewed up. Millie took a cup and saucer up and came back down with the one from earlier and a slice of uneaten toast.

'Still no response?' Alice asked, shaking her head worriedly.

'Nothing, but she's breathing. She's probably just exhausted with grief. It does funny things to you. I'd get the doctor in. I think she may need help.'

Alice sighed. 'Terry's mam will be here soon for Madam and then I think I'll nip to the surgery and see if he'll come out to her. She's eaten nothing for days and hardly touched a drink.'

'I'll stay here while you go,' Millie offered. 'Just in case she wakes up for the lavvy or something. We don't want her falling downstairs because she's so weak.'

'Thanks Millie. What would I do without you?'

❁

Doctor Marshall beckoned Alice to follow him downstairs after examining Mam. She hadn't even acknowledged him, just continued to lie on her side with her eyes tight shut.

'Alice, I'm going to send for an ambulance. Your mother is very dehydrated so we need to get her on a drip, and she needs feeding up as she's eaten hardly a thing since your brother's death was confirmed. We can't let this go on or she'll start to have problems with her kidneys and other organs. She's very depressed and I honestly think she's in the middle of a complete nervous breakdown. Hospital is the best place for her right now and maybe a nursing home for a few weeks when she shows signs of recovering. Her mental state will be assessed properly. This isn't something we can do at home; she needs specialist care. I know you've done your best to look after her, but it's time to let us take over.'

He patted Alice on the shoulder. 'Pack a bag for her and I'll go back to the surgery and make the arrangements to have her admitted right away. The ambulance will be with you shortly.'

Alice saw Doctor Marshall to the door and thanked him. She went back into the sitting room, where Millie stood by the fireplace chewing her lip. She gave Alice a hug.

'God, Alice, I'm so sorry. Thank goodness you went to fetch him. She'll be in the right place to get the help she needs now. I'll come and baby-sit Cathy while you and Brian go and visit her any time you want. I'm here to help you as much as I can.'

White-faced, Alice nodded. 'She's much worse than when Dad died. I need to go back to work. I've got Cathy and our Brian to support now, so like you say, she'll be better in hospital than on her own here.'

'I'll clear up in the kitchen while you go and get her a bag packed and I'll wait here with you until the ambulance comes. Shall I go and let Mrs Lomax know? And would you like me to meet Brian from school and take him to my mam's for some tea? You may be ages waiting until she's admitted and you've seen she's settled and everything.'

Alice flung her arms around Millie and burst into tears. 'Thank you so much. I really need your support right now.'

'I'm always here for you, Alice, just like you are for me.'

'Tell Mrs Lomax I'll be back for Cathy as soon as I can. And will you keep our Brian with you until I get home? Make sure he does his homework if he has any.'

Alice made her way to pick up Brian from Millie's house after making sure her mam was settled in. She'd left her sleeping comfortably with a drip in her arm to stop any further dehydration. The ward sister had reassured Alice that great care would be taken of her and she would be assessed by the doctor tomorrow morning. Alice had told the sister about her mam's forgetfulness, which seemed to have been getting worse even before Rodney's death.

She'd felt a bit easier in her mind as she'd got on the bus outside the hospital gates. Though how she was going to manage to work and look after Cathy and Brian, as well as visit Mam regularly, she didn't know. It would all need careful thinking about. Perhaps she should give up her Legion job, but then if she did that there would only just be enough money coming in to survive and she'd have nothing left over to save. For a few brief moments she almost wished she'd said no to Terry when he'd asked her to marry him. They should have waited, just got engaged maybe, which they would have done by now without this flipping war making people rush into things just in case. Then she wouldn't have had Cathy and would be able to work full-time at Rootes. She immediately felt guilty for having such thoughts. Her baby meant the world to her, and so did Terry. She'd manage. She had no choice.

Brian was sitting in the back room at Millie's with his school books spread out on the table.

'How's Mam?' he asked as Alice came into the room. 'She's not gonna die, is she, Alice?'

Alice put her arms around him and gave him a hug. 'No, love. She just needs a little time being looked after properly. She has to learn to eat again and look after herself. It was the shock of losing Rodney that made her go a bit unbalanced. But the hospital will help her to get right. Best pack your books away in your satchel and then we can go and pick up Cathy from Granny Lomax's house. Hope you've been a good boy for Millie and her mam.'

'He's been as good as gold,' Millie's mam said, coming into the room. 'Polished his tea off in a flash and had seconds.'

'We had sausage and mash with loads of gravy.' Brian rolled his eyes in ecstasy.

Alice laughed. Nothing dented her brother's appetite, not even the wartime sausages with hardly any meat.

'Thank you so much for looking after him. I really appreciate it.'

'Any time,' Millie said. 'We've done his spellings for the test tomorrow; I think he's got a twenty out of twenty there, all his own work as well. He knows his ten, eleven and twelve times tables off to a T. And we've done the page of fractions the teacher set him. Wouldn't surprise me if he passes his eleven plus next year.'

Brian beamed at the praise. He put on his jacket and school cap and picked up his satchel and gas mask box.

'Come on then, our Alice,' he said, marching to the door. 'Thank you for having me,' he said to Millie and her mam.

'I'll see you in the morning, Alice,' Millie said, seeing them to the door. 'I'll come round when I'm up and ready.'

❦

Alice sighed with relief when she saw that Granny Lomax had a stack of sandwiches and slices of cake waiting on plates on the table. She could eat a scabby horse between two bread vans, as her dad used to say.

'You must be starving, love. Bet you missed out at dinnertime as well. Has Brian had his tea? Get those down you and I'll make a brew,' Granny said as Brian nodded his head. 'Cathy's bathed and fed and I've tucked her in the little cot in Terry's room. I know she's getting a bit too big for it now, but she was falling asleep as she finished her bottle. How did it go at the hospital? What did they say?'

Alice told her what the doctor at home, and then the hospital, had said.

'Oh dear, you are having a time of it, aren't you,' Granny said. 'She could be away for some time. I've been thinking. We need to make life as easy as we can for us all over the next few weeks. I know this is a bungalow and there's only two bedrooms, but there is a loft room that you get up to by a big ladder that pulls down. Terry used to play with his clockwork trains up there when he was a little lad. My husband boarded the floor so you can walk around and there's a little window that overlooks the back garden so it can be aired. We could make it into a temporary bedroom for Brian. I've a camp bed we can put up and a little cupboard he can put his things in. Then you and Cathy can have Terry's room again. My neighbour can go and pick up her big cot from your mam's and then we can lock your house up safely until she's ready to come home and take charge again. It's quicker for Brian to walk to school from here and between us we can look after Cathy while you do both your jobs. What do you think?'

Cathy smiled as Brian's face lit up. He knew the food would be good, at least.

'Is Terry's train set still up there?' he asked, a hopeful expression on his face.

'It is, and there's a station and lots of tracks and engines. You could set it all out at one end and sleep at the other.'

Alice felt the weight of the world lift from her shoulders. She could pay for their keep and also save a bit if she wasn't running the house solely on her wages.

She smiled. 'Yes please. We would all love that, wouldn't we, Brian?'

'We would,' Brian agreed. 'Thank you, Granny. And Cathy loves me, so we'll be a dead good baby-sitting team, you and me.'

'We will indeed,' Granny said. 'It will be my pleasure. Now, as Cathy is settled, why don't you stay tonight? Brian can have a sleeping bag on the sofa and Terry's bed is made up as always. Finish your tea and then you can nip home, Alice, and get a change of clothes for you both and make sure all is locked up. And don't forget to draw the curtains before you turn the lights on while you get your stuff together, and then turn the gas, electric and water off at the main, as well, to be on the safe side.'

As Alice dashed up Linnet Lane and turned the corner towards Lark Lane she bumped into a man hurrying in the opposite direction. He put out his hand to the nearest wall to steady himself and began to apologise at the same time as she recognised him.

'Oh, Jack, I'm so sorry. I nearly knocked you flying. Are you okay?' She felt awful for rushing along with her head down. Poor Jack was unsteady on his feet to begin with, without her knocking him over.

'Alice, where's the fire?' he teased.

She smiled and told him where she was going and why.

'Sorry to hear that,' he said. 'Tough time for you lately.'

She nodded. 'It is, but hopefully it will get a bit easier now. All being well I'll be in work at the weekend. Have we got any beer to sell yet?'

'We have, thank goodness. I'm on my way there now, just for a drink and to meet a couple of mates.'

'You not seeing Maisie then tonight?'

He shook his head. 'No. I took her to the pictures a couple of times, but she's not really my type. Bit gobby, and a bit too clingy for me.' He laughed. 'Right, I'll maybe see you on Saturday then. Good luck with everything and I hope your mam gets well soon. Oh, by the way, you might want to tell your mates at Rootes that we're putting on a big dance for the Yanks from Burtonwood at the end of next month. We've booked a good band, that Glenn Miller act we had at the last do. We'll have a raffle, and we might just have a talent contest, so if you know anybody that wants to do a turn, let me know. We've got our lads from the convalescent home coming along as well. Should be a great night, hopefully.'

He waved and limped off up the road as Alice waved back.

She went on her way towards Lucerne Street, a little smile on her face, cheered up by the thought of a good night at the Legion to look forward to.

Chapter Seventeen

September 1942

Her daughter had just drifted off to sleep as Alice crept out of the bedroom, her black court shoes in hand, and moved quietly down the hall into the sitting room. Granny Lomax and Brian were finishing a game of snakes and ladders, with the wireless playing quietly in the background. Alice smiled. Her little brother had settled in well here and Granny was enjoying looking after him. The loft bedroom was now his temporary home and he'd spent ages arranging and rearranging Terry's train sets and hours playing up there, talking to himself and his imaginary train drivers, passengers and guards. Mam had spent the first two weeks in hospital while they stabilised her and they had got her eating again and gaining a bit of weight. She was now in a convalescent home over in Crosby; it was the nearest place with a vacant bed that they could get her into, as most of the local homes were looking after injured military staff. They'd been lucky to get somewhere still in Merseyside. But the distance meant that her children could only visit on a Sunday due to Alice's work and Brian's school commitments.

'I'll be quite late coming home so I'll see you two tomorrow,' Alice said, slipping her shoes and black fitted jacket on. 'Do I look okay?'

'You look lovely, our Alice,' Brian said, nodding with approval. 'Like a proper posh lady.'

'Very smart indeed,' Granny said. 'That skirt is a good fit.'

Alice looked down at the bar uniform the Legion steward had presented her with last weekend. The black skirt was a similar fitted style to what she usually wore, but this one had kick pleats at the front and the neat white blouse had a logo embroidered on the breast pocket with the club name. They'd been made especially for the important event tonight and she'd even been given a pair of silky black stockings that she'd treasure with her life.

'We're going a bit posh for this do tonight,' Alice said. 'There are flight commanders and lieutenants expected as well as the regular airmen, so the boss wants to create a good impression.'

'Well I'm sure you'll do them proud. And good luck to Millie with the talent contest. Ah, there's the gate squeaking. See you later, Alice.'

Alice dashed to the door and whipped it open before Millie knocked. They linked arms as they hurried up Linnet Lane. Millie had settled back into the routine of working full-time at Rootes and helping her mam out in the evenings with the salon. Alice had adjusted back to her part-time hours and her Legion job. She sometimes worried that she was relying on Granny Lomax too much with all the child-care now falling on her shoulders, but Terry's mam had told her to stop worrying as she was enjoying having a family to look after again. She said it was good to get up in the morning and feel a sense of purpose about the day, instead of wallowing in self-pity about being widowed and having her only child putting his life on the line daily.

'At least it's not raining,' Millie said. 'I've just spent ages doing my hair and didn't want to flatten it with a scarf.'

Alice smiled. 'It looks lovely. Are you nervous about singing later?'

'A bit,' Millie admitted. 'I've been practising though, so I hope I'm not too rusty.'

'Has anyone else from Rootes said they're going to have a go?' Alice asked. She rarely got time to chat with her workmates these days, apart from the morning breaks. She left for home when they all clocked off for dinner. She knew that she could stay and eat with them, but didn't like to take too much advantage of her mother-in-law's time.

'Not sure. Norman, one of the janitors, says he's bringing his squeezebox, so he might give us a turn. Have you sold many tickets?'

Alice nodded. 'Jack said we'd sold out when I was in last Sunday. The American air force sent a box over last weekend in a jeep with a couple of their young men. They gave us loads of really nice things for the buffet supper: tins of ham and salmon for the sarnies and a couple of boxes of chocolates, silk stockings and cigars for the raffle. They even sent a good bottle of liquor called bourbon. Jack had his eye on it, but the boss locked it in the safe.' Alice laughed. 'It should be a really good night. I'm looking forward to it.'

'Me too,' Millie said as they walked up to the entrance doors of the club. 'I'll give you a hand with the tables seeing as I'll be in before any other customers tonight.'

Jack waved to them as they made their way across to the bar and hung their coats on the back of the staffroom door.

'Can you give Winnie a hand in the kitchen please, Millie? She's struggling to get everything plated up for later. She's made a mountain of sarnies and they're in danger of toppling onto the floor.'

'On my way.' Millie gave him a mock salute and dashed to help Winnie, the wife of Arnold, the steward.

The band was setting up on the stage and Alice looked around the large room to see where she could be of help. But everything looked as though Jack had it all in hand.

'What can I do?'

'Just stand behind the bar and look beautiful,' Jack teased.

'Cheeky.' Alice flapped a tea towel at him. 'You look very smart in your new uniform.'

He did and his black boots were so highly polished Alice would bet she'd see her face in them if she tried.

'So do you, but more sexy than smart.'

'Jack!' She giggled but could feel her cheeks heating at his bold comment, and as he came closer she caught the smell of whisky on his breath. 'Behave yourself. I'm a married woman.'

'Yeah, more's the pity,' Jack said as the band started to do a sound check.

Alice sighed and swayed from side to side. She'd always loved 'Moonlight Serenade'. She and Terry had danced to the tune a few times and she closed her eyes and imagined his arms holding her tight right now. She blinked rapidly to stop the tears that suddenly threatened.

'You okay, Alice?' Jack frowned. 'Sorry if I offended you. I was only pulling your leg, chuck.'

'I'm fine.' She smiled. 'I'm missing my Terry. This tune reminds me of him. I just wish this flipping war was over. It seems to be taking forever.'

Jack patted her shoulder. 'I know. But we're all in it together. Let's make sure everyone has a great time tonight and give them some good memories to take home.'

Alice took a breather for a few minutes as a temporary lull hit the bar. She glanced around the crowded room; everyone seemed to be really enjoying themselves. Jack was out on the floor collecting empty glasses and Millie was going around the concert room selling raffle tickets. People were digging deep in their pockets to be in with a chance of winning one of the wonderful prizes laid out on a table. There was even an early Christmas hamper in pride of place, centre of the table, containing tinned and packet goods that had been handed in by the American contingent as they'd arrived on the packed coach from Burtonwood. The huge basket was filled to the brim with luxuries most local people could never afford or even find in the shops at the moment. Ham, salmon, tinned veg and fruit, evaporated milk and a large round tin with a full rich fruit cake, according to the label, as well as bars of assorted chocolate and a box of Christmas crackers. Whoever won that would be able to feed their family well for the festive season. The basket was topped with red ribbon bows that would probably grace a lucky little girl's hair in time.

Millie came back to the bar, her borrowed apron pockets full of money. She tipped it out onto a small table.

'Can you count that, Alice? I've still got some more tickets to sell but my pockets were in danger of bursting at the seams. Won't be a minute and then I'll come and do a stint for you and you can have a dance and catch up with the Rootes crowd.'

Alice found a spare money bag under the bar where they kept the takings bags and proceeded to count up the coins Millie had tipped out. There was a good few pounds here towards the Legion's benevolent fund that would go towards a Christmas treat for the injured soldiers.

Jack came back with the glasses and proceeded to wash them.

'You go and get a break, gel. Take a drink with you. Millie said she'd come and give me a hand when she's done selling the tickets. The boss and his wife are going to put the food out in a few minutes, so it'll be chaos again as they'll all want a drink to wash it down with.'

Alice wasted no time in helping herself to a schooner of sherry and made her way over to the Rootes table. Marlene made a space for her next to Freddie and his wife. It was good to see everyone all dressed up in their best for the occasion instead of in overalls and turbans.

'There's some right good prizes up for grabs in that raffle,' Marlene shouted above the noise of the music and people all talking at once. 'I fancy that nice 'amper. Do my lot very nicely for Christmas, that would.'

Alice smiled. 'I think they've all got their eyes on it,' she said. 'There's some lovely silk stockings and chocolates up there too.'

'It's a smashing night,' Freddie said, looking around at the couples dancing on the floor. 'The Yanks are enjoying themselves anyway. Plenty of spare women to choose from. That's what they like.' He nodded towards Maisie, who was in the arms of a uniformed airman, being waltzed around the room. 'She ain't wasted any time getting off with one anyway.'

Alice took a sip of her sherry, enjoying the few minutes of relaxation that was probably all she'd get tonight. The music ended and the handsome young airman brought Maisie back to the table.

'Thank you, Brad,' she gushed as he smiled, showing even white teeth. He thanked her politely and walked to a table occupied by several other young men. 'Catch up with you later,' she yelled at his back and picked up a glass, downing the contents.

'Take it easy, Maisie,' Freddie warned. 'You'll be too drunk to stand up, never mind dance, if you don't go a bit slower.'

Maisie rolled her eyes. 'It's a party, Freddie. I wanna just enjoy myself for once. Let your hair down, not that you've got much.' She grinned cheekily. 'And I want to show *him* that he's not the only fella on the planet who can show me a good time.'

Alice followed her gaze and saw that the *him* she was referring to was Jack. Oh dear. Maisie didn't look too happy about being dropped by him. But then, he said he'd only taken her out to the pictures twice. It was hardly the romance of the century.

'No,' Maisie carried on, '*he's* only got eyes for one woman, and she knows it. Some people are just plain greedy.'

'Maisie,' Freddie shouted. 'Watch your mouth.' He turned to Alice, who was looking at him questioningly. 'Sorry, chuck.'

'Why are you sorry, Freddie? What's wrong?'

Freddie beckoned her to one side. 'She's jealous and putting rumours about that Jack Dawson dumped her because he's seeing you on the sly,' he whispered. 'I've told her not to be so bloody ridiculous, that you're happily married, like. But the drink is loosening her tongue, so you best know what's in her head, and then you can deal with it if she says anything else. She said earlier that he can't take his eyes off you and it's obvious why he dumped her.'

Alice stared at him and shook her head. 'But that's just stupid. I work with Jack. He's a mate and he walks me back to my mother-in-law's in the blackout to be safe. There's nothing going on with us at all. Why didn't Millie tell me she's spreading rumours?'

Freddie shook his head. 'She keeps her trap shut in the canteen when Millie is around. Millie'd slap her face if she heard her, believe me. Anyway, just ignore her, chuck. I'll try and stop her drinking too much more and hopefully she'll dance her socks off and burn herself out.'

Alice nodded, feeling stunned. 'I'd better go back now; the bar's getting busy again. Buffet's on in a minute, then the raffle and then the talent contest, so we'll be busy. Get some food down her to soak up the drink. I'll just ignore her, or I might be tempted to slap her one myself, the cheeky mare.'

Alice walked back to the bar, her mind working overtime. She felt really annoyed now. If Maisie was spreading rumours like that, how long before they got back to Terry's mam and eventually reached Terry's ears? Not that he'd believe them, she hoped, but still, it wasn't a very nice thing to happen. Scorned women were the worst; she'd read about them in romance books from the library. They could be dangerous and cause all sorts of trouble, so she'd watch her step from now on with Jack. She took her place behind the bar and Jack smiled.

'What's up? You look mithered to death.'

'Nothing.' She smiled back and turned to the next person waiting to be served. It was the handsome Brad. 'What can I get you?' she asked as he caught her eye.

'Ten pints, Ma'am,' he said, waving a wad of notes in her direction.

'Ten? Right, you'll have to bear with me while I get enough glasses together,' she said, concentrating on the job in hand and putting Maisie, Jack and everything else to the back of her mind for now. By the time she'd finished serving Brad and he and two members of his squadron had cleared the bar counter of full glasses, Alice had a queue of impatient customers waiting.

Jack got up on stage in front of the microphone and announced the buffet was ready and for everyone to form an orderly queue and help themselves. There was a mad rush to the tables where the generous spread was laid out. The band put down their instruments and joined everyone else for a well-earned snack; the peace and quiet, apart from general chit-chat, was overwhelming as the food was consumed and enjoyed. Alice tucked into a ham sandwich and rolled her eyes. What a treat. Jack poured her and Millie a sherry each and they sat down on a couple of stools behind the bar while the steward kept his eye open for any customers that needed serving.

There wasn't a crumb left over as Millie and Alice collected the empty plates and tidied the buffet tables away. Jack announced that the raffle was to be drawn and he and Arnold, the steward, took to the stage. Cheers went up as each lucky number was drawn. To her delight, Marlene's ticket was the first number out and she burst into tears as Jack told her she could have the pick of the table.

'I'll take the 'amper, chuck,' she choked out. 'I can give me mam an' dad a good Christmas this year now. Thank you, lads,' she called out to the young airmen who clapped and cheered as she carried the basket back to her table.

'Bless her, I'm glad she's won that,' Millie said. 'She deserves it, looking after her mam and dad like she does. All her wages go on keeping the roof over their heads and they are both getting on a bit.'

Alice smiled. 'Then it's gone to the right person,' she said. 'I know she likes a gossip, but she's got a heart of gold deep down and I'll never forget how she delivered my Cathy in that air raid shelter.'

Millie whooped loudly as her number came up next.

'Jack,' she yelled from her place behind the bar, 'I'll have a pair of stockings, you choose them.'

She grinned as wolf-whistles from the troops were sent in her direction.

The prizes went down quickly. When Alice's ticket came out she chose a box of chocolates to take home to her mother-in-law, who would be thrilled to bits and would no doubt take great pleasure in sharing them with Brian.

'Haven't we done well?' Millie said, putting their prizes in the back room for later.

'You two have,' Jack said, coming behind the bar. 'I wanted that bottle of bourbon. But it went to one of the wounded soldiers. Ah well, I'm sure he'll enjoy it.'

'I'm sure he will,' Alice said as the band started to play again.

'What time are we starting the talent contest?' Millie asked.

Jack looked at his watch. 'About twenty minutes,' he said. 'Let 'em have a few dances first. I've only got five names down on the list, so you're in with a good chance, Millie, and it'll be nice for you to sing with a full band.'

Millie smiled gleefully. 'And now I've had a couple of drinks I'm feeling more relaxed.' She looked up as a young airman came over and asked her to dance. 'Is that okay, can you manage without me?'

'You go and enjoy yourself,' Arnold said. 'You giving us a hand tonight has been a big help, chuck. But you're here to have fun as well. Go on. And you, Jack, take Alice for a dance and me and the missus will see to things here for a few minutes.'

'Oh, but I…' Alice faltered as Jack grabbed her hand and limped onto the dance floor. The band was playing Glenn Miller's 'In the Mood' and the couples around them were jitterbugging. Alice felt her cheeks heating as Jack smiled at her and spun her around and around the best he could with his disability. He smelled of whisky and something spicy and there was a glint of devilment in his eyes. Alice tried to keep her own eyes averted from his as they danced. She saw him glance across the room towards where Maisie was sitting on her own at the Rootes table, glaring at them. Jack smirked and inclined his head in Maisie's direction.

'The face on it,' he said. 'And she wonders why I let her go.'

Alice pulled away from him. 'Stop it, Jack. You have no idea of what she's been saying and the damage she could cause.'

She ran towards the ladies' toilets and locked herself in a cubicle, leaning her back against the door, her eyes closed. She felt sick and took a couple of deep breaths. She heard the outer door opening.

'Alice, are you in here?' Millie called out. 'Jack sent me to find you. What's wrong? He thinks he's upset you.'

Alice unlocked the door and came out of the cubicle. 'He has – well not him so much as what Maisie is saying.'

She told Millie what Freddie had said earlier and then Jack's reaction to Maisie's glaring at them.

Millie shook her head. 'Ignore Maisie and her bloody big gob. I don't blame Jack for dumping her. She's a tart. He's probably had his wicked way with her and she expects a ring on her finger in return. He wouldn't be the first. She's making a right holy show of herself over that Brad now. He's dancing with a lovely girl out there and Maisie's making eyes at him and calling out to him every time he dances past. He's trying to ignore her. She won't dare cause trouble for you if she knows what's good for her. She'd lose the few friends she's got. And Jack wouldn't jeopardise your marriage, you know that, but if you want to keep on working here you need him to walk you home to be safe.'

Alice nodded. 'You're right. She's not getting the better of me. It's nowt to do with her what I do. I'm not even doing anything wrong. One little dance is all it was, and it wouldn't matter which man I danced with, would it? That's what tonight is all about, to enjoy ourselves. I'm going out there now and I'm telling Jack what she's saying about us.'

'Wait until we're on our way home,' Millie advised. 'Don't give her any reason to kick off and spoil what's left of the evening. Jack was getting organised for the talent contest. Let's go and see what's happening and just ignore her.'

❁

Back behind the bar Alice and Millie clapped as Jack introduced the first contestant to take part in the talent contest. Joe Shaw, the elderly caretaker from Rootes, marched proudly up to the stage with his piano accordion. He began his two-tune spot with an energetic Swedish polka that had the troops on the floor, pulling any willing girl up to join them. As everyone clapped and cheered, Joe took a bow and began his final tune, 'The Cuckoo Waltz', with everyone joining in the 'Cuckoo' bit. Again the dancers were up, waltzing around this time in a two-four step. Once more the applause and whistling and cheering had Joe beaming from ear to ear with pride.

Jack jumped back up on stage and consulted his list. 'We've had a few more talented folks add their names to my list tonight. And following a consultation with our band here, to make sure they are familiar with the chosen tune, I'd like you to welcome on stage one of our visiting US airmen, Mr Brad Edwards, who is giving us a rendition of Cole Porter's "Night and Day", Frank Sinatra style. Take it away, Brad.'

Brad took to the stage and bowed to the cheers that went up from his troop, then stood in front of the microphone and waited for the intro.

'Hey.' Millie nudged Alice as Brad began to sing; his voice was powerful and clear. 'He's good. What a fabulous voice.'

Alice nodded and turned to serve Freddie with his order of a pint of mild and two small sherries.

'You not doing your Max Miller impersonations tonight, Freddie?' she asked him.

'Not with the missus in the building,' Freddie replied and rolled his eyes. 'She doesn't appreciate risqué. What goes on at Rootes stays at Rootes as far as she's concerned.' He handed over a ten-bob note and Alice gave him his change.

Whistling and loud applause followed Brad's performance as he finished his song.

Jack thanked him and consulted his list. 'And now we have two young ladies doing us a comedy spot. Please welcome on stage Sadie Romano and Jenny Baines as Elsie and Doris Waters, otherwise known as Gert and Daisy, with a *Workers' Playtime* sketch.'

Millie nudged Alice as the band launched into the signature tune 'Daisy, Daisy' to welcome the girls on stage. They giggled nervously as they launched into a routine about working in a munitions factory. Everybody laughed and their nervousness disappeared as they got going.

'What?' Alice said, frowning as Millie pointed at one of the girls.

'That's Sadie who was in our class at school,' Millie said. 'I'm sure it is. But her surname wasn't Romano, was it? That sounds Italian.'

Alice nodded. 'She was Sadie Wright at school. Don't you remember though, she ran away from home, caused her mam and dad loads of trouble and went off with that boy from the travelling fair that used to pitch up on Sefton Park before the war. That was it, Romano's fair. She must have married him. Wonder how it's affected her now though, with him being Italian. Loads of them have been rounded up and taken as prisoners of war. The fair hasn't been here since she went off in 1938.'

'Blimey, I'd forgotten all about that,' Millie said. 'Maybe he's back in Italy with his family. We'll have to ask her. Call them over when they've finished and we'll offer them a drink.'

As the girls finished their spot and everyone clapped, Sadie led Jenny across to the bar.

Millie grabbed her arm. 'I'm due on stage right now, but it is you, Sadie, isn't it? I'm Millie and that's Alice about to serve you. From school, remember?'

Sadie's mouth fell open. 'Oh my God, Millie, Alice, of course I remember. How nice to see you. How are you both?'

'We're fine,' Alice said as Jack called Millie up on stage. 'Let her go and do her spot and then we'll join you for a drink when Jack comes back behind the bar. We've a lot to catch up on. It's years, in fact.'

Sadie nodded. 'I'll say; a lot of water's gone under the bridge since that final year at school. I see you're married, Alice? Don't tell me. Terry Lomax, by any chance? You and he were always together.'

Alice laughed. 'Yep, I'm Mrs Lomax now but Terry's away in God knows where and I'm left holding the baby.'

'Aren't we all?' Sadie rolled her eyes. 'Better let Millie get on with her turn and we'll catch up later. We're sitting right by the back wall over there.'

Sadie picked up the two glasses of gin and orange she'd ordered and she and Jenny made their way back to their table.

Millie's 'White Cliffs of Dover' received a standing ovation. She beckoned to Alice to come on the stage with her and whispered, '"Boogie Woogie Bugle Boy of Company C" for an encore – with you.'

Alice nodded and took her place next to Millie. She couldn't sing for toffee compared to her friend, but she could harmonise and let Millie carry the song. The audience joined in and the floor filled with dancers. Alice felt a rush of adrenaline as they neared the end of the song and wished her Terry could see her now. He'd be proud that she was making an effort to get on with her life and bringing up Cathy the best she could.

The clapping and cheering that heralded the end of their performance had Millie in tears and Alice gave her a hug before they jumped off the stage and hurried back behind the bar. Jack got up on stage and announced that, according to his observations, and the amount of cheering and clapping and shouting for more, Millie was the out and out winner of tonight's talent contest. He beckoned Millie back on stage and asked her if she'd do another song. She whispered in his ear and he nodded and spoke to the band leader.

Alice felt a little shiver go down her spine as Millie sang their favourite song of the moment. You could have heard a pin drop as her beautiful rendition of 'Over the Rainbow' silenced the room. In that moment Alice felt certain that her best friend was destined for a future on the stage. With a voice like that, Millie could go far. Again the applause and cheering rocked the room and Millie curtsied and came off stage, only to be beckoned back again by Jack and the band leader.

By the time the evening came to an end and most of the empties had been collected and washed, the band wound down the festivities with a final waltz. Brad claimed Millie, and Jack asked Alice if she'd like to dance.

Alice hesitated for a moment, thoughts of Maisie and her nasty comments rearing their head, but Arnold's whispered, 'Go on, queen. Make his night. He's in a bit of pain, I can see it in his face; he's worked hard tonight, but I reckon he could manage a waltz with you,' made her feel she couldn't refuse.

Jack took her hand and slowly waltzed her around the floor. There were loads of wives and girlfriends dancing with servicemen tonight; she wasn't alone – and they weren't doing anything wrong. Life had to go on. Maisie could say what she liked on Monday.

As they got ready to go home Millie made an announcement to Alice. 'The band leader wants to know if I'll sing with them permanently. I said I'd have a think about it. They travel around the country entertaining the troops at the base camps, so it would mean leaving home and my job again. I feel all of a dither. I'm not sure what to do. But isn't it exciting that they feel I'm good enough to perform with them?'

Alice swallowed the lump in her throat that threatened to choke her. 'You have to do what's best for you, Millie. It's a wonderful opportunity and you don't know where it may lead for the future.'

Millie nodded. 'It's a lot to take in. I'll have to see what my mam and dad say.'

As they left the building with Jack someone yoo-hooed them. Alice whipped around and saw it was Sadie and her friend Jenny.

'Just wanted to say well done to Millie,' Sadie began. 'Also we didn't get a chance to catch up. Me and Jenny are going into town tomorrow afternoon and wondered if you two fancied meeting us for a cuppa in Lyons Corner Café, say about three-ish?'

Millie nodded. 'I'm sure the afternoon will be okay. Need to give my mam a hand in the salon in the morning. What about you, Alice?'

'If Terry's mam can look after Cathy for a couple of hours, it'll be fine by me. I'm not working tomorrow night with tonight being a late one. The boss said it will be quiet as they'll all have spent up tonight.'

'Well I'm in, just in case,' Jack said, 'so hopefully you'll both get a bit of time to catch up with your mates.'

'See you tomorrow, then,' Sadie called as she and Jenny hurried away into the pitch black night.

'Right, you two; let's get you home,' Jack said, slinging his gas mask box over his shoulder and offering them an arm each.

'I need to tell you something,' Alice began as they walked away arm-in-arm from the Legion towards Linnet Lane. 'It's about something Maisie said earlier.'

She told Jack what had been said. His jaw tightened and Alice saw an angry glint in his eyes.

'Right, leave it with me,' he muttered. 'I'll pay her a quick visit on my way into work tomorrow night. Don't you worry; she won't dare say anything else out of turn.'

Chapter Eighteen

On Saturday afternoon, Alice and Millie sat open-mouthed as Sadie told them the tale of her whirlwind romance and subsequent hasty marriage to Luca Romano, her dark and handsome Italian lover. Their young son Gianni was three years old; exactly two years older than Cathy. The four girls were enjoying catching up with the tales of each other's lives since their schooldays.

'Oh my goodness, and don't you miss him?' Alice asked. 'You must have been really in love to run away with him like that.'

'I was,' Sadie admitted wistfully. 'I loved him to bits. He was a good-looking charmer and I couldn't resist him. I ended up pregnant and threw everything away to be with him. But I soon discovered the fairground was a dangerous place to bring up a child. Well in my opinion it was, anyway. The rides, wild dogs that roamed around, loud noises and smells that got into everything. I never felt clean. Luca knew I was unhappy, but there was no way he would leave and get a normal job; he'd been born into that lifestyle, it was in his blood and he loved it. The final straw came when he and his brother Marco started a Wall of Death ride with the motorbikes. I'd had enough by then. It terrified me that he could risk his neck in such a way, knowing he'd got a wife and baby to support. Then the war got underway, and with him being Italian, there was always the risk he'd be taken away as a prisoner of war – all of his family too, not just him.

'We were headed back to Italy via Dover, and then one day when we were parked up not too far from the Bristol area, near to Temple Meads station, I snuck away in the early hours of the morning while everyone else was sleeping, with Gianni and a small bag of belongings. I had hardly any money; just enough to get us back to Liverpool. I was worried to death about coming back to my mam's place, but she just opened the door at my knock, said, "Well, well, look who's here," and took us both in immediately. She adores Gianni, he's her first grandchild, and she's never given me a hard time over what went wrong. Just lets me get on with making amends in the best way I can.'

'And does Luca have no idea where you are now?' Alice asked. She couldn't possibly imagine roaming the country with Cathy, trying to get home; it must have been scary, especially with the war in full swing and no one to turn to.

'He wrote to me at my mam's address a few days after I left him – he'd have known I had nowhere else to go – but I haven't replied. The fair was still in England then, making its way down south, but I have no idea where he is now. It's best he gets on with his own life and I'll just get on with mine. I can't go back to that lifestyle, and like I say, he would never leave the fair and it would be wrong of me to nag him to do that. Once the war is over he may come and look for us, but until then I want our son to have a normal upbringing: live in a house, not a caravan, and go to a proper school. The travelling was very tiring. We never stopped anywhere for more than a few days at a time. And there's some shady characters work on fairgrounds. I just didn't feel safe, for myself or for Gianni.'

'It doesn't sound ideal for family life. Motorbikes scare the life out of *me*,' Alice admitted with a shudder. 'Never mind anything else. Terry has a Harley-Davidson and I wouldn't get on the back for a hundred pounds and a gold clock. I'm hoping he'll get rid of it when, and if, he comes home safely. A little car would be nicer, and then he could take me and Cathy out at the weekends.'

'We'll have to meet up with the little ones when you have a spare afternoon,' Sadie suggested. 'Mam said I should send Gianni to be evacuated, but I couldn't bear it. Be really nice for him to have a friend close by.'

'It's getting a bit too cold for Sefton Park at the minute,' Alice said. 'But come over to Terry's mam's place one afternoon and they can have a play together.'

'I'd love to. Thank you. Do you just work the weekends at the Legion?'

'Yes, but I also do a morning shift at Rootes during the week. I'm trying to save up for when Terry gets home. So I'm free in the afternoons. Where do you two work?'

'Well, we were working at Blacklers,' Sadie's friend Jenny replied. 'But it's closed for repairs following the Blitz. We've been taken on part-time at the Utility clothing company for now. Bit boring, the clothes, I mean; not much style, needless to say. But at least people know where to come to get the best deals for their clothing coupons. We're hoping to get jobs in the new Lewis's if and when they rebuild it.'

Millie smiled. 'I loved Lewis's. Wouldn't have minded a job on the cosmetics counter for myself when the new store is ready, but I might be off to pastures new. I'm still trying to decide.' She told Sadie and Jenny what had happened after last night's dance.

Now it was their turn to stare open-mouthed.

'What's there to decide?' Sadie said. 'A chance like that only comes once in a lifetime.'

Millie laughed. 'I'm not as impulsive as you are, Sadie. I'm going to talk it over with my mam and dad this weekend, see what they think. Thing is, I do like my job at Rootes, doing my bit for the war effort. Alice and I do the riveting on the wings for the Halifax bombers.'

'It will be so much nicer for you doing the base camps and singing for the troops,' Sadie said. 'It's still helping the war effort. Keeping up their morale. You might meet a handsome American and get swept off your feet.'

Millie laughed again. 'Not sure about that. Although that bloke who sang like Frank Sinatra last night was lovely.'

'You could do some duets with him,' Alice suggested.

'Now you're just getting carried away,' Millie said, grinning. 'I'll probably never see him again.'

'More's the pity. But who knows? What will be, will be, and all that!' Alice said, looking up as the middle-aged waitress, smartly attired in the black and white uniform worn by all Lyons' Nippy waitresses, came to the table clutching a pad and pencil. 'Now then, are we all having tea and a slice of whatever cake they have?'

'That'll do nicely for me, cake is such a treat,' Sadie said and Jenny and Millie nodded.

'So, four teas and four slices of cake?' the Nippy said. 'We have a lovely fatless Victoria sponge or a marble cake, which has a small swirl of chocolate running through it. Quite a luxury in these times.'

Four heads nodded at the marble cake and the Nippy went away to see to their order.

'Hope you find your mam a bit better tomorrow,' Sadie said to Alice. 'It's been an awful time for you, with losing your brother. No wonder she's ill. I remember your Rodney from school. He was a nice-looking boy; popular with the girls and a good footballer too. Such a waste of a young life.'

'It is,' Alice said, blinking a sudden rush of tears away. 'I really can't believe that he'll never walk through the door again, shouting, "What's for tea, Mam?"'

'Him and thousands of others,' Jenny said sadly. 'Our next-doors have lost two of their four sons. Half the family just wiped out like that. *Their* mam is in a bit of a state as well. She tries to put on a brave face and told my mam that she thinks they're still alive as they can't show her proof they're dead without a body. She's sure they'll come home with all the others when the war is over and they'll all be able to laugh at the telegrams and the stupid mistakes that were made. God help her, I hope she's right, but I doubt it.'

'If only.' Alice sighed and looked up as the Nippy wheeled a trolley across to their table and proceeded to place their orders in front of them.

'What about you, Jenny?' Alice asked as they tucked in. 'Are you courting anyone?'

Jenny shook her head. 'I split up with my boyfriend last year after he told me he didn't think we were working out. He's away with his regiment somewhere in the Middle East, according to his sister who I'm still friends with. I worry about him, obviously, and he sent me a card at Christmas, but it wasn't a special card or anything. That man you work with at the Legion, Jack who did the raffle and the talent show; he seems nice. Is he married or anything?'

Alice felt her face heating. Another one that fancied Jack. 'Er, he's single. He was going out with a girl from Rootes but not for long. Just a word of warning though, he likes being footloose and fancy-free. Doesn't stay with anyone for too long.'

Jenny blushed. 'Oh, I'm not looking for anything serious. Just company really. It would be nice to have someone take me out now and again. To the pictures or a dance and what-have-you.'

Alice nodded. 'Well, he works all weekend and part of the week. But I suppose if you come in on one of the nights he's there you can smile sweetly at him and see what happens.'

'We'll go in next weekend,' Sadie suggested. 'Do they have any music if they don't have a band playing? We like to have a dance.'

'There's a regular chap plays the piano, and we have a sing-song,' Alice said. 'It's always a good night in there, even in the event of an air raid warning!'

❀

'It's time we made tracks,' Millie said, looking at her wristwatch. 'Finish your tea, Alice, I need to get home. I promised my mam

I'd be back for six so we can have the "should I, shouldn't I go with the band" talk.'

'Yes, *we'd* better be making tracks too,' Sadie said. 'Don't like to put on my mam too much with Gianni. She baby-sat last night until late. Maybe we'll see you next Saturday.'

'You will,' Alice said. 'But do come over one afternoon with your little boy. What about Wednesday?'

'Smashing,' Sadie replied. 'We'll see you then.'

Millie and Alice linked arms as they made their way back to the tram stop.

'Can I ask you something?' Millie asked. 'And don't bite my head off.'

'Course you can,' Alice said, wondering what Millie had on her mind that was causing her to frown.

'Are you a bit sweet on Jack Dawson?'

'Am I heck! What makes you say that?'

'Just something, oh, I don't know. When Jenny asked about him you had a "look" on your face, like she was asking after your fella, like. And it seemed to me like you were trying to put her off.'

'Not at all. Anyway, I'm a married woman. I don't need to be sweet on anyone other than my Terry. I suppose I feel a bit sorry for Jack, a bit protective of him, like I would a brother. Because of his accident and the fact it's left him lame and he doesn't have much to call his own; just lodgings in someone else's house. He's been so nice to me at work and it would be good for him to find a woman who would look after him. But he doesn't seem to want commitment and, like Marlene told me, he definitely *does* like his booze. He always smells of whisky or something when he comes to work and that's *before* he has anything to drink there. I don't think he's the settling-down type and I remember when we first went to that dance and I told him I had a teething baby at home, he was quite scathing and said, "Rather you than me." I doubt he's the husband and family-man type.'

'Hmm, best avoided then if Jenny's looking for more than she says she is.'

'Maybe,' Alice said as the crowded tram trundled into view, its brakes squealing as it jerked to a stop. They jumped onto the platform and found seats upstairs. 'Good luck talking things over with your mam and dad later. I'll really miss you if you go away, but I've got to admit it's a wonderful opportunity for you and we don't get many of those these days.'

'True.' Millie nodded. 'I'll miss you too if I go, and my little god-daughter. But you'll have Sadie to knock about with, and Cathy will have a new little friend to play with.'

Alice sighed. 'It won't be the same without you though.'

They got off at the stop on Aigburth Road and linked arms as they turned onto Lark Lane.

'Shall we see if there's any chocolate in the newsagent's for you to take to your mam tomorrow?' Millie suggested. 'Hopefully she's showing signs of improvement this week and will soon be home.'

'Good idea. I'll get her a *Woman's Weekly* as well. She'll be missing it.'

❀

Mam looked smart in a white cardigan over a navy blue soft wool dress. Her hair had been trimmed and set and she greeted Alice, Brian and Cathy with a wave as they walked into the lounge at the convalescent home. She held her arms out for Cathy, who pulled back shyly, plugging her thumb firmly into her mouth and hiding behind Alice's skirt. She peered shyly out from beneath her fringe.

'I think she's forgotten me,' Mam said. 'It's been a long time and they soon forget at that age.'

'She's just being clingy, Mam,' Alice said reassuringly. 'Give her a bit of time and she'll soon come round.'

'Well, our Brian will give me a hug, won't you, my love.'

Brian smiled and moved forwards, allowing a brief hug and a peck on the cheek. Boys of his age didn't go around kissing their mams all over the shop. It was a sissy thing to do.

'Feeling better, Mam?'

'I think so, chuck. Some days I'm okay, and others I can't even face getting out of bed in the mornings. I feel I've nothing to get up for, like it's all so pointless.'

Alice frowned. 'Mam, you've got us three. Have you talked to your doctor about these feelings?'

Mam shook her head. 'They've enough to do here without me mithering them. I'll be all right, eventually.'

'They are here to be mithered,' Alice said firmly. 'You need to talk to them. Do you want *me* to say something?'

'No, no I don't want that. Leave it. I'll do it when I feel up to it.'

'Okay.' Alice chewed her lip. 'Do you promise me? They won't let you home until you are able to cope again.'

Mam stared at a place above Alice's head and smiled, a serene expression on her face.

'I don't want to go home, back to that house. They're here you know, your dad and Rodney. I can feel them with me. They're not there at home and I don't want to leave them alone here.'

Brian frowned and pulled Alice to one side. 'What does she mean?' he whispered, looking worried. 'Can she really see ghosts? Won't that be a bit scary for her? And me dad and Rodney wouldn't come and haunt her, would they?'

Alice smiled and rubbed his arm. 'No, of course not. I think she's just imagining how it was when they were both alive. If it gives her comfort then that's no bad thing, is it?'

Brian screwed his face up. 'I s'pose not. The lads at my school say she's gone mental. She's not though, has she, Alice? I punched Albert Dobbs last week for saying that she's crackers and he's kept his gob shut since. But there are others who say things, not to my face though because they're scared of me now that I'm doing my Saturday club boxing. They think I might knock 'em out.'

Alice tried not to laugh at his earnest face. Poor little lad. He'd endured so much lately. Thank God for Granny Lomax, who treated him like a son. She spoiled him rotten and Brian loved it.

'She's not mental, love,' she whispered. 'Her mind is a bit disturbed, that's all. They'll make her right here and we'll get her home soon.'

Her mam was still staring at a spot above Alice's head, a smile fixed on her face. Alice shook her head. Coming home was not an option she could see happening in the foreseeable future. The visits to Crosby on a Sunday took a whole chunk out of the day. Granny Lomax's neighbour had brought them today and he was having a stroll up the promenade with his little dog while they did their visiting. Although she was missing her mam, Alice didn't feel Mam was missing her family in quite the same way.

'Mam, put your coat and hat on and let's have a little stroll in the gardens,' she suggested.

Mam got to her feet and Alice asked one of the nurses to help her get ready for a walk outside. Brian grabbed Cathy's hand and she squealed and lifted her feet off the floor. Alice grabbed the other hand and Cathy swung back and forth while they waited.

'Little monkey, aren't you?' Alice said as Cathy squealed and kicked her legs out so that she swung higher and higher. 'Right, put her down now, here's Grandma.'

Mam walked towards them with the nurse and raised her hand in a wave.

'Hello, Alice love, fancy seeing you three,' she said, genuine surprise registering on her face. 'I didn't know you were coming today.'

The nurse patted Alice's hand, shook her head and smiled sympathetically. 'The memory comes and goes,' she whispered.

Alice nodded. She swallowed a sob and took her mam's arm as they followed Brian and Cathy out into the gardens to pass a bit more time.

Chapter Nineteen

December 1942

As they waited for the works' bus on Monday morning, Alice hugged Millie when her friend excitedly told her that her parents thought she should give singing with the band a go.

'Mam said I might be famous one day if I'm discovered, like Vera and Gracie were. Tommy, the band leader, gave me a phone number to ring if I decided to do it and he said the person I would speak to is called Don Robinson. He's the manager of the band and will tell me where to go to meet up with them. I phoned him yesterday afternoon and he's making the arrangements for me. I'm to give a week's notice at Rootes today and be ready to go with him next weekend. He's picking me up in his car on Saturday morning. I'm so excited, Alice, I could burst.'

'Oh God, I bet you are,' Alice said, choking back tears. 'But I'm really going to miss you so much.'

'And I'll miss you, you know I will, but if I don't take this opportunity while I can, I might regret it forever. And like Sadie says, it's still doing something good for the war effort. The troops need a bit of entertainment and cheering up to keep their morale up. Don't say anything to anyone when we get on the bus. I'll tell Freddie privately.'

'I won't,' Alice said as the bus lumbered into view. 'Here we go. Plaster a smile on your face.'

Marlene called them over as they clambered aboard. 'Saved you some seats,' she yelled up the aisle, gesturing to the two seats in front of her and Maisie, who half-smiled at them.

'Morning,' Alice said and sat down next to the grimy window. Millie took the aisle seat and turned to nod a greeting.

'Was your mam pleased with your raffle winnings, Marlene?' Alice asked, ignoring Maisie, who looked decidedly sheepish. She wondered if Jack had said anything to her like he'd promised he would.

'Thrilled to bits, chuck. We 'ad a tin of salmon for our tea last night with some bread an' butter, and the rest's been put away for Christmas. Not too long to wait, an' it will all 'elp to make a special day even more so this year. 'Ow was your mam yesterday, Alice?'

Alice shook her head. 'Not great, I'm afraid. I can't see her coming home any time in the near future, and certainly not for Christmas. She's well enough in herself, but her mind is all over the place. I wouldn't be able to leave her on her own and go to work if they let her home, and without me working we'd never survive. She's safer being looked after for the time being.'

'It's a bloody shame,' Marlene said. 'You've all 'ad enough to put up with, losing your dad not that long ago an' now your Rodney. An' you getting caught with the babby so soon after the wedding as well. It's a job an' a 'alf looking after yourself in times like this, but you've the little lad as well as your Cathy. Some folk don't know 'ow well off they are.'

She glared at Maisie beside her. 'Only got themselves to think about. Gadding about at the weekend an' drinking most of their wages away, an' then causing bother for people who are just trying to earn an honest bob or two extra for their families.' Marlene pursed her lips. 'An' not a word of an apology, never mind a good morning.' She snorted as Maisie got up and made her way to an empty seat further down the bus.

Alice felt uncomfortable as the sulky-faced woman stared at her. She was certain Jack must have said something. Well, it served her right. Going around tittle-tattling about something that wasn't true anyway. She looked up as Freddie made his way to the empty seat next to Marlene.

'Morning, ladies,' he said, offering his cigarettes around. They all shook their heads. Freddie lit up and puffed contentedly. 'Soon be Christmas again. Do you think we should put on another revue show?'

Alice raised an eyebrow at Millie, who chewed her lip. 'Maybe,' Alice said, 'although we're all very busy with family stuff at the moment, Freddie. I can't really spare any evenings to rehearse with the baby to look after.'

She knew she was waffling, but it saved Millie from having to say anything and at that point the bus driver began whistling Bing Crosby's 'White Christmas', and all the passengers joined in, including Freddie.

They all got off the bus inside the factory gates and Millie linked her arm in Alice's and muttered, 'Saved by the sleigh bells. I'll collar Freddie as soon as we get inside, before he comes to put my name on his list for singing.'

She stopped and frowned as Maisie barged past them, almost knocking Alice flying. 'Oi, you, watch where you're going. Has anyone ever told you you're out of order, Maisie? You upset Alice on Friday night, didn't apologise, and then you act as though she's the one in the wrong.'

Maisie stopped dead and turned to face them. 'When that boyfriend of yours apologises to *me* for coming banging on my mam's front door and threatening me if I didn't keep away from you, that's when I'll apologise to you and not before.'

Alice frowned. 'Jack's not my boyfriend. I work with him, that's all. And you've only got yourself to blame if he told you to stop saying things that were untrue and could cause trouble. I'm a married woman with a family to think about. You shouting your drunken mouth off on Friday was wrong and you know it. I doubt Jack would threaten you, that's just you exaggerating things.'

'Is it?' Maisie said as they reached the locker room. She pulled her coat off and showed a bruised right arm to Alice. 'Look at them finger marks then. That's where he grabbed me. He didn't need to do that. I was trying to shut the door on him and he put his foot out to stop me and nearly fell inside. He grabbed my arm and he really dug his fingers in, as you can see.'

Alice chewed her lip, remembering Marlene's comments a few months ago about Jack being handy with his fists, but Millie was quick to point out: 'Jack probably grabbed hold of you to stop himself falling over, you idiot. He only has one good foot and if you tried to shut the door on it he probably lost his balance. Serves you bloody well right that he bruised you, you could have hurt him badly.'

Alice shook her head to stop Millie from saying anything else as Marlene popped her head around the door. Maisie flounced past her, pulling on her overalls and carrying her turban.

'Earrings,' Marlene called out. 'Take 'em off now.'

Maisie snatched at her earlobes and flung the diamanté clip-on earrings in Marlene's direction. 'Shove them in my locker for me, please.'

Marlene shrugged. 'Now what's up with 'er?'

'Nothing,' Millie replied, fastening her turban. 'Right, I'm off to find Freddie,' she mouthed to Alice and slipped out of the locker room.

❋

Alice put down her riveting gun as Millie joined her on the bench. 'What did he say?'

'That I'm a very lucky girl and shouldn't let my talent go to waste,' Millie said with a big grin. 'He told me to go for it.'

Alice nodded, trying her best to look and sound enthusiastic. 'I'll miss you, but this is your big chance to make a name for yourself. Go for it, as Freddie says.'

'I'm a nervous wreck thinking about it, but I know I'll regret it forever if I don't give it a try.'

'You'll be fine. You'll knock 'em dead. Come back to us when the war is over and make sure you always let me know if you are singing in Liverpool. I'll come and see you. Maybe Sadie and Jenny will come with me.'

'And if you bring Jack along as well, I'll have my own audience. Right,' Millie said, picking up her gun, 'I'd better do a bit of work. They can name this plane after me.'

Alice couldn't shake off the feeling of gloom that descended on her as the morning got underway. Not even the thought of hot buttered toast and a decent brew cheered her up as the break bell rang out. She put down her gun and linked Millie's arm as they walked to the canteen just ahead of the shell girls. She ignored Maisie, who tried to catch her eye while they queued at the counter. Millie also saw her looking over and turned her back on the girl.

'Let's sit near the window,' Alice suggested. 'It's a bit quieter and this is the only chance I get to have you to myself.'

As they shared a plate of toast and a tiny dish of mixed-berry jam, Freddie came rushing over.

'Alice, I just had your mother-in-law on the blower. Nothing to worry about,' he assured her as Alice jumped to her feet, hand on her chest. 'It's not bad news but she thought you should know in case you hear something on the way home and start to panic.' Freddie pulled out a chair and sat down next to Millie. 'Seems the school your Brian goes to has been evacuated and the kids sent home for the rest of the day while they deal with an incident.'

'What sort of an incident?' Alice asked.

'Some of the lads were on the school playing field collecting shrapnel as kids do, and they came across an unexploded bomb.

Bloody lucky it didn't go off in their faces – apparently one was standing on it, showing off. Fortunately the brighter ones in the bunch ran to tell a teacher and they were all told to run. They were sent into the shelters until a bomb squad attended and made it safe. But there's a search of the area going on now to make sure there are no more, so they've sent the kids home. Good job there's only a handful, with most of them being evacuated.'

Alice felt herself go faint at the thought of the bomb exploding and killing all those innocent little lads who thought they'd found a treasure. If only her mam had used a bit of common sense and left Brian in Wales where he was safe. It had been a selfish act really, to bring him home, no matter how much they all missed him. He could have been blown to smithereens this morning. Who knew how many more unexploded bombs were lying around the city at any given time? Liverpool, like all major cities with a port, was a dangerous place to be at the moment. She wished she was in a position to take both children somewhere deep into the countryside away from all the bombs and air raids. She wondered if there was a chance she could do that, but then there was her mam to visit each week, and Granny Lomax would be heartbroken if they all upped sticks and went away. It was hard knowing what to do for the best sometimes.

Brian was full of it when Alice arrived home, excitement written all over his face, in spite of the danger he'd been in. Alice gave him a hug, just thankful he was still in one piece.

'It was me what said it were a bomb that hadn't gone off, you know,' he boasted. 'The others were about to pick it up, and Johnny Owens wanted to stand on it like the king of the castle, daft fool. I shouted at him that it was a bomb and he laughed and said what did I know anyway. I ran to tell the teacher and he blew his whistle and ordered everyone off the field and into the shelters. I probably saved a few lives, our Alice.'

'You probably did, sweetheart,' Alice said, giving him another hug and saying a silent prayer of thanks that he was a sensible kid. She turned to greet a pale-faced Granny Lomax, who had walked into the sitting room with Cathy in her arms.

'That was a close call,' Granny Lomax muttered to Alice. 'She's just woken up. Here, Brian, take hold of Cathy for me while I make your sister a cuppa. She looks like she could do with one.'

Brian took Cathy to sit on the rug and got her bricks out to play with. Alice watched as he sat beside her, building a tower and talking to his niece, who looked at him with adoring eyes. Granny Lomax beckoned for Alice to follow her into the kitchen, where she filled the kettle and put it on the gas hob to boil.

'Since Brian got home earlier I've been thinking. Before I married Terry's father I was a primary school teacher for a number of years. How would you feel if I offered to teach Brian here at home for the duration of the war? He told me that he's had problems with some of the boys calling your mother mental and it upsets him. He's a sensitive child at the best of times. I think one-to-one teaching with me would be ideal for him.'

Alice stared open-mouthed at her mother-in-law. 'Would you really do that for him? Would the school allow it?'

'Well there's only one way to find out, dear. I'll phone them later and see what they say. I expect the headmaster will still be there while the grounds are being searched and if he's not then tomorrow will do. I'd be delighted to put myself into a teacher's role again. Brian is a clever boy and I reckon he'll get into grammar school with a bit of extra help. He'll miss his chance if he keeps getting distracted by the naughtier element of his class, not to mention the bullies.'

'If it's possible, then yes, I'm very happy for you to teach him. Maybe the school will provide textbooks and what-have-you. But can you manage the pair of them while I'm at Rootes in the morning?'

'Of course I can. Once I've set Brian his lessons I can see to Cathy while he gets on with his work. We won't have that mad rush of getting him out of the door on time in the mornings either, and with the winter fast approaching it will be much nicer for him that he doesn't have to go out on freezing days. Let's ask him what he thinks of the idea.'

Brian's face lit up as they explained the plan of him being taught at home. 'Will I still get a morning snack and me dinner at dinnertime?'

Granny Lomax laughed and nodded her head. 'Of course, Brian. That's one of the most important elements of being taught at home. You'll get decent food to feed the brain.'

A look of delight crossed his face.

'Then I think it's a smashing idea,' he declared as Alice breathed a sigh of relief. It was one worry off her mind and the air raid shelter was close to hand if and when they needed it too.

Chapter Twenty

The poster for the Christmas Eve do at the Legion had attracted a lot of attention and all the tickets had now been sold. Alice was really excited and proud as punch that the entertainment that night, brought back by popular demand, was the Tommy Jones band with Millie Markham, and her friend's name was plastered all over the poster. The money raised at the last social night the Americans had attended was being put towards giving the local wounded soldiers a hot meal to be served earlier than the evening do, and a nice Christmas present each.

Alice had been asked if she could do a shift that night. Christmas Eve fell on a Thursday, not her usual day of working, but Granny Lomax had told her to do what she could to help out and that she and Brian would get their Christmas Day preparations underway once Cathy was in bed. The tree was already up in the sitting room and this year it was a slightly taller one than usual, from Granny's farmer friend's land. He had also brought round a fat, plucked and prepared chicken, a large bag of fresh vegetables and six newly laid eggs this morning. They were looking forward to a lovely family Christmas. It was just a pity that Mam wouldn't be with them to celebrate.

Alice was hoping to go over to Crosby on Boxing Day to visit her, but so far there was no one available who could take her there. Very few buses, trams and trains would be running and the next-door neighbour, who had taken them on other occasions, was busy with his family all over the Christmas period. But Alice had promised her mam she would see her, so would need to find a way of getting there somehow or other. Brian wouldn't be joining her; his school friend's family had invited him over for tea and he was looking forward to going as he missed spending time with his old pal now he was being taught at home.

Granny Lomax had told Alice that he was a pleasure to teach, constantly thirsty for knowledge and dedicated to getting his learnings down on paper. School had agreed it would be a good idea, and safer, for Brian to be taught at home. Someone would call in once a week to check on his progress and to bring the lessons round for him to work on. Alice felt very proud of him and what he was achieving. He certainly seemed happier and more settled in himself and even Cathy, young as she was, was learning colours and shapes and recognising numbers thanks to Granny Lomax. She'd be way ahead by the time she started school. Hopefully the war would be well over and done with by then and Terry would be home and they could be a complete family once more. Alice hoped for a bright future for her little daughter, the chance to fulfil her dreams. Maybe she'd even want to be a nurse, like Alice had longed to be before both this flipping war, and the need to be around to look after her mam when Dad died, had put paid to her chances.

Alice arrived at the Legion with a flurry of snow that she hoped had no intention of sticking. A crowd of people were already queuing outside in the hope of getting the best seats. She'd had to work that morning at Rootes, dash home to help do her bit with present-wrapping and then have a quick bath and rush to get ready for her Legion night shift. The soldiers were just finishing their Christmas meal and the rich aroma of roast chicken and stuffing hung in the air, making her mouth water. Jack was waiting to clear away the tables and chairs in readiness for the evening's entertainments. Millie and the band hadn't arrived yet, so Alice joined Arnold's wife Winnie in the kitchen. Winnie was up to her elbows in hot sudsy water, on washing-up duties.

'There's a dinner saved for you and Jack in the oven, for when you have your breaks,' she said, nodding towards the large stove in the corner. 'Put a pinny on, then you won't splash water on your nice uniform.'

'I will, and thank you, it smells delicious.' Alice had only had time for a quick sandwich before she left home and a hot roast dinner would go down very well later. She took a wrapover pinny off the back of the kitchen door, slipped into it and picked up a clean tea towel from the stack on the work top near the sink.

'There's a cuppa in the pot and a mince pie if you want summat to be going on with,' Winnie announced after a few minutes of silent pot-washing and wiping. 'You can pour me one as well, while you're at it.'

Alice put down the damp tea towel and poured two mugs of hot strong tea. She milked and sugared them and took a mince pie from a plate on the table where several other plates were waiting for tonight's Christmas supper, piled high with sandwiches, and covered in greaseproof paper. Winnie certainly knew how to feed a crowd. No wonder the club was popular and always full.

'You've been really busy. I wish I could have made it in earlier to help.'

'Don't worry, love, Jack's been here all day and he's been a great help to me. It was his idea to scrape all the left-over chicken meat from the bones and mix it in a bowl with some stuffing. It's made a lovely filling for the sandwiches, gone much further than we expected as well. Those big pans on the stove are full of stripped bones now boiling up for stock and I'll make soup for Boxing Day supper as we've quite a few that'll come in. Some poor folk have got no one at home to spend the festive season with. It's a bit of company coming in here and having a bite to eat as well. But I'm definitely having tomorrow off, although Arnold has asked Jack over for his dinner or *he'd* have been on his own, poor lad. It's the least we can do for him. He's a good help and he's like a son to us.'

Alice frowned. 'Doesn't he have any family of his own?' It dawned on her that she knew very little about Jack and his background, apart from the details of his accident, and those were sketchy.

Winnie shook her head. 'His mam and dad died a few years ago and he fell out with his only brother not long before the war began. He's now away fighting God knows where. Jack could do with meeting a nice girl and settling down, like.'

Alice raised an eyebrow. She didn't think that was in Jack's immediate future plans.

'I'm sure he will do, one day when he's ready.' She took a sip of tea and bit into her mince pie, savouring the tasty mincemeat that, in spite of rationing, Winnie had made herself. She had done a good job of it as well.

Jack popped his head around the door, looking smart in his black and white waiting-on uniform that matched her own, apart from the skirt, that was.

'The band has arrived and they're just setting up on stage. Any chance of a hot drink for them? They've come a long way in that old van and they're freezing.'

Winnie nodded. 'Of course. Will you see to that, Alice love? Take a plate of mince pies out to them as well.'

'I'll start to let the punters in now,' Jack said as Alice filled the big kettle and put it on the gas hob to boil. 'It's a bit too cold out there to keep 'em waiting any longer. The soldiers are all settled now and said to say thank you for a fantastic dinner, Winnie.'

Winnie blushed. 'Bless them. Somebody needs to mother them in the absence of their own mothers. Tell them thank you and I'll be out later to speak to them all.'

Dying to see Millie, Alice whipped off her pinny, brewed the tea in a large catering pot and carried it through to the concert room. She dashed back into the kitchen for mugs, milk and connie-onnie, as sugar was scarce; there was little left in the sugar bowl and no fresh packets in the cupboard to open either. She looked proudly around the concert room, which looked lovely and festive, decorated with red and green crepe paper streamers. A large tree decorated with tinsel, baubles and lights stood at the side of the stage. A few bunches of holly hung from the beams and Alice smiled as she saw the inevitable bunch of mistletoe hanging as close to the centre of the dance floor as Jack – as there was no doubt it was his idea – could have hung it.

Millie squealed as she spotted Alice near the tea pot and hurried across to say hello.

'I'm so excited we're here tonight,' she began. 'I couldn't believe it when I was given a list of places we were playing this month. I didn't think I'd be back this way for Christmas. And we're all off tomorrow so I'm staying at my mam and dad's. Is it okay if I dash round tomorrow afternoon to see you and Cathy? I've got a little present for her.'

'We'd love that,' Alice said, giving Millie a hug. 'And how nice for your mam and dad that you're home for Christmas.'

'It is. Mam was thrilled when I rang her. They're coming here tonight so you can catch up with them. I'll be off again Boxing Day morning as we're playing somewhere in Cheshire that night. How's your mam?'

'Not great.' Alice sighed. 'Away with the fairies, for want of a better way of putting it. I'm going to try and get over to Crosby to see her on Boxing Day, if I can get transport, but that's not looking promising at the moment.' She stopped, aware of Jack standing behind her, starting to fill the mugs with tea.

'Thought I'd give you a hand as I knew you'd be chin-wagging with Millie and forget about the poor frozen boys in the band,' he teased, tipping a drop of whisky into each filled mug. 'That'll see them right,' he finished. 'Right, lads, tea's up and help yourselves to a mince pie. Enjoy.'

❋

The night flew by. Alice felt like her feet hadn't touched the ground from the minute the bar opened until her break time. The band had played background music while everyone did their catching up and drinks ordering. Millie would be on stage later. Alice couldn't wait.

'You and Jack go and eat your dinner,' Arnold said. 'Me and Winnie will see to this lot. We'll put the buffet out as soon as you come back. Go and sit in the kitchen, and Jack, pour Alice a big glass of sherry, she deserves it.'

Alice sat at the kitchen table and eased her shoes off her aching feet as Jack folded a tea towel and lifted two plates from the oven.

'Be careful,' he said. 'The plates are very hot. Smells bloody lovely though.'

Alice tucked in with relish, savouring every tasty mouthful. She drank her sherry and sat back feeling relaxed as Jack supped his pint, staring at her over the top of his tankard.

She frowned. 'What's up?'

'Nothing.' He shook his head. 'I overheard you telling Millie that you need transport to go and see your mam on Boxing Day.'

She sighed. 'Yes, I do, but God knows what or how. I hate letting her down, but it may well be that I can't get there. And then even if I do, there's the problem of getting back safely in the blackout.'

Jack nodded slowly and finished his pint. He put the tankard down on the table and folded his arms.

'Well, in that case I just might be your knight in un-shiny armour, although I do promise to polish my boots first.'

Alice frowned. 'What are you on about?'

'I told Arnold that you needed to try and get to Crosby and when and why, and he's offered the use of his car. They've got visitors coming on Boxing Day, Winnie's sister and niece, so he won't need it as they live in walking distance to here. So he's suggested I take you. How does that sound? I've got nothing else on, just working here at night from seven, but we'll be back long before then if we spend a couple of hours with her.'

'Oh, Jack, that's wonderful, thank you.' Alice's eyes filled. 'Arnold is very kind to offer his car and so are you for offering your time. That's a huge weight off my mind. She's a bit odd, my mam,' she warned, 'but I'm sure she'll be okay with you.'

Jack grinned. 'Don't worry. Mine used to be the same. I'll go for a walk outside if she doesn't want me there. The important thing is that you get there and back safely. Right, we'd best get back out there and give Arnold and Winnie a break. Millie will be singing soon, once the supper has been served.'

Various members of the Rootes workforce were in the club tonight: Freddie and his wife, and Marlene, all excited to see their Millie performing in her official capacity. Sadie and Jenny were also here and Alice had seen Jenny eyeing up the mistletoe and then gazing longingly over at Jack as he announced the buffet was served. There was no bingo or raffle tonight; Arnold had said not to bother when Jack had brought up the subject of getting prizes. He'd said people would be watching the pennies and he'd rather they put money over the bar. The young soldiers from the convalescent home were eyeing up the available girls in readiness for the dance spot.

As the buffet tables were cleared away and Jack re-introduced the band and Millie, everyone stood up to clap and cheer. None louder than Freddie, who whistled through his fingers as she walked on stage dressed in a sparkly strappy dress with a full skirt, matching silver shoes on her feet. Her long dark blonde hair curled softly on her shoulders and around her face. Alice thought her friend looked every bit the star as she confidently strode up to the microphone and announced the first song.

As Millie launched into 'You Made Me Love You', a couple of the wounded soldiers approached Sadie and Jenny and invited them to dance. Jenny looked across to the side of the stage where Jack was nodding in time to the music, oblivious to her wistful glance in his direction. She accepted the young soldier's hand and followed Sadie and her soldier onto the floor. A few more couples got up and joined in. Alice smiled throughout Millie's performance and clapped enthusiastically as the song came to an end.

Freddie came dashing over for refills for his wife and Marlene and himself. Alice apologised for not spending any time with them this evening.

'There just hasn't been a minute,' she said, pulling his pint of mild ale. 'We've been rushed off our feet.'

'Don't you worry, Alice; I can see how busy the place is. Isn't our Millie the best turn to have on tonight though? I feel that damn proud of her. Her mam and dad are sitting just behind us and her mam keeps wiping her eyes. I'm glad they've got her back for Christmas Day. Her being an only one, it's really nice for them. Right, best get this lot over to my ladies.' He handed her a ten-bob note. 'Keep the change, gel, put it in your tips.'

'Thank you, Freddie,' Alice called after him, slipping the coins into a glass behind the counter where she and Jack pooled all their tips before splitting them at the end of the night. Millie was singing 'That Old Black Magic' now and the audience loved her; she certainly had *them* in her spell. Next, she had them wiping their eyes with her rendition of Vera Lynn's 'White Cliffs of Dover'. Millie could do no wrong and Alice was certain this was just the tip of the iceberg; her friend was going to be a star, no doubt about it. As the band drew the set to a close and the audience shouted for more, stamping their feet and whistling, Millie beckoned to Alice. Arnold pushed her out from behind the bar.

'Go on, chuck, she gave us fair warning she'd want you to join her for the encore.'

Alice ran up on stage and Millie grabbed her hand. 'Tonight, just imagine that Alice and I are the Andrews Sisters,' she announced. The band struck up with 'Don't Sit Under the Apple Tree' and they finished with 'Boogie Woogie Bugle Boy' to cheers and shouts and whistles. Alice looked around and saw Jack staring at her, a big smile on his face. She smiled back, feeling elated. Millie must feel like this every time she performed, Alice thought. They hugged each other and Millie thanked her and hugged her again.

Back behind the bar Alice came down to earth with a bump as Jack and Arnold brought empty glasses over to be washed. Winnie had gone upstairs half an hour ago, saying her feet couldn't take much more as she'd been on them since the crack of dawn. She'd wished Alice a very merry Christmas and said she'd see her again on New Year's Eve, if she could work. Alice was sure Granny Lomax wouldn't mind. The pay was double tonight and would be on New Year's Eve, and the tips had been plentiful. A few coppers here and there soon mounted up, so she didn't need to do her weekend shifts as she'd earned enough money to make up for it.

Jack came to help her with the glasses and between them they soon had the bar area looking shipshape. The punters were starting to leave the club, calling out their thanks for another great night, and Merry Christmas, as they left. Alice hung the tea towels up to dry and went to talk to Millie while the band packed away their instruments. Millie's parents came over to say goodnight.

'My case and everything is in the van, so I'll get dropped off in a short while, Mam,' Millie said. 'I'll see you tomorrow, Alice. It'll just be a flying visit, but it's better than nothing and I wasn't expecting to be in Liverpool today so it's a bonus for me to get to see all my favourite people in one go.'

'Hope you include me in that,' Jack teased. 'Brilliant night. You'll go far, you will.'

'Of course I include you, and thank you, Jack.' Millie stood up on tiptoe and gave him a kiss.

'I knew I should have reached that mistletoe down,' Jack said with a grin. 'Enjoy your day with your mam and dad. I'm going to walk Alice home now and leave Arnold to lock up once the lads have finished loading their gear. Get your coat on, gel,' he said to Alice.

Outside the snow had fallen, lightly, but enough to make the pavements slippery. Alice felt her feet going from beneath her and Jack grabbed hold of her and slid his arm around her waist to catch her before she went down.

'Whoops, don't want you breaking anything.'

Alice blew out her cheeks. Jack's arm around her felt a bit too intimate, but at least he had saved her from falling. They walked down the road as quickly as they could, him limping and Alice slithering along. She could smell the drink on him and hoped he wouldn't fall over himself before he got home. He'd certainly knocked a good few back tonight and he'd had a few before he came into work, as seemed to be his usual practice. Alice worried about him spending a lot of time alone. Maybe drinking was his way of coping with having no one to care about him and coming to terms with his disability. They were soon outside the Linnet Lane bungalow and as she turned to thank him his lips brushed her cheek.

'Just a little Christmas kiss,' he whispered. 'Your Terry's a lucky bugger. Pity he's away. I mean, one day of marriage and that was it? Why didn't you wait to tie the knot until after the war?'

Alice frowned. 'Terry didn't want to wait.'

'Well I can't say as I blame him, but it's tied you to a life of hard work and the responsibility of a kid and not having a clue what the future will bring. You're too young; you should be free and having fun, Alice.'

'I enjoy my life,' she muttered. 'It's not exactly how I *imagined* married life would be, but I'm not the only one with a husband abroad. There are thousands of us.'

Jack laughed. 'Well, Terry made sure he staked his claim on you by knocking you up right away. Having a kid could have waited until after the war, surely. What if he doesn't come back? You're lumbered for life now.'

Alice chewed her lip, wondering where all this was coming from. Too much drink probably; Jack wasn't usually a one for talking about relationships.

'But I love my baby, Jack. You'll understand one day when you've got a family of your own.'

He shrugged. 'I doubt it. Kids are not my thing. Give me a dog any day.'

'It's different when they're your own.'

'If you say so, Alice. Right, you'd best get in before your ma-in-law looks out the window. She'll think we're canoodling, me with my arm still around you. Don't want to start rumours, do we? I'll see you about one o'clock on Boxing Day. Pick you up here. Enjoy your day tomorrow.'

'And you enjoy yours with Arnold and Winnie.'

'I'm sure I will. Goodnight.'

Alice watched him limp away into the cold dark night. Shivering, she crept indoors and into the warm sitting room, where the lights on the tree twinkled. She smiled at the presents nestling underneath the lower branches, waiting to be opened tomorrow. She couldn't wait until Cathy was old enough to know what it was all about, hanging her stocking up for Father Christmas to fill. Terry would play that role so well, she just knew it. She sighed and wished there had been some news from him this month but she'd had nothing, not even a card, since she'd written and told him about Jack walking her home after her Legion shifts. She'd sent *him* a Christmas card, a photo of Cathy and a small parcel with socks and hankies, a couple of weeks ago. There was probably a big backlog of post sitting in a sorting office somewhere in the back of beyond with all the forces cards waiting to be shipped to anxious sweethearts everywhere. Damn this war and bloody Hitler. She wanted and needed her husband badly, especially right now, to put his arms around her, to love her and to celebrate Cathy's second Christmas with them all.

Chapter Twenty-One

Millie dashed round to Linnet Lane just after the King's three o'clock speech to the nation finished. She came indoors with a blast of cold air and a large bag of parcels. Alice led her into the sitting room, where Brian and Granny Lomax were about to play a game of snakes and ladders and where Cathy was sitting on the rug nursing her new teddy bear, a present from Freddie and his wife. She got to her feet and toddled across to Millie, a big smile on her face.

'Look who's come to see you,' Alice said as Millie scooped up Cathy and gave her a cuddle.

'Shall we see what I've got in my bag?' Millie said, carrying Cathy across to the sofa and sitting her on her knee. She dug into her bag and pulled out a small parcel. 'Now, this is for Brian. You take it to him,' she instructed as Cathy grabbed the parcel, said, 'Mine' and held it to her chest.

'Maybe not the best idea,' Alice said, laughing and prising her daughter's fingers off the parcel. She handed it to Brian, whose eyes lit up.

He ripped off the paper and gasped. 'Wow, a real fountain pen in a box and some ink, look, Granny and Alice. Thank you, Millie. It's a Parker too, a right posh one. Just what I need for my schoolwork.' He jumped up and gave a delighted Millie a hug.

'I expect you to pass your eleven plus next year now, Brian,' Millie teased. 'With your brains and a posh pen, there's no excuse not to.'

'I'll do my best,' he said, cheeks going red with pleasure.

Millie handed over wrapped boxes of chocolates and silk stockings to Granny and Alice. She tapped the side of her nose when they asked how on earth she had managed to get her hands on such luxuries with all the shortages.

'It's not what you know, but *who* you know.' She laughed. 'The Yanks at the bases have a large stash of all sorts and they're a generous bunch. When I told a couple of the band I needed to do my Christmas shopping soon, they showed me the way. And this one,' she held out a large, brightly wrapped parcel, reading from the label, 'it says this is for Miss Cathy Lomax.'

'Oh, that's for you, sweetie,' Alice said as Cathy squealed excitedly. She wriggled off Millie's knee and snatched the parcel, flopping down onto the floor to open it. 'Sorry, Millie, she's got absolutely no finesse when it comes to accepting gifts gracefully.'

Millie laughed. 'No surprise, at her age.' She smiled as Cathy held up a box containing a small dressed dolly in a wooden crib, covered with a white blanket. 'Open the other box,' Millie instructed. Cathy did as she was told and revealed a toddler-sized nurse's outfit of a blue dress, white apron and white lace cap. There was also a toy fob watch to fasten to the apron and a stethoscope to wear around her neck.

'Oh, look at this,' Alice said. 'Nurse Cathy. How lovely is that? You lucky girl. Mammy always wanted to be a nurse. Shall we put your uniform on and then you can see to the poorly dolly and make her better? I think she's got a bad cough, don't you?'

Cathy got to her feet and began to tug the dress she was wearing over her head.

'Come here, Madam.' Alice laughed. 'Let's get you sorted out.'

Granny Lomax got to her feet. 'I think this calls for a cuppa and mince pies all round.' Brian followed her into the kitchen, leaving Millie and Alice to catch up.

'Thank you so much for all of this,' Alice began. 'We have a couple of things under the tree for you, but it seems like nothing in comparison.'

'Alice, it's the thought that counts. And believe me, I haven't spent a fortune. Like I told you, the Yanks are more than generous. I was just lucky to be in the right place at the right time last week.' She delved once more into the bag. 'There's chocs for your mam for tomorrow and can you give Jack these parcels when you see him, please? It's a small box of cigars and a half-bottle of bourbon. If he hadn't set up that talent contest I wouldn't be doing the best job in the world right now. I've got a lot to thank him for.'

'Of course I will. I'm seeing him tomorrow. He's taking me to Crosby to see Mam.' Alice bit her lip. She hadn't thought to get Jack anything and now wished she had. After all, who was there to buy him gifts, other than friends? And he didn't seem to have a lot of those as he kept himself to himself, apart from when he was with Arnold, Winnie and herself. There was a spare pair of black socks and three white gents' hankies upstairs that she'd kept back from sending to Terry as the parcel would have been too expensive to post if she'd included everything in it. She'd put them away for when he came home, but she could wrap them up instead and give them to Jack. It was better than nothing and she knew he liked a clean hanky in his pocket, so at least he would use them.

As Granny Lomax and Brian carried the tea things into the lounge, Alice pushed Millie's gifts for Mam and Jack back into the carrier bag that Millie had brought everything in.

'I'll take these to my bedroom and then I won't forget them tomorrow when I visit Mam,' she said, hurrying from the room. She felt almost embarrassed at the thought of giving gifts to another man and she didn't know why. After all, Jack was a good friend to both her and Millie and a little gift would be much appreciated by him, she was sure of that. But she'd rather her mother-in-law didn't know about it, although Granny Lomax knew Jack was taking Alice to Crosby and had said how kind it was of Arnold to lend Jack his car to help out.

Alice gave Millie a hug goodbye as her friend hesitated in the hall before opening the door.

'What is it?' Alice asked, frowning as Millie's eyes filled with tears.

'It's Alan,' Millie whispered. 'I got a letter. It was waiting for me when I got home after the do last night. It's over. He met a nurse when he hurt his arm a few months ago and was hospitalised for a few days. Said he loves her and she loves him. She's from London way. Nice of him to drop it on me at Christmas, isn't it?' She half-smiled. 'I knew it was on the cards, but it still hurts. He could have told me weeks ago.'

'Oh, Millie,' Alice said, giving her a hug. 'I'm so sorry.'

'Good job I've got my singing to keep me occupied.'

'And Jimmy. You will still write to him?'

Millie smiled. 'I will. He's a nice boy and I won't feel so guilty now. I'll just enjoy being the someone he writes to and see what happens.'

Alice lay back in the lavender-scented regulation six inches of hot water and closed her eyes, relaxing at long last. Cathy was fast asleep after a screaming battle to get her out of her nurse's uniform and into a nightdress, and Granny and Brian were tackling the compendium of games Brian had received from their next-door neighbours. When they'd tried to persuade Alice to play a game of tiddlywinks she had told them she had a bit of a headache starting, so was plumping for a soak in the bath and an early night instead. She honestly felt like she could fall asleep if she let herself. What a busy last few days she'd had; it had been non-stop. She'd been sad saying goodbye to Millie again, but had wished her well for tomorrow's show in Cheshire and then on the journey down to Portsmouth with the band for the New Year's Eve show they were the stars of.

It would have made Christmas much better for Alice if only there had been some word from Terry, but Millie had told her that there was nothing waiting for her from Jimmy either when she'd gone back to her mam's place, just Alan's bombshell letter. Millie had written to Jimmy to let him know about her new job and that she may be delayed in writing back to him from now on as she was never in one place for long and her letters would still need to be picked up from home on her probably infrequent visits to Liverpool. So it wasn't just Terry's letters that were delayed, which was a comfort in a way.

She wondered how her mam would be tomorrow and hoped there would be a bit of a change in her, at least.

The following day Jack was outside the bungalow in Arnold's shiny black Ford Anglia dead on the dot of one o'clock. He looked smart in a navy pinstripe suit and white shirt and was even wearing a navy blue tie. He got out of the car and, like a gentleman, opened the passenger door for Alice. And true to his words of Christmas Eve, his highly polished boots shone brightly. Alice had been waiting by the window for the car to arrive and was hoping her mother-in-law wouldn't ask Jack inside. But as she'd opened the front door to dash out, Granny had called out to invite Jack in for a cup of tea when they came back as it was the least they could do.

'I will, if he doesn't need to dash straight back,' Alice said. 'See you later.'

'You look very nice, Jack,' she said as he helped her into the car.

'I scrub up well when I need to,' he said with a grin. 'You look nice too.'

'Oh, thank you.' She looked down at her knee-length black and red plaid skirt with a kick-pleated hemline that she'd teamed with a red angora sweater, knitted and presented to her by Granny Lomax on Christmas Day. She'd put Millie's gift of stockings on and her black court shoes. As she'd got ready she'd told herself that she was just making an effort to look nice for Mam, but lurking in the back of her mind was the fact that she wanted Jack to see her in something other than her Legion uniform and this outfit was the newest she possessed. She'd topped it with a warm black jacket and felt she looked quite smart. She put the carrier bag of gifts down by her feet and held her handbag on her knee.

'Ready for off then?' Jack asked. 'By the way, Arnold told me to ask if you can definitely do the New Year's Eve shift for him. Otherwise he'll need to collar one of the other staff, but he said he'd prefer to have you behind the bar.'

'Yes, it's fine, I can do it,' Alice replied. 'I'm looking forward to it. Pity we haven't got the band and Millie again though.'

'Not to worry. We've got the fella who plays piano and Arnold bought his wife a gramophone for Christmas. Think it was for him as well, but he got away with it because he bought her a few favourite records too. So he said we can bring it down and use it for dancing. I've asked around and a few people I know will bring their records in, so we can use them. One of the injured soldiers is a piper in the regiment band and he's going to pipe in the New Year at midnight. So all in all it should be a great night. Will you let the Rootes crowd know when you go in tomorrow? No tickets this time, just first come first served, but it's pay on the door and Arnold hasn't decided how much yet. It'll be on a poster when he gets round to doing it tomorrow.'

'I'll tell them. I'm sure some will be coming and I'll let my pals Sadie and Jenny know as well.'

'Just don't invite that Maisie one,' Jack said. 'She drives me mad. Shut the bloody door on me foot and nearly knocked me flying when I had a go at her for saying things out of turn about you and me.'

'Yes, she told me,' Alice said. 'She also showed me bruises on her arm that she said you did.'

'I grabbed hold of her to stop me falling. Serves her right if she bruised. Stupid girl could have done me a right mischief.' Jack frowned and Alice saw his jaw clench. 'Anyway, enough about her. What did Father Christmas bring you?'

Alice smiled. She knew deep down that Jack wouldn't have deliberately hurt Maisie, and like he said, she could have injured him badly if he'd fallen.

'I got this sweater, stockings, chocs, bath cubes and a new hairbrush. Useful things, you know. Not a lot of choices in the shops right now.'

'I wouldn't know. I don't have anyone to buy gifts for. Although I did manage to get some chocolates a few weeks ago off the Yanks and some cigars too. I hung on to them just in case, and Arnold and Winnie loved their pressies.' He inclined his head towards the back seat. 'There's a box for you too. You can have them later.'

Alice's eyes widened. Thank goodness she'd wrapped up the left-over things from Terry for him.

'I've got some surprises in here for you too. You can have yours later as well.'

'If I'm a good boy,' he teased.

She laughed. 'Yes.'

She wondered how he was managing to drive with only half a right foot, but he seemed to be doing okay. Maybe his boots had been adapted especially to fit. She didn't feel she knew him well enough to ask though. The road was quiet, with very little traffic, and there was hardly a soul about. They passed a few bombed-out and boarded-up houses, making Alice realise how lucky they were that they all still had a roof over their heads. There'd been no air raid warnings for almost a week now, but that wouldn't last.

She stared out of the window until they came to the sign and turn-off for Crosby.

'It's just down the main street and second left,' she said. 'There's a visitors' car park and it's usually fairly empty.'

Jack pulled in at the entrance, where previously a pair of tall, double iron gates had hung. But they'd been removed to be melted

down for the war effort, as had most iron gates in Liverpool. Alice
was thankful that Granny Lomax's garden gate was wooden; she'd
have been inclined to aim a right hook at anyone who tried to take
her gate away. Brian had been teaching her some moves he'd learnt
at his Saturday-morning boxing lessons that he was still attending.

'Just in case any stray Germans are hiding in the bushes in the
garden, you need to know how to stick up for yourself,' he'd told her.

'Right,' Alice said as Jack switched off the engine. She picked
up the carrier bag from the floor. 'I might as well as give you your
presents now – there's no point in taking them in there. This one
is from Millie.' She handed him Millie's gaily wrapped package
and watched his face light up as he took the paper off.

'Smashing,' he said, clearly delighted that Millie had thought
of him. 'My favourites. Makes up for not winning that bottle of
bourbon on the raffle the other week. I shall enjoy this *and* the
cigars when I'm sitting with my feet up at home tomorrow, listening to the wireless. I'll feel like a king.'

Alice handed him her small wrapped package and wished that
she'd made more of an effort, but his smile was genuine when he
unwrapped the socks and hankies.

'Thank you so much. It's years since I've had any presents at
Christmas and now I feel really spoiled. I got this nice shirt off
the boss and his wife and a pot of Brylcreem, and now these gifts
from you two.' He reached over to the back seat and presented
Alice with a box of American chocolates; the box was decorated
with a lavish red satin ribbon bow.

'Thank you, those look lovely, and I'll save the ribbon for
Cathy's hair when it grows a bit more.'

'Use it in yours,' Jack said, leaning forward to lift a curl that
had fallen over her face. 'You can tie back your curls and it will go
with that nice jumper. Be a shame to waste it on the kid.'

Alice felt her cheeks heating as he looked at her intently. She'd
been about to give him a peck on the cheek for his present, but the

look in his eyes told her not to. He still had hold of her curl and she put up her hand to free it and brushed his with her own. This wasn't right; she shouldn't have accepted his offer of a lift. Alice felt that the least bit of encouragement from her would be wrong. She felt flattered by his attentions, but a bit worried about them at the same time.

'So what did Terry send you?' Jack asked, breaking the moment.

'Oh, er, nothing yet. We've had no post from him for nearly three weeks. It's terrible. I hope our parcels have got through to him.'

'Yeah,' Jack said and lit a cigarette. He got out of the car and came around to the passenger side to help her out. 'It must be hard, waiting for something that never arrives.'

'Oh it will, eventually,' Alice said. 'He always writes, but for some reason there's no letters or parcels coming through at the moment. Millie had nothing from Jimmy this time either, so it's not just me. Anyway, shall we go in?'

She led the way through the reception area, which was festively decorated with streamers and a tall, well-lit tree, and was directed to the communal lounge, where she was told her mam was waiting for her. Thank goodness for Jack, because without him, Mam would have been sitting there all day.

'Hello, Mam,' Alice greeted her and turned to Jack to introduce him.

But Mam got there before her. 'Hello, chuck, and oh you've brought Terry to see me. That's nice. You two will be getting married soon, I expect. Sit down, both of you. I'll make you a cuppa in a minute.'

Alice chewed her lip and looked at Jack, who shrugged and sat down. Mam got to her feet and shuffled away, calling over her shoulder that she was just waiting for the kettle to boil.

Alice's eyes filled and Jack stood up and put his arms around her.

'Look, I know this is hard to take but she's gone like my mam did. Just follow her lead, Alice, play along with her. She doesn't know what she's doing or saying by the sound of it. I'll be Terry for the afternoon if needs must.'

Alice leant against him, glad of his support and that he was there with her. Nothing seemed to go right lately. She needed a friend, a shoulder to cry on, and at the moment, in the absence of Millie, that friend was Jack and the shoulder belonged to him. They sat side by side, Jack holding her hand in a comforting way. Eventually Mam shuffled back into the room and smiled as she sat down in front of them.

'Hello, love, fancy seeing you here. And who's this?'

Alice caught her breath. What was happening to her mam? She didn't even realise that she'd just spoken to them five minutes ago. Jack spoke up for them both, still holding onto Alice's hand.

'Hello Mrs Turner. I'm, er, Alice's friend.' Jack didn't give a name. 'I've driven Alice over to see you as there are no regular trams and buses today. It's Boxing Day, you see.'

Mam nodded. 'Oh yes. It was Christmas Day, wasn't it. I told them I had to get home to see to my little boy. He's only a baby, you know. Where is he, Alice? They wouldn't let me go home yesterday. They said I had to wait to see you. So where is he?'

'Brian is fine, Mam. He's with a school friend today. The family invited him for tea.'

'Don't be silly. Brian's not at school, he's only three. And where's our Rodney and your father? They said they'd take me home today but I haven't seen either of them since last night.'

'I don't know, Mam.' Alice looked at Jack in despair. 'What shall I do?'

'Just go along with her,' Jack whispered. 'If you can't beat 'em, join 'em. We could do with speaking to a nurse or someone. Bet there are no doctors on duty today. Shall I go and ask at reception?'

'Would you, please? Thanks Jack, I'll stay here with her.'

Mam grabbed her hand as Jack went in search of someone to speak to. 'He's nice, your young man. Don't let him get away, see that you marry him as soon as he asks you, he looks a good one. Terry, did you say his name was?'

Alice took a deep breath and nodded. 'That's right, Mam. And I'll take your advice when he asks me.'

She gave her mam the wrapped presents and watched as she unwrapped them, smiling at the framed photo of Brian and Cathy that they'd had taken together.

'Who are these children? They look very nice. Do I know them?'

Alice almost choked on a sob. 'That's Brian, your little boy, and that baby is my Cathy, your granddaughter.'

Mam stared at the photo for a while and then smiled, but not with recognition. 'Are you married then, love?'

'Yes, Mam.' This was awful. Did her mother even know there was a war going on? She clearly had forgotten that Dad and Rodney were dead. The door opened and Jack came back in with an older man in a suit.

'This is Doctor Forbes, Alice,' Jack said. 'I'll take your mam for a cup of tea while he talks to you.' He patted her shoulder and helped Mam to her feet. 'Oh, what have you got there? Shall we go and look at your pressies while Alice has a chat to the doctor?'

He led her away and Alice felt grateful that Jack was with her today. It was a good job he was, because she had a feeling that what she was about to hear wasn't going to be pleasant in any way. Doctor Forbes sat down in the chair Mam had vacated.

'Is it serious?' she began, her voice faltering.

'I'm afraid it is, Alice,' he replied. 'We've seen a real decline in your mother's state of mental health since she's been with us. She's rather young, at nearly fifty, for the diagnosis, but we've assessed her and done tests since she's been here and her condition deteriorates as the days go by. I'm afraid that we will be unable to keep her here in the convalescent home for much longer and she is of course unable to go home and live independently. We are looking to transfer her in early January to a mental health hospital in the city where she will get the help and treatment that she needs.'

'You mean an institution?' Alice said, her voice barely more than a whisper. 'Oh no, my poor mam. Is there anything she can take that will make her get well again? She's missing out on her little lad growing up and my baby girl, her granddaughter.'

The doctor shook his head. 'There's nothing, I'm afraid. Her brain is in decline and her condition will only worsen over time. She has a brain disease that we believe to be dementia and she also suffers from psychosis. She is a very sick woman and needs specialist care that only a hospital dealing with mental health patients can help with.'

Alice sighed. 'And will she die of this brain disease?'

He nodded slowly. 'The brain eventually stops functioning and communicating with parts of the body. I'll make sure you get as much information as we can give you to keep you informed. We'll let you know where we are sending her, and when, as soon as we know ourselves. Meantime, I can assure you that we will do our best to care for your mother here and keep her comfortable until that time arrives. Now I'll take you to find her and your husband and you can enjoy the rest of your visit with her.'

Alice nodded, not bothering to correct him, and followed him to the dining room, where Jack and Mam were sitting at a table chatting like they were old pals, a plate of cake and a tray of tea things in front of them. The doctor shook Alice's hand and she joined them, feeling stunned at what she'd just been told.

'Okay?' Jack asked, pouring her a cuppa from the green tea pot on the tray. 'Sugar?'

'Just one please. I'm in a spin, I really am.'

'I know, I've been in the place you're in right now. We'll talk about it on the way home. Meantime let's get back to that Blackpool holiday your mam was telling me about. When you fell in the sea and wet your clothes and had to be taken dripping wet back to the boarding house to get changed.'

Alice half-smiled at the long-ago seaside holiday memory that seemed clear as a bell to her mam, who was chatting happily to Jack. She still seemed to think he was Terry.

Chapter Twenty-Two

February 1943

Mam had been transferred to Rainhill Hospital in mid-January, and although it wasn't an ideal solution as it was still quite a journey to visit, it was the only hospital place available right now that could cope with her mental health, which was worsening as the days went by. Alice wished she could care for her at home but it would be impossible for her to continue to work, and without her working they would starve. She knew she was in a better position than a lot of girls her age who were married to soldiers and had the responsibility of children to look after, but sometimes she thought about what Jack had said, about her being tied when she could have been free until Terry came home. He was right, but it had been her choice and what she'd wanted more than anything at the time. After all, no one had expected the war to last all this time and still with no end in sight.

The daily slog of working at Rootes was getting harder and occasionally Alice had been asked to do overtime, as the demand for Halifax bombers was overwhelming. So many planes had been lost in battle along with their crew and the need to replace them was urgent. It meant extra money in her wage packet, but gave her less free time to spend with Cathy and Brian. She was still working on Friday and Saturday nights at the Legion and then trying to visit her mam each Sunday, transport permitting. To say she felt worn out was an understatement.

Granny Lomax and Brian were supporting the Dig for Victory campaign and had dug half of the large back lawn over ready for growing vegetables. The last few days had been frosty and had halted the dig and preparation as the ground was too hard, but the pair was determined to have it ready for spring and the new planting season. Granny's farmer friend had promised a couple of chickens too, so Brian was excited about the prospect of looking after them and having fresh eggs. He'd collected all the government pamphlets about what to grow and how, and had painstakingly written out lists of seasonal planting times, and how to grow things in stages, so that as they harvested one lot another would go in the ground and they would have fresh vegetables and salad throughout the late spring and summer months. Granny was in charge of fruit-growing, he'd told them. The planning was keeping him busy and, along with his studies and helping with Cathy, he never gave Alice a moment's trouble, unlike some of the unruly boys he'd been at school with. Boys who, if she'd been their parents, she'd have been glad to see the back of during the mass evacuation.

Alice yawned and dragged her frozen feet as she walked the short distance from the tram stop to the bungalow. It was bitter cold and icy underfoot. She felt tired and her shoulders were aching from being hunched over the factory benches all day. She'd done five hours' overtime and was looking forward to soaking her weary bones in a hot bath after tea. Production on the Halifax bombers had stepped up even further to keep in line with demand. But it seemed to Alice that the more they produced the more they lost, not to mention all the young lives that went down with them.

As she let herself into the bungalow the aroma of something tasty wafted down the hallway. Rabbit pie? Certainly smelled like it anyway. Her stomach rumbled with anticipation as she hung her coat on the hallstand and went into the kitchen, where Granny Lomax was draining potatoes over the sink, steam engulfing her face and hair.

She put the pan down on the wooden draining board and wafted the steam away with a tea towel.

'Smells good,' Alice said, reaching for the dish of butter from the cold slab in the pantry. She cut a sliver and dropped it into the pan. Granny poured in a drop of milk and got to work with the masher.

'I long for the day when we can throw as much milk and butter into the spuds as we used to,' Granny muttered as the potatoes fluffed up slightly. 'How can we enjoy really creamy mash when we can scarcely butter the toast with our rations? It's ridiculous.'

'We could always get a goat,' Brian said, coming up behind Alice and giving her a quick hug. 'I'll learn how to milk it and I might be able to make butter as well. I think there's something about it in my pamphlets.'

Granny raised an eyebrow. 'I think we'll have quite enough livestock with the chickens when they arrive.'

'So do I,' Alice said, giving her brother a hug back. 'And I'm not even sure what goats' milk tastes like. We might not like it and then we'll be stuck with an animal we still need to feed.'

'Set the table, Brian love,' Granny ordered. 'Have you finished all your schoolwork? Put your books away in the sideboard if you have.'

Brian nodded and went off to do his chores.

'Where's little Madam?' Alice asked, peeking round the kitchen door for signs of her daughter. 'She usually comes to greet me.'

'Playing with her dollies on the rug and struggling to stay awake. Can you just lift the pie out of the oven for me, Alice love?'

Alice savoured the aroma as she lifted the pie up onto the work top next to the gas stove.

'Mmm, smells wonderful. I'm starving tonight. It's all those extra hours I'm putting in. Makes me really hungry.'

Granny smiled. 'My neighbour dropped some bits of wood off earlier for Brian to have a go at making the chicken coop. We need some nails but we can get them at the weekend from the ironmongers on Lark Lane. He's drawn a plan for Brian to follow and it looks quite straightforward. Once it's ready he'll bring the chickens round. We've got some more plant pots outside as well to put seeds in, to get things going so that we can then replant into the beds we'll finish digging over when the weather improves and the ground's not so hard. By the way, two letters arrived earlier for you. One from Terry and the other looks like Millie's writing with a London postmark. They're on the mantelpiece. I'll dish up while you have a read,' she finished, as Alice's eyes lit up.

Lying in her bed, stomach full and feeling relaxed and fresh from her lavender-bath-cube-scented soak, Alice took Terry's letter from its envelope and re-read his words. Her eyes filled as she read how much he was missing her and that he couldn't wait to hold her in his arms again. He wrote that he still couldn't tell her where he was stationed, but that he was doing his best to stay safe, not to worry, and he hoped that she and Cathy were staying safe too. He'd already told her that he knew who Jack Dawson was, from her earlier letter, and to thank him for escorting her home at night from the Legion. He said he would buy him a pint when he got home and to ask if he was still keen on motorbikes. She'd written back that he was. Terry's missing Christmas card had finally arrived in the middle of January, much to her relief, swiftly followed by another that Alice assumed had been stuck in the seasonal backlog too. Since then there had been nothing until now. Terry wrote that he'd be keen to ask Jack if he'd help him sort out his Harley on his return. Alice smiled as she got her pad and pen out of the bedside table drawer to write back to him. She was certain that Jack would be thrilled to be involved with the motorbike repairs.

Millie's short letter had been written at RAF Biggin Hill, where the band had played a few shows before moving on to RAF Benson in Berkshire for a brief time. She said she was fine, still enjoying herself, and she hoped all was well with Alice and her family. She was missing them and hoped to be back in Liverpool as soon as the band worked its way up the country. She would write again when she had any further information. Alice wished she could write back to her friend, but there was little point, as all Millie's letters went straight to her mother's for collecting when she was home. She would just have to wait and catch up with all the news then. Not that much was happening. It was the same routine, day in and day out.

Alice finished her letter to Terry and put it to one side to post tomorrow. She took a quick look at Cathy, who was flat on her back, fast asleep in her cot under the window, crept back into bed and switched off the lamp. She shivered and pulled the blankets tightly around her. What was the betting the windows would be iced up tomorrow, both here in the bedroom and on the bus to work?

❦

'So 'ow's she doing?' Marlene asked when Alice told her that she'd had a letter off Millie. The pair were on the works' bus bumping along towards Speke, and just as Alice had predicted, the windows had ice on them. She picked at it with her fingernail and shivered.

'She's fine. Enjoying herself and the band seems to be doing plenty of shows.'

'Lucky Millie,' Marlene said. 'Wish I could sing an' 'ad a figure like she does. I'd be off with that band an' all like a shot. Nice life if you can get it.'

'It certainly is,' Alice agreed as the bus pulled up in front of the factory. 'Here we go. No singing driver today. Pity because I always feel happier going in when we've had a sing-song.'

Marlene laughed and linked her arm through Alice's. ''E'll be back on tomorrow. Everybody needs a day off.'

'Tell me about it,' Alice said. 'At the moment I'm working every single day. The extra money is handy, but I'm falling asleep on my feet at the Legion. Hopefully things will be a bit less fraught here when we take on more staff.'

'Aye, maybe,' Marlene said. 'Freddie's interviewing today so fingers crossed. Meantime keep saving that extra money for when your Terry gets home. It'll stand you in good stead for getting a nice place of your own.'

The pair followed the other workers inside and changed into their overalls, turbans and rubber-soled footwear. Alice placed her wedding ring inside her coin purse and pushed it to the bottom of her handbag before stashing everything in her locker. She still hated taking off her ring each day, but needs must.

As she sat down at the bench and flexed her fingers in readiness to pick up her riveting gun, Freddie appeared beside her looking anxious.

'Would you mind giving me a hand this morning, gel? I've twelve coming in for interviews and the office girl's phoned in ill so there's no one to do the paperwork.'

'Of course I will, Freddie. It'll make a nice change from here.'

He nodded. 'Smashing. Go and get back into your own clothes and then you'll look more the part.'

Alice smiled, looking down at her unfeminine, baggy attire and flat, ungainly shoes. She dashed back out to the locker rooms again and changed into her smart black skirt, white blouse and black court shoes. Thank goodness she'd put stockings on today to help keep her legs a bit warmer on the bus. She'd be sitting behind a desk most likely, so the fact that she had a small ladder running up the back of one of them wouldn't matter too much and it was above knee height anyway. She ran a comb through her hair and touched up her lips with the worn-down stub of Tangee lippy she kept in her handbag. She really must try to get another, but the shops were in short supply of most cosmetics. She glanced in the cracked mirror on the back of the door and smiled at her distorted reflection. She ran a comb through her hair, now freed from the turban. There, she'd do. Not quite as smart as the usual girl who worked in the office, but better than nothing.

Freddie was waiting for her in the corridor and they walked into a small room that was simply furnished with a desk, chair and a tall filing cabinet. It was freezing cold with ice on the windows. Alice shivered and Freddie switched on a two-bar electric fire that sparked and fizzled as it glowed red.

'I'll get you a hot drink in a minute but that fire will soon warm the place up a bit if you keep the door closed. The list of applicants is there on the desk.' He pointed to a clipboard. 'The ladies will wait out in the corridor. If you call them in one at a time and take down their particulars, and then bring them and the paperwork in to me in the office next door, I'll do the interview while you sort out the next lass. It shouldn't take us too long. I can usually suss out who I think is suitable for the job or not. Then letters will need to go out to the ones we take on. Right, I'll nip down to the canteen and get us a brew. Won't be a minute.'

As he left Alice looked around the office and spotted a fluffy black cardigan draped over the back of the chair. She picked it up and popped it around her shoulders. It smelled of Soir de Paris perfume and would help keep her warm for a while. Gloria, the office girl it belonged to, was similar in size and Alice didn't think she'd mind an unauthorised borrowing of her garment in a time of need.

Freddie came back with two steaming mugs. He handed one to Alice and perched himself on the corner of the desk with the other. He looked up at the wall clock and nodded.

'Ten minutes and they'll start rolling in. I believe one of the girls is the cousin of young Avril who set off that explosion upstairs. Let's hope she's got a bit more nous about her than *she* had, eh?'

'How is Avril doing?' Alice sat on the chair behind the desk and wrapped her hands around the mug of tea.

'Not great. But she's at home with her mother now, so it's much better for her than being in the institution. She has to have a lot of help with having no hands. I don't suppose she'll ever work again, poor kid.'

Alice sighed. 'But at least she's still alive.'

'Aye. Poor Josie.'

They finished their tea in thoughtful silence and then Freddie jumped to his feet. 'Right, gel, let's get on with it.'

The morning flew by as Alice called in the applicants one by one and took down their details. As she showed the final girl in to Freddie and went back to her own office, she thought that, given a chance, she might take to office work quite easily once the war was over. Maybe even do something in a hospital, reception work perhaps. But when Freddie came in later with a list of the successful applicants and asked her to type up letters to go out in that night's post, Alice quickly changed her mind. Although she'd had a few typing lessons in school, she had to do the letters with one finger and it took her ages. She decided it was easier to rivet plane wings and pull pints. But at least it had made a nice enough change and added a bit of variety to her working day, and it would be something new to tell Granny and Brian when she arrived home.

Easter Sunday, near the end of April, dawned bright and sunny and Alice, Granny Lomax, Brian and Cathy made their way to St Michael's Church for the morning service. Brian was clutching a bunch of daffodils he'd grown himself to put on their dad's grave.

The church was packed and it was heartening to see people dressed in bright spring clothes. As they took a pew down near the front, Alice straightened the ribbons on Cathy's straw bonnet and wiped her nose. They were meeting up with Sadie and Gianni later in Sefton Park for a stroll and a teatime picnic before it got dark.

Granny Lomax had left a small chicken in the oven to roast while they were out. Although there had been no Easter chocolate eggs in the shops to buy, Millie had sent a parcel of chocolate treats for the children, who this morning had excitedly unwrapped the package that had been hidden away from prying eyes for the last few days. There was a letter for Alice too, telling her the Yanks the band had entertained had been more than generous again and helped her put the parcel together. Alice was as thrilled as Brian and Cathy with their treats to receive a box of chocolates tied up with yellow ribbon to share with her mother-in-law. There would be few families as lucky as theirs on Merseyside today.

After the service, followed by tea and Easter biscuits in the church hall, Brian laid his flowers on their dad's grave. Alice wiped away a tear and said a silent prayer for Dad and Rodney, whose name was now engraved in gold lettering on the headstone. She blew them a kiss as they left to walk home.

❀

'Any more, Brian?' Alice held out a roast potato and her brother nodded. 'Might as well, it's the last one,' she said. 'Well, that was a lovely dinner and those tiny carrots were just perfect.'

Brian beamed. Granny Lomax had told him they were too small to harvest yet, but he'd been determined that they would have at least some of his crop for dinner.

'My like baby carrots,' Cathy said, swiping her hand across her chin where gravy had dribbled. Alice leapt up and wiped it away before it dripped onto her clean dress.

'Are we ready for some rhubarb crumble then?' Granny got to her feet and helped Alice to clear the table.

'Yes please,' Cathy shouted after them. 'Wiv custard.'

'Cut a bit of that left-over chicken up to put on sandwiches to take to the park,' Granny said. 'And there's a few scones in the tin, plain though, no fruit, as you know. But sliced and buttered with a bit of jam on, the kids will enjoy them.'

Alice filled the sink with hot soapy water and put the plates and cutlery in to soak. 'Are you coming with us to the park?' she asked as she got the bread out of the breadbin.

'No, love, I'm going to sit with my feet up and read the paper,' Granny replied, dishing up the crumble. 'You and Sadie have some catching up to do and Brian can keep his eye on the little ones. I'll probably have forty winks as well while it's peaceful.'

❈

After a stroll around the crowded boating lake, and while their mothers relaxed on a grassy mound, enjoying the sunshine, Gianni chased after Cathy with a wriggling worm in his hands. She screamed at the top of her voice as he giggled helplessly.

'Gianni, put it down and come here,' Sadie ordered. 'No ice-cream for you later if you don't stop that.'

Gianni stuck his bottom lip out and threw the poor worm into a nearby flower bed.

Cathy ran over to Alice and dropped down beside her. 'Naughty Gianni,' she cried. 'No like worms.'

'I'm sorry, Cathy, he's a little monkey,' Sadie said with a sigh. 'Typical boy, always up to mischief lately.'

Alice laughed. 'I remember Brian being fascinated with worms and daddy-long-legs when he was little. And our Rodney once put a spider in my bed when I was about ten. I screamed the house down. Dad didn't half clobber him for it. He was always into mischief too, until he grew up and discovered girls. Poor Rod, he'd only just found his feet with life when he was called up.'

'Yes, it's very sad,' Sadie said, grabbing Gianni by the arm. 'So many lost, before their lives began properly. We need to go and wash your hands, Gianni, and then we can eat our picnic. I'll nip in the toilets with him,' she said to Alice.

'Give Brian a shout as you go past,' Alice said. Brian was over near the Palm House talking to some boys he used to go to school with. She looked across to the bandstand. 'The brass band are setting up as well, so we can go and watch them later and you can have a little dance, Cathy. How about that?' she finished as Cathy nodded and smiled, the worm incident quickly forgotten.

Alice set the picnic out on a checked cloth that she pulled from her bag and by the time everyone was back she'd poured tea from the flask for her and Sadie and orange juice for the youngsters.

'Now sit down and eat up and then we'll have ice-cream and go and watch the band. Millie's dad might be playing today. Fingers crossed there's no air raids tonight,' she whispered to Sadie, glancing up at the sky as two military planes flew over. 'We deserve a peaceful Easter.'

Chapter Twenty-Three

July 1943

On a Saturday morning in early July, Alice had just turned over for another five minutes' snooze, relishing the feeling of not getting up to rush for the Rootes bus, when a hammering on the bedroom door pulled her back to consciousness.

'Alice, Alice. Wake up. It's come. I've passed,' Brian called out.

Forcing her eyes to focus, Alice slid out of bed, pulled on her dressing gown and opened the door a fraction, slipping out into the hallway before Cathy woke up.

'What is it?' she asked, bleary-eyed, as he waved a sheet of paper in front of her face.

'I've passed the eleven plus,' he yelled excitedly. 'I can go to grammar school in September.'

'Oh, well done, love.' Alice hugged her brother, tears streaming down her face. 'I'm so proud of you, Brian.'

Granny Lomax came out of her room. 'What's all the noise about?'

'He's only gone and passed his eleven plus,' Alice said, choking on her words. 'This is all thanks to you for taking the time to teach him well.'

'Nonsense,' Granny said, beaming from ear to ear. 'It's all down to the genius that is our Brian. Well done, young man. I'm thrilled to bits for you.'

'I can't believe it,' Brian said, waving the letter in the air. 'I'm going to grammar school.'

'We'll need to think about getting your uniform sorted out,' Granny Lomax said. 'Let's hope there are places open that will have them in stock.'

'There's a list with this letter,' Brian said. 'It tells you all the things I need and where to get them.'

'At a cost I'll bet, but we'll manage. You're not losing that place, you've worked hard for it. Right, well I think this calls for a nice celebration breakfast, don't you?' Granny said. 'Good job our chickens laid well this week. Scrambled eggs on toast all round. Come on Brian, let's get cracking while Alice sorts little Madam out. I can hear her shouting Mammy.'

Alice hurried back into the bedroom as Brian followed her mother-in-law down the hallway to the kitchen.

Cathy was hanging out of her cot, one leg dangling over the side. She'd need to buy a bed soon or she'd be climbing out properly and hurting herself, little monkey that she was, Alice thought as she lifted her wriggling daughter down. She took Cathy into the bathroom and washed and dressed her. Alice sighed. Brian's uniform would cost a fair bit, never mind a new bed for Cathy. It was never-ending and she was finding it harder to save as the months went by. The overtime at Rootes had slowed down a bit now the new full-time staff had been taken on. Her plans to have enough put away by the time Terry arrived home were not going too well as every few weeks one or other of the children needed shoes or something else. By the time she'd paid her way here with bills and food, a few shillings into the Lloyd George insurance scheme in case they needed to see a doctor and her bus or tram fares home from work each day, there wasn't much left. Her Legion job was the only real spare money she had and she tried to put at least half of it into the post office account each week.

The cost of going to see Mam over at Rainhill Hospital every Sunday was expensive too, and even if Arnold let Jack take her in his car, there was still petrol to pay for. It wasn't fair to let that cost go to either Jack or Arnold; Alice insisted on paying her share. The responsibility of caring for two young children, even with the help of Granny Lomax, was overwhelming at times and Alice always had the worry hanging over her that, if anything happened to Terry, this was how her life would be forever, or anyway until Brian grew up and could stand on his own two feet. It was a daunting prospect and at not even twenty-one until November, Alice wondered how she'd continue to cope if this war went on for much longer.

If only Mam could get better and come home, she would be over the moon for Brian and his good news. But it wasn't to be. There was no getting better from her condition. The hospital doctors had made that quite clear. The family home on Lucerne Street was falling into a state of disrepair. Alice checked on it regularly when she went to the shops on Lark Lane, but it needed money spending on it to fix the roof where several slates had slipped and rain had poured in, damaging the ceilings. A broken downstairs window had been boarded up by the kindly neighbours, who did their best to keep an eye on the place. They could do with selling it really now there was no chance of Mam ever coming home, but she was in no fit state of mind to sign any papers and while she was still alive Alice had no power to do anything. Granny Lomax had made enquiries with her own solicitor about the matter, and he had told her that Mam would have needed to give something called power of attorney to Alice while her mind was still sound.

This year had passed in much the same vein as the last three. Air raid warnings were slightly less frequent than they'd been during the Blitz, but they still happened on an all too regular basis and continued to put the fear of God in everyone. Shortages in food and all but the most important essentials were ongoing; repairs to damaged buildings seemed to be a waste of time when bombs were still dropping, but the city was doing its best to pull together.

Alice and Sadie had become good friends and Sadie often popped round with Gianni to play with Cathy. The two children nearly always got on well together and Cathy didn't even seem to mind sharing her bricks with the dark-haired, dark-eyed little boy, who, Sadie said, was the image of his Italian father. Letters from abroad were still infrequent, although Alice had been amazed that a birthday card for Cathy had made it through from Terry last week along with a letter. Millie wrote as often as she could and her letters were always cheerful and a joy to read. She was due back in Liverpool in August, so would be here for her god-daughter's birthday, and was looking forward to seeing them all again. The band was booked to play at the Legion again on the Saturday night; something for Alice to look forward to.

Cathy's second birthday on the twenty-ninth was celebrated in the garden on a sunny Sunday August afternoon with her granny, Uncle Brian, Sadie and Gianni and her godparents, Millie, Freddie and Marlene, in attendance. Dressed in a hand-smocked pink and white gingham dress made by Granny Lomax, her dark hair now falling into ringlets with a bit of careful coaxing, Cathy made a pretty picture and posed happily for Freddie and his box camera as he took photos of her. Her little friend, Gianni, held her hand as they stood side by side in front of the neat border of rose bushes.

'I'll get them developed next week and you can send some to your Terry,' Freddie told Alice. 'She's making a right pretty little thing, isn't she? He'll be that proud; I know I am and I'm only her godfather.'

'You're the best she's got though, Freddie.' Alice said. 'I couldn't have wished for a better one for her.'

'Thank you.' Freddie's eyes looked moist as he turned to Brian. 'And what about you, young fella? Passing that eleven plus, eh? Clever lad. What school will you be going to?'

Brian's cheeks flushed and his blue eyes danced with excitement. He drew himself up to his full height of just over five foot. He'd slimmed down with the exercise he got at his boxing lessons and had recently joined a cross-country running club also held at the church hall.

'I've won a place at the Liverpool Institute for Boys,' he said proudly. 'I start the second week of September and I'll be nearly twelve by then.'

'Smashing. Good school, that. You'll do well there. Bet Alice is real proud of you, son.'

'I am,' Alice said. 'I just hope he can find his way to and from the city without getting lost.'

'The tram goes straight past it. Get on it at Aigburth Road and stay on until the conductor shouts "Institute",' Freddie said. 'He can't go wrong.'

'Famous last words,' Granny said, raising an eyebrow. 'He's not used to doing trams on his own. We can do a dummy run next week, Brian. We'll have to take Cathy with us because Alice will be going to work, but we'll treat ourselves to a walk around the city afterwards, what's left of it, and have tea and toast in the Kardomah as a special treat.'

Brian nodded. 'Sounds like a good plan to me. Can we go to the docks and see what's happening down there?'

'We can. Right, now that's all sorted you can help me to carry out the party food and we'll settle on the lawn for a picnic.'

Seated on the grass beside Alice, Millie nudged her with an elbow. Alice followed her gaze and saw her daughter open her mouth as Gianni smiled and offered her a bite of his apple.

'Adam and Eve,' Millie said with a grin. 'Aren't they sweet together? True love, if you ask me.'

Alice laughed. 'Give them time. They're only babies and only the other week he was scaring her half to death by chasing after her with a wriggly worm!'

'Even so, he's giving her the look of love now, wouldn't you say?'

Alice nodded. 'But wasn't it the other way round? Eve gave Adam the apple.'

'Ah, maybe. I never quite got that right,' Millie said, smiling at the little ones, who were oblivious to everyone else as they shared the apple. 'Whatever, Gianni seems smitten and very protective right now. Just how a man should be.'

'You're fanciful; I'll give you that, Millie,' Alice said. 'They'll probably fight like cat and dog when they go to school.'

In mid-September, two weeks after Brian had started at his new school, Jack drove Alice to Rainhill to see her mam. Brian had refused to come with them as the last time he'd visited he'd been frightened by the wailing and moaning coming from some of the other patients. Alice phoned the hospital on Saturday morning, her regular time for checking on Mam's welfare. The nurse who answered told Alice that her mam had been transferred within the hospital to a unit for patients with breathing problems. Mam had developed a severe chest infection and needed oxygen to help her breathe. Alice felt worried. She'd been unable to concentrate on her job last night and Winnie had taken her upstairs for a cuppa and a chat. Arnold and Jack had managed the bar between them and Arnold had suggested Jack take Alice to visit today.

'Did you manage to get any sleep?' Jack asked as he drove out of Linnet Lane and onto Aigburth Road.

'Not much,' Alice admitted. 'I can't stop worrying. Mam's never been a strong woman, but until Rodney died she was making an effort to pull herself together and get on with things. She just went downhill from that day.'

Jack nodded. 'The trouble with senility setting in, it's not reversible, and there's no pills that can cure it. As bits of the brain die off the mind shuts down and parts of the body that are no longer controlled by them bits of dead brain start to fail. That's the way I understood it when my mam was like this. Just a shame that your mam is so much younger than mine was for this to happen to her.'

Alice sighed. 'I know. I just don't have a good feeling about it, Jack.'

He reached over and squeezed her hand. 'Try and be brave. It'll help get you through it, and I'm right there for you to help as well.'

'And I'm so grateful for your support. I always will be. Thank you.'

He smiled. 'It's what mates are for.'

Alice chewed her lip as she stared out of the car window. Jack *was* a good mate, there was no denying it, but Terry was the one who should be here right now by her side; supporting her. It's what husbands were supposed to do. So much had happened since their wedding day and, apart from that one day and night with him, she'd dealt with it all on her own. The effects of the war, the air raids and Cathy's traumatic air raid shelter birth. Rodney's going missing and then the subsequent news of his death, supporting Brian through it all and then having to agree that her sick mam should be institutionalised. It was a lot for anyone to cope with in such a short space of time. She'd grown stronger through her experiences, and although she missed Terry, and his letters home told her that he was missing her too, were they just words he thought she needed to hear? Did he still mean them? He felt like a stranger now, someone she used to know, and she felt herself getting closer to Jack, though she knew deep down that it was probably just because she needed a shoulder to cry on. He'd been there for her through most of it, the shoulder to cry on, the arms to hold her, doing nothing inappropriate, apart from stroking her hair on Boxing Day when they'd gone to see her mam. In spite of that, she was grateful for the constant support he gave her when she felt she couldn't carry on.

But she was married, for better or for worse, even though at times she didn't feel it could get any worse than it already was. Since Alan had told Millie that he'd met someone else, there was always that niggling thought at the back of her mind that the same thing might happen to Terry, that he'd get injured and fall in love with his nurse. She told herself not to be so stupid; Alan and Millie weren't married and she and Terry were. They'd made vows and promises to each other. It still didn't stop her hopes and dreams of a happy ever after from fading slightly. But maybe that's how every woman whose husband was away felt: bereft at being left behind holding the babies. It was a hard life for all concerned and hopefully would start to get better once the war was over, which at the moment felt like it would never happen.

At Rainhill Hospital Alice and Jack were taken to a side room in a clinically clean ward, where Mam was lying perfectly still on crisp white linen. Her cheeks were highly flushed in her grey face, as though fighting a temperature, and her breathing behind the oxygen mask sounded laboured. Alice broke down and clung to Jack, who held her close. The woman in the bed didn't even look like her mam.

The sister who'd spoken to them said not to expect too much and to only stay about half an hour. Jack brought two chairs in from the corridor and they sat side by side.

'What will I do if she dies?' Alice whispered.

Jack looked at her and frowned. 'I'm gonna be blunt here, Alice. Don't think badly of me, but this is no life for your mam. She's got no existence in here. She's getting weaker by the day and she'll pick up any germs going. Something will see her off eventually. She's peaceful right now. Be glad of that, chuck. It was a relief when my mam just slipped away. I couldn't stand seeing her suffer.'

Alice swallowed hard. 'I'm sure you're right, but it's still horrible to think about it. When she was at the other place she once told us she didn't want to come home because Dad and Rodney were there with her and she didn't want to leave them behind. I guess that's about the time her mind started to leave me and Brian behind. Maybe she's at peace with herself now she knows she's going to join them soon.'

'Aye, maybe. She'll know when she's ready to go.'

Chapter Twenty-Four

October 1943

Mam lingered until the middle of October, getting weaker, until Alice, sitting by her bed, prayed for her ending to come peacefully. She felt guilty while she was doing it, but knew deep down it was time for them all to release her. In these final days she spent as much time with her mam as working would allow. Jack kindly brought her and Brian to Rainhill after work and school as often as he could borrow Arnold's car.

Brian and Alice held Mam's hands, sitting either side of the bed, as she took her final breath. Alice looked across at her brother, his cheeks flushed and his eyes red-rimmed. He was trying so hard not to cry and to be strong for them both. It broke her heart to see him like this. He was too young to suffer so many losses in so short a space of time. She put her arms around him as he got to his feet and convulsed into sobs on her shoulder. She silently vowed to do whatever she could to look after him properly, to give him a good future and to make sure he would never want for anything.

❀

The kindly Lark Lane shop proprietors had a collection for Edith Turner, who had been one of their regular customers since the day she'd married and moved into Lucerne Street with her new husband. Arnold and Winnie offered to put on a small wake at the Legion and wouldn't accept any contribution from Alice towards it.

The funeral cortège moved slowly down Lucerne Street, the shiny black car carrying Alice, Brian and Granny Lomax following the hearse. Granny's next-door neighbour was looking after Cathy for a few hours. The residents of the terraced houses had closed their curtains as a mark of respect. The small procession pulled up outside St Michael's Church, where Mam had worshipped for most of her life. Alice was touched to see all the neighbours and Mam's old workmates from the Princess Laundry and the sock-knitting circle, standing outside waiting. They would do her proud and Alice knew she would have been thrilled to bits to know it.

Millie and her mam were waiting by the church door and Millie waved her hand in greeting. Alice lifted her hand in acknowledgement. Jack was standing beside them with Arnold and Winnie and they nodded at her as she linked her arm through Brian's and followed the coffin bearers inside.

The vicar welcomed them all and, following prayers, Mam's favourite hymns were sung.

During 'Morning Has Broken' Alice could feel tears coursing down her cheeks. She didn't bother to wipe them away; after all, no one would mind. Brian pulled on her sleeve as the vicar began his eulogy.

'What?' she whispered as he turned red-rimmed eyes to her. She took his hand and squeezed it.

He reached into his jacket pocket and handed her a sheet of lined paper torn from a school exercise book.

'I couldn't sleep so I wrote a little poem for Mam last night. It's just about some memories. Do you think the vicar will let me read it?' he whispered back.

Alice chewed her lip as she took a quick look at his lengthy scribblings. 'Are you sure you can manage all this? It may make you feel very sad.'

'I want to. It's not just sad. I've tried to make it a bit happy as well.'

Alice sighed and caught the vicar's eye as he finished the eulogy and made his way out of the pulpit. He walked over to her and she whispered to him. He smiled and nodded and addressed the packed church.

'Edith's youngest son Brian would like to read a few words he has written for his mother.' He smiled encouragingly at Brian, who got to his feet and went to stand beside Mam's flower-bedecked coffin in front of the altar.

Brian studied his piece of paper for a few seconds and then, glancing at Alice, who smiled and gave him a nod of reassurance, he cleared his throat and began to read, his young voice clear, precise and growing with confidence in the silent church.

'My poem is called "Our Mam",' he began.

Dear Mam, we're missing you so much
And I'm sure you're missing us
But I know you are at peace now
Instead of running for t'next bus

One cold and frosty morning
You looked at me and frowned
Then wrapped a scarf around me neck
And took me into town

We went to Paddy's Market
And you bought me some nice new clothes
We had tea and toast in the Kardomah
And you wiped me snotty nose

We called in Lewis's toy shop
And we looked at cars and games
And my favourite Meccano set
But you shook your head in shame

We'd lost our dad and we was poor
But it didn't matter, Mam
Because we still had Alice and Rodney
And white bread with strawberry jam

And then Hitler made the war begin
And they made me an evacuee
I missed you Mam, but I was okay
Because they took good care of me

My parcel from home at Christmas
Made me cry with surprise and joy
Wrapped up in fancy paper
Was me favourite Meccano toy

Thank you for all you did for us
You were the best mam in the world
Now it's my turn to look after our Alice
And her lovely little girl

Brian put his fingers to his lips and placed a kiss on Mam's coffin before walking back to his seat as the congregation got to its feet and applauded him.

'Well done, Brian,' the vicar said. 'There's not a dry eye in the house. That was very brave and you were word-perfect. You did your mother proud.'

'Bravo, Brian,' Granny Lomax said, giving him a hug. 'Very well done.'

'That was wonderful, Brian,' Alice said, wiping her eyes as the clapping congregation sat back down. 'Mam would be so thrilled.'

Brian smiled shyly, folded his paper and put it back in his pocket.

❁

After Mam had been laid to rest alongside her husband, Alice and Brian invited people back to the Legion to join them for refreshments. After offering their condolences following the service, Jack, Arnold and Winnie had left to get organised for the wake.

Freddie and Marlene arrived at the Legion after their shift at Rootes had finished, apologising that they'd been unable to get the afternoon off as the company rules were strict about taking time off only for relatives' funerals. Alice was just glad to see them and was touched when Freddie handed her an envelope. Just as he had done after they lost Rodney.

'We had a whip-round,' he whispered. 'To help you with the cost.' He gave Alice a hug.

'Thank you so much. It will be a big help as Mam had no money at all to her name. Just a couple of penny policies I can claim on.'

Freddie nodded. 'Those'll help you a bit. And you'll inherit the house now, you and your Brian. That should see you both okay for the future, chuck. It'll give you a roof over your heads and you can get it ready for when Terry comes back. Make a lovely home for you all, that will. Use a bit of that money you've been saving up and get the roof fixed. And once it's watertight I'll rally up some of the blokes that are still around to give you a hand to get the place put right.'

Alice stared at him as the penny dropped. She'd been so consumed with grief at losing Mam and trying to get everything arranged for the funeral that she'd been unable to think straight. The fact that the house now legally belonged to her and Brian hadn't even entered her head. Her own place; and one that she could make nice in readiness for Terry's eventual homecoming.

After all, it was her family home and all her precious memories of Mam, Dad and Rodney were there. It would be a struggle, but she could make it a real home again for Cathy and Brian too. But what would her mother-in-law say to that idea? She dreaded to think and turned her attention to the guests, who were offering their commiserations to her and Brian as they tucked into the plates of sandwiches made by Winnie.

❧

Alice and Freddie walked around the house on Lucerne Street on a Saturday afternoon in late November, making notes. Well, Freddie was pointing out things that needed urgent attention and Alice was writing them down in her notebook. The loose slates on the roof had been secured by Freddie's brother Albert and the bedroom ceilings were drying out now. Large brown water stains were apparent, but Freddie assured her they would be fine with a couple of coats of distemper. Most of her mam's neighbours who were still able had offered to help when she was ready. She only had to ask, she was told over and again.

'So where will we get paint from at the moment?' Alice asked. She couldn't recall seeing any on the shelves of the little hardware shop on Lark Lane when she'd gone in with Brian to get some nails to make the chicken coop for Rosie and Betty, the adopted chickens.

Freddie tapped the side of his nose. 'There are three big cans of white distemper at work. It's left over from when we set up the munitions floor upstairs. Can't see as we'll need it now. It's just standing in the store cupboard taking up room. I'll have a word with the boss tomorrow. See if he'll let us have it. I'll offer a few bob, but I reckon we'll get it for nowt.'

'Oh, well that will be a huge help,' Alice said, smiling. 'Your brother took up the old carpet squares when he did the roof as they were sodden. So there's nothing to stop me tearing off all the old paper now and then it's ready to paint upstairs. Once the bedrooms are done I can see how much money I've got left to buy some new carpets or oilcloth and rugs. We might not be able to move in for quite some time, until I can afford to refurnish the lot, but at least it's going to be taking shape nicely.'

Freddie nodded. 'How did Terry's mam take it? That you intend to move in here, I mean.'

Alice sighed. 'Not very well. She suggested I sell it and stay there with her, but it's our family home and I'd like to make it nice again for me and Brian and Cathy. I know it won't be easy, but I'm not afraid of hard work and neither is Brian. His main worry is his veg garden and the chickens, but he can walk round each day after school and do his bit.'

'You need your own space, chuck. I wouldn't have lived with my ma-in-law for a gold clock. Not saying yours isn't very nice, but when Terry comes home you'll all be squashed in up at that bungalow. You'll have a lot more space here. That little box room at the back will be grand for Cathy, Brian can have the middle one and then you and Terry can have the big front bedroom. An ideal home for all of you. I presume you've told him of your plans?'

'I have, yes. He says to go ahead and do what I can afford to do. He'll send money as and when he can to help me.'

'We'll soon have it shipshape and Bristol fashion, as my mother used to say, though Lord knows what she meant by that!'

Alice laughed. 'Shall we go down to the little café on Lark Lane?' she suggested. 'I think you deserve a nice brew and a sticky bun if they've got any.'

'You're on, gel. Lead the way.'

Chapter Twenty-Five

April 1944

Alice, Brian and Cathy moved into their house on Lucerne Street the third week of April, just in time for Brian going back to school after the Easter holidays. In the true Lark Lane community spirit of helping, all the neighbours had been on the job to restore the house to a habitable state. A neighbour had replaced the broken pane in the front living room window and the whole inside had been freshly distempered in white with the paint donated by the kindly boss at Rootes. All the interior woodwork had been washed down and given a coat of white gloss-paint that another neighbour had produced from his garden shed.

'If it's out of the way the wife won't nag me to do ours,' he told Alice as he handed over the two tins, with a cheeky wink.

Alice had been outside finishing donkey-stoning the front step and windowsill when he arrived. When she came back outside after carrying the tins through to the kitchen, several tell-tale paw prints on the sill, courtesy of Blackie or Ginger next door, brought a smile to her face. Bessie came out and shooed them away and took over from Alice, re-stoning and wiping.

'I'm sorry, chuck,' she said and shook her fist at the two naughty cats, who sat warily watching her every move.

The front door had been given a new coat of shiny black paint – by whom, Alice had no idea, but it looked lovely. The doorknocker and letterbox had been polished up with Brasso and looked sparkling. Everywhere was fresh and clean and another neighbour had brought curtains round that she'd picked up at Paddy's Market and altered to fit. They replaced the old faded curtains that had been up for donkey's years. The criss-cross tape and blackout linings still remained at the windows as standard for the time being. Alice was moved to tears time and again by her neighbours' kind deeds.

The old beds had been ruined by the rain that had leaked through the ceilings. Those had now been removed and burned in someone's back garden and Granny Lomax had given her the beds they had been using from the bungalow. There had been a few more cross words over Alice's wish to move back home, but eventually her mother-in-law reluctantly agreed that it would be best for them all and that she understood Alice's wish to be in charge of her own family home for when Terry came back. And at least this way they had a good start in that they didn't need to rent or borrow money to buy a house.

'How will you do your weekend job at the Legion now though? I can't come here each night at the weekend,' she'd said as she looked round the house on the day they moved in. 'I'd have to walk home alone in the blackout and it's not safe. Cathy and Brian can't stay with me as you've got their beds here now and I don't really want to buy any more, besides which, I probably wouldn't be able to get my hands on any at the moment.'

Alice chewed her lip. She hadn't thought this out very well and she would need the money from both jobs still, as there would be bills to pay and food to put on the table. Saving wasn't as important any more as she had used up all her carefully saved post office money to buy things for here – she now had the home she'd been planning on having – but the day-to-day living costs would take every penny she earned.

'Of course,' Granny Lomax continued, 'I can still look after Cathy while you work at Rootes.'

Alice nodded, relieved. 'Thank you. I'll think of something. Brian is sensible enough to leave alone with Cathy on Friday and Saturday nights and I'm sure Bessie next door will keep an eye on them both. I'll just have to see how it goes.'

She was determined to make this work now she'd come this far. Standing on her own two feet and being independent was important to her. If the unthinkable happened and Terry didn't come home she would have had to do it anyway. They couldn't have stayed at the bungalow forever.

'But Brian is only twelve,' Granny protested. 'He's far too young for that sort of responsibility.'

'He's thirteen in October and he's a very sensible boy for his age,' Alice said. 'Besides which, I really have no choice. It's not my fault I've got all this responsibility on my shoulders. Blame the war for that one, robbing me of my big brother's life, my husband's time and my mother too, in a way.'

Alice choked back a sob. She didn't want to argue with her mother-in-law, who had shown her nothing but kindness so far, but she'd expected a bit more support from her with this. She'd always had the feeling that Granny Lomax was a bit on the possessive side, first with Terry and then taking over looking after Cathy and Brian, making Alice feel a bit redundant at times. She'd pushed any uncharitable thoughts to the back of her mind as she'd been really grateful for all the help she'd received from her. But it couldn't go on forever. The children would miss having her around all the time, but rules could be relaxed slightly now they were under their own roof, and they could invite Granny over for tea as Alice would be at home in the afternoon to cook for them all. They would still see a lot of her, but not be living in one another's pockets all the time. Hopefully it would all work out eventually.

Granny Lomax nodded. 'I can see how much this means to you, Alice. I still think you've rushed into it, but I'll do what I can to help, when I can.' She patted Alice's arm and picked up her handbag, ready to leave.

❧

'If you need a sitter any time I could always nip round to 'elp out for a couple of hours,' Marlene offered when Alice told her how she was fixed while they were having their morning break in the canteen at work. 'I can bring a book with me to read an' a bottle of milk stout to sup. Me an' young Brian can 'ave a game of cards an' listen to the wireless, an' Cathy will be asleep most likely. I don't usually go out on a Saturday night unless the Legion's got a special do on. But it'd be good to get away from me own responsibilities now an' again. Me dad's taken to grinding 'is bloody teeth non-stop and it drives me mad. It doesn't bother me mam – she can't 'ear him on account of 'er being deaf as a post.'

'Oh that would be great, Marlene, thank you. I'm sure Jack would offer to walk home with you after he drops me off.'

'No need. I won't stop all night, 'cos I'm up early an' needs me kip, but a couple of hours will keep them company an' make sure they're safe. You tell your Brian to knock on for Bessie next door if 'e's worried about anything after I'm gone. An' if there 'appens to be an air raid warning you've got the shelter in the back yard. You'll just 'ave to make sure they know what to do.'

Alice nodded, feeling better about the situation already. 'Yes, we have a shelter, and Bessie and Bert next door share it with us so they will look after the children for me, I'm sure.'

'Course they will. Everybody likes to 'elp out in times of need. It's what we do around Lark Lane area. An' youse doing a good job taking on the mother role for your young brother, Alice. Brian's a smashing kid an' a credit to you.'

'He is, and that's why it's important I work as much as I can so that he can stay at school and not have to leave early like a lot of lads do. I want to do all I can for him to make sure he gets a good education and the best life possible. He's lost so much, poor little soul, he's an orphan now.'

Marlene nodded. 'So are a lot of kids with this bloody war, an' not many are lucky enough to 'ave a good sister to look out for them either.'

Alice took a sip of her rapidly cooling tea. 'Surely to God it can't go on much longer now? What do you reckon, Freddie?' she asked as he came to join them. 'I mean, it's been five years. Five years! It's ridiculous. My Terry hasn't even had any leave since our wedding day. But then I don't suppose anybody else has either since they've been sent abroad.'

Freddie tapped the side of his nose. 'Well, summat's afoot, but I'm not sure what. We've been asked to keep up production and so has shells. The powers that be have got summat big planned, I think. But Mr Churchill isn't likely to call me up and keep me in the loop; we'll just have to see what happens next.'

Alice chewed her lip. 'So you think it might soon be over?'

'Oh I'm not saying that, chuck, but Hitler's losing out from what I can make of it all. Like I say, we'll just have to wait and see what happens in the next few weeks.'

Marlene frowned. 'But then we'll all be out of a job.'

'Aye, we will, but the country will need to rebuild itself and there'll be plenty of work. If the war does end soon all the lads will be coming home and they'll want their jobs back anyway. You ladies will be second in line for anything going once they get home.'

'I don't like the sound of that,' Marlene said, pulling a face. 'We women 'ave kept this country going an' we'll still expect to be able to earn a few bob of our own. I don't want to go back to relying on my Stan for 'andouts.'

'Well I won't mind just being a mother who stays at home and looks after the family, for a change,' Alice said. 'But I see where you're coming from, Marlene. Your kids are grown up and you had the time spare to spend with them while they were little and before they were evacuated. So it's quite right that you want to work now they're older.'

If Alice was honest with herself, she'd give her right arm to not have to come to work at all. The only thing she'd miss would be working with Jack at the weekends. He was good company and he made her laugh. But he might still stay in touch with them both as he was Terry's friend from the past, well, acquaintance anyway, and in his letter Terry had said he'd buy him a pint for looking after her on the walks home in the blackout. He'd said nothing else that would make her wary of Jack; the stories that had been bandied around earlier about his handy fists seemed to have faded away and the tale Maisie had spun about the bruises on her arm had never been mentioned again. The only thing Alice wasn't sure about was his drinking, but it didn't stop him from working hard and he seemed to be in control. It wasn't her business what he did in his spare time anyway. He was sometimes in a lot of pain from his injured foot, or so he said, and maybe the drink took the edge off. Everyone at the Legion seemed to hold him in high regard, and so did she after the way he'd supported her over her mam's illness and subsequent death. She felt the occasional spark between them when he pretended to tease her or caught hold of her and she knew that, if she wasn't already married, they might have taken up with one another. But her vows had meant the world to her and she'd never be unfaithful to her Terry, even though she felt distanced from him most of the time.

True to Freddie's warnings, things were heating up in Europe and with the news that Hitler had now placed Field Marshal Erwin Rommel in command, in anticipation of an Allied invasion, every-one was glued to their wireless sets for regular updates. Rumours abounded that the war was almost over, but on the 6th of June the Allied operation to liberate German-occupied north-western

Europe from Nazi control began. Twenty-four thousand troops from the UK, Canada and America were deployed on amphibian crafts to target a fifty-mile stretch of the Normandy coastline. Many would never return.

The wireless was switched on all the time in the factory as the workers listened anxiously to reports of attacks and drowning. The weather was bad and caused delays and accidents. Strong winds were reported to have blown several craft east of their intended positions and the men landed under heavy fire from gun placements overlooking the beaches. Alice listened with her heart in her mouth and a sick feeling in her guts at the thought of all those brave young men who were being killed just because of one 'out-of-control lunatic', as Freddie called Hitler. All those innocent boys, like her brother, who would never see their home and family again. She prayed that Terry was safe, wherever he may be, and willed him to come home soon.

By some miracle – and, Alice thought, the prayers and good wishes coming from the people at home may have helped – over the next few weeks the Allies eventually gained a foothold. By the 21st of July the casualties from D-Day, as the invasion was now being called in all the news bulletins, were high, with an estimated nine thousand German fatalities and an even higher ten thousand Allies killed.

'Does this mean the war is over now, Freddie?' Alice asked as they all sat, riveting guns in hand, on a hot summer's day in July, listening to the updates on the wireless.

'Not quite, chuck, but we're winning,' Freddie told her. 'Let's hope it stays that way, girls.'

Chapter Twenty-Six

October 1944

On a Saturday afternoon in mid-October, Alice wrapped a couple of plates of neatly cut egg sarnies with greaseproof paper and did the same with the sausage rolls she'd made that morning. Not that there was much meat in them, but she'd done her best. There was a bowl of salad on the table from their own produce-growing venture, as well as some fruitless scones and a pot of apple and blackberry jam. She and Brian were throwing a small party for his thirteenth birthday and a bit of a house-warming, and had invited Millie, who was home for the weekend, and Sadie and Gianni, as well as Freddie and his wife and Marlene. It was a way of saying thank you to the friends who had been there for them at the hardest of times. Granny Lomax had also been invited and said she might pop in for an hour later as she had things to do in the city centre that afternoon. She'd given Brian a card and present yesterday.

Alice knew her mother-in-law was still unhappy that they had all moved out of the bungalow, but looking around her spotless little back sitting room she knew she had made the right decision, and Granny was welcome any time she liked. Life was so short and unpredictable, and although it had been a bit of a struggle financially while she got used to juggling her wages around, having her little family under their own roof was the most important thing to Alice. It was what her mam would have wanted. Alice was determined that they would manage, no matter how hard it was.

She plumped up the floral-patterned cushions on the sofa and fireside chair and straightened the clock on the mantelpiece. Rodney smiled at her from his framed photo to the right of the clock and she blew him a kiss. She still found it hard to believe that he would never walk through the front door again. Her wedding photo was at the other side of the clock and the two black poodle ornaments with red collars that she'd received as wedding presents from Rootes were out of their wrappings for the first time and sat either end of the mantelshelf. The rag rug Mam had proudly made for Cathy to sit on had been salvaged from the house renovations and given a good beating over the washing line in the back garden, and now sat in pride of place in front of the hearth.

The front door opened and Brian came in holding Cathy by the hand. They'd been down to the shops on Lark Lane to get a sponge cake from the bakery. Alice had ordered it on Thursday, knowing she didn't have enough ingredients in of her own to make a birthday cake, and had been hoping the order would be fulfilled as the bakery was awaiting a delivery of flour and sugar, both still in short supply.

'Any luck?' she asked hopefully as Brian handed her a small brown paper carrier bag. She peeped inside, beamed and lifted out a perfect sponge cake sandwiched together with red jam, a fine white icing sugar dusting on the top. Icing sugar was in short supply, so fancy iced cakes were hard to get.

'Oh, that looks and smells lovely. I've found a box of white cake candles in the cupboard; they're used, but we can at least light them while we sing to you.' She got her mam's best glass cake stand from out of the sideboard cupboard and a white doily from the drawer. The cake looked lovely on the stand and Alice put it on the table towards the back and brought the small wax candles through from the kitchen. She inserted thirteen of them around the edge of the cake and smiled. 'There we are. Better than no cake at all.'

Brian nodded. 'Can't wait to have a slice.'

'Me too,' Cathy said, hopping from foot to foot. 'It looks luvverly, Mammy.'

Alice laughed. 'Let's get you upstairs and ready for the party, Madam. We'll put you a pretty dress on and a ribbon in your hair. Brian, you can go and put a clean shirt on. There's a white one freshly ironed hanging from the picture rail in your bedroom.'

'Do I need to wear a tie?' He pulled a face.

'No, love. It's Saturday. You can leave the top button undone. But that shirt you're wearing is a bit grubby round the collar. Don't want people thinking I'm neglecting you, do we?'

❀

Pretty as a picture in a red woollen dress with her dark hair fastened up into ringlets with red ribbons, Cathy laughed with delight as Sadie and Gianni arrived. She quickly led her little friend into the front room to play with her crayons and colouring book.

'That's them two sorted,' Alice said. 'Brian, take Sadie's coat upstairs and put it on my bed. How are you?' she asked, turning to Sadie and giving her a hug and a peck on the cheek.

'Okay, thanks. Well, sort of.' She glanced over her shoulder to make sure the little ones weren't eavesdropping and whispered, 'I got a letter from Luca yesterday. It came from Italy. He says as soon as the war is over he's coming to find me and wants to see his son. I might have to move away in case he wants to take him.'

'Oh, Sadie. Surely that won't happen. He can't take him without your permission.'

Sadie shook her head. 'Just let him try. I may go away to my auntie's for a few days when I know he's coming.'

'Play it by ear. But don't worry. I'm sure it won't happen. He can't look after Gianni while he's working on the rides. Anyway, have a seat while I brew up. And can you get the door if anyone comes while I'm in the kitchen? Brian, will you keep an eye on the little ones, love?' she said as he came back down the stairs. 'Read them a story or something.'

'Oh, Brian. Happy birthday. Here you are, chuck,' Sadie said and handed him a parcel. 'A bit of something from me and his little lordship.'

'Thank you,' Brian said. 'I'll go and open it with them two.' He smiled and went into the front room, closing the door behind him.

Sadie sat down on the back sitting room sofa and eyed the laden table. 'This looks good. You've been busy.'

'Just a bit,' Alice said, going into the adjacent kitchen. 'The cake's from down the bakery though, not one of my own.'

'You look quite the little housewife with your frilly pinny on.' Sadie laughed. 'Are you enjoying being in your own home?'

'I am,' Alice called through. 'I'm loving it.'

'Well you've got it very nice.' Sadie looked around at the fresh, clean room. 'It's really lovely and homely.'

Alice smiled with pride as she came back into the sitting room. 'I could do with replacing the sofa and chair, but I can't afford to do that just yet. I'll have to wait until Terry comes home and starts working again. Bessie next door knitted those two stripy blankets that are covering them. Brightens them up a bit, all them rainbow colours, and with the cushions Mam made a while ago, they'll do for now.'

'Well I think they look very nice,' said Sadie. 'I wish I could find somewhere for me and Gianni to call our own. I've been putting a bit away each week and when this war's over I'm hoping to get a better job or at least my old job back at Lewis's. Might even be able to buy a little house somewhere one day. I bet a lot of people will want to sell up and leave the city eventually. I may find a bargain. We'll have to see.' She stopped as someone rapped on the front door. 'More guests. I'll let them in.'

As Freddie, his wife Rose, Marlene and Millie, who'd all arrived together filled the hall, Cathy squealed and flew out of the front room, flinging herself at Freddie's legs. He picked her up and gave her a cuddle.

'Come through, everyone,' Alice said, bringing the tea pot to the table.

'Where's the birthday boy?' Freddie asked. Brian popped his head around the door of the front room. 'Ah, there he is.' He handed Brian a parcel and card and Millie and Marlene did likewise. Brian flushed with pleasure as he thanked them all.

Freddie's wife handed Alice a large and colourful bunch of sweet william flowers and Millie produced a tin of iced buns made by her mam, who'd found half a packet of icing sugar up the pantry when she was having a root for something. Marlene had brought a half-bottle of sherry that she'd been saving for a special occasion.

'Them flowers are hand-grown by yours truly,' Freddie said. 'We've turned some of the garden over to regulation veg and stuff, but I likes me flowers.'

'So do I, and they are beautiful, thank you so much,' Alice said. 'Oh this is lovely, It's like Christmas, isn't it, Brian? Thank you, everyone. I'll just put the flowers in water and then we'll get stuck in.' She found a vase under the sink, arranged the flowers and put them on the sideboard. 'There, those look gorgeous and they brighten up the room. Right, hope you're all hungry, let's eat.'

Sadie removed the greaseproof wrappings and handed out side plates. Alice poured tea into Mam's treasured china cups that were still in service, and everyone tucked in.

'Them sarnies are smashing,' Freddie said.

'Eggs from my chickens,' Brian said. 'I've been saving them for today and Alice has mashed them with a bit of milk and butter and salt and pepper. Very tasty.'

'And nice and fresh. None of your powdered rubbish. Good work, Brian.' Freddie patted the young boy's shoulder and he flushed with pride.

Alice smiled. Brian was growing up to be a lovely young lad. He was so thoughtful and helped her a lot with Cathy, always teaching her things, and Cathy was his willing pupil. Since going to grammar school his manners were impeccable and he spoke well. Their mam would have been so very proud of her youngest son.

As the last crumb was eaten, bar the cake, Alice brewed more tea and quickly washed the side plates. She also brought in some sherry glasses and handed them to Marlene.

'You do the honours and we'll drink a toast,' she said. 'Then I'll light the candles on the cake before Cathy and Gianni burst with impatience.'

Marlene divided the sherry between the glasses. She picked one up and nodded at the other adults to do the same. Freddie cleared his throat and began to speak.

'Raise your glasses to Brian on his birthday, Alice's mam Edith, Rodney and all who've suffered as a consequence of this war. And let's hope our lads are soon home safe and sound. And also to Alice, Brian and Cathy for their hospitality today. Wishing you all the very best for the future and I can see you're well settled in your lovely new home. I'm sure you all enjoy living here. It feels a really happy place to me. Cheers.'

'Happy birthday, Brian, and cheers,' everyone said and raised their glasses. Millie poured more tea and the candles were lit. A rousing 'Happy Birthday to You' was sung and Brian blew out his candles to loud cheers.

'I hope you made a wish, Brian,' Alice said as she sliced the cake and offered it round.

'Oh I did.' Brian smiled secretively as the cake was demolished. It disappeared within seconds.

'Well, that made short work of that.' Alice laughed.

Marlene nodded. 'I'll stay 'ere when the others go, Alice, if that's all right.' She was looking after Cathy and Brian tonight while Alice went to the Legion.

'Of course. No point in you going home to have to come all the way back again.'

Millie smiled. 'I'm going to nip home and put my new frock on and then I'll come back here and go to the club with you, Alice. Might as well, with having the weekend off.'

'Jack will have you up singing,' Alice said.

'Oh I don't mind that. Coals to Newcastle, as they say.'

'We'll get off now then,' Freddie announced. 'We'll see you in the Legion later. Thanks for a lovely afternoon, chuck.'

'You're all very welcome,' Alice said, giving everyone a hug.

'If my mam will look after Gianni, I'll pop down to the club later as well,' Sadie said. 'Carry the party on there.'

'Sounds like a good plan to me.' Alice laughed as she showed everyone but Marlene out. 'See you all later.'

Cathy pushed through her legs and grabbed Gianni from behind. She gave him a hug and a sloppy kiss on his cheek, which he promptly wiped away and blushed.

'Won't be wiping her kisses away in a few years,' Freddie teased. 'The lads'll be fighting over her.' He laughed and waved goodbye, his wife linking his arm as they strolled up the street towards Lark Lane.

Alice closed the door and leant against it. She had the nicest bunch of friends anyone could wish for. They were more like family and treated Brian and Cathy as their own. She went into the front room, where Brian was opening his presents with Cathy and Marlene. He held up *The Boy's Own Annual*, a gift from Marlene, a smart sleeveless pullover from Millie in a nice shade of light blue and a boxed game called Monopoly from Freddie and his wife.

'Oh, that looks interesting,' Alice said. 'Bet Granny would enjoy playing that with you.'

Brian nodded. 'Wonder why she didn't come today?'

Alice shrugged. 'Who knows, eh?'

Alice felt disappointed that she hadn't accepted their invite and shown her face. Maybe it would take a bit of time for her mother-in-law to step back from being in charge and let them get on with their own lives.

❀

As they strolled to the Legion, Millie told Alice that Jimmy had confessed in his last letter that he thought he was falling in love with her.

'I don't know what to think. I mean, we've only met each other the one time, but we've grown very close in our letter-writing and I get butterflies in my tummy when I know I've got another letter from him. He says the nicest things, like he's going to marry me when he gets home. But he hasn't actually asked me yet.'

'And do you love him?'

Millie chewed her lip. 'Maybe I do, and I don't realise it. It all feels a bit unreal. Once I see him again, I'm sure I'll know.'

Alice laughed. 'I'm sure you will. Hopefully it won't be too long now before it's all over and they come home. I can't wait. I'm fed up now. Another Christmas in a few weeks' time and still no husband to share it with. Surely the end is close now.'

'Well, at least you've got a nice home for him to come back to,' Millie said.

'Yes, he said he can't wait to see what we've done to the place. I wish his mother would come round a bit more often though. We do ask her over several times a week, but she hardly ever takes us up on it and the kids miss her – and I'm sure she misses them. But this year I want Christmas on Lucerne Street, so I'm hoping she will join us. Are you in Liverpool this year?'

'Not for Christmas Eve but we are at New Year,' Millie said. 'We're doing the Legion.'

'Oh, that's something to really look forward to,' Alice said.

'I'll be back up here on Christmas Day. The band will drop me off at home, so I can pop over in the evening if you like.'

'I *would* like,' Alice said. 'We'll have another little party at mine.'

Chapter Twenty-Seven

December 1944

Alice looked up from the oven where she was basting the lovely plump chicken that Granny's kindly neighbour had given them for dinner. Thankfully her mother-in-law had recently admitted to missing the children and said that she wanted to see more of them. She had accepted the invitation to join them today, offering the chicken, which Alice had been more than glad to receive. She turned over the roast potatoes surrounding it, and blew her hair off her face as her little daughter held out a dolly for her inspection.

'Oh, she looks beautiful. Very pretty.' Alice admired the pink knitted outfit the dolly was dressed in. 'Isn't Granny clever to make such lovely things?'

Cathy nodded and ran back to the front room, where Brian was chatting to Granny Lomax, the wireless set playing carols quietly in the background. Alice popped her head inside and looked around with pride. The room felt so cosy, with a small decorated Christmas tree in the window and the fire blazing up the chimney. She'd treated herself to a nice red half-moon hearth rug and some red velvet cushion covers on a recent trip over to Paddy's Market. They were almost new too; you wouldn't know the difference. They brightened the room up no end and they'd been such a bargain. She was so glad Terry's mother had joined them today. Alice wanted to show her that she too was capable of producing a nice roast dinner in exchange for all the lovely dinners her mother-in-law had cooked for them.

'Would you like a cuppa to be going on with? Dinner will be ready in half an hour. Just waiting for the potatoes to finish roasting.'

'No thank you, Alice. I'm fine. I'll wait until we're at the table.'

Alice nodded and went back into the kitchen, pausing to tweak the cutlery into place on the table that Brian had set earlier. He and Cathy had made a little table decoration from some pine cones and bits of holly and fir tree off-cuts they'd picked up from the floor in the greengrocers. A candle sat in the middle of it all. The pair had also made four crackers from red crepe paper and the inside cardboard tubes of toilet rolls. Cathy's red hair ribbons had been borrowed to make bows around the middle. It had kept the two of them busy for a couple of evenings this week while Alice had hidden herself away in her bedroom and wrapped up their presents in secret.

There'd been great excitement as the two had rushed down the stairs at seven this morning to see if Father Christmas had really been. Brian had excelled himself at keeping the secret for his little niece, and had told her he'd definitely heard sleigh bells in the middle of the night and reindeer hooves on the roof, exclaiming to a giddy Cathy that the carrot she'd left out for Rudolph was gone. Alice smiled now as she checked the sliced carrots in the pan on the stove, Rudolph's among them. They'd had scrambled eggs for breakfast from Brian's chickens and then she'd hurried them along to church for the early service. Alice had felt sad that Mam wasn't with them; she'd loved the Christmas morning service and the tea and biscuits in the church hall afterwards, greeting friends and neighbours and catching up on all the gossip. Before the war it was always warm mince pies that were served with the tea, donated by members of the congregation.

Tonight they were hosting a little buffet party for Freddie and his wife. Marlene was popping along once she'd sorted her ageing parents out, and Sadie, Gianni and Millie were also coming. Alice had worked last night at the Legion while Marlene baby-sat for the first couple of hours and then Bessie had popped in until Alice arrived home with Jack. It had been a cold night so they'd hurried along, Jack limping badly after being on his feet for hours. Alice had felt sorry for him as Arnold and his wife were going to her sister's for dinner this Christmas. She'd paused on the path as he'd said goodnight to her and turned to walk away.

'Jack,' she'd called after him. 'Would you like to come for tea tomorrow night? Millie and everyone will be here. I'm sorry I can't ask you for dinner but Terry's mam's coming. But she's going after the King's speech to visit her friend.'

Jack's face had lit up and he'd smiled. 'I'd love that, Alice. Thank you very much. What time about?'

'Five-ish.'

'I'll be here.' He'd limped away and she was glad she'd made the offer as he'd been a bit quiet all night and looked miserable on the walk home. It was no fun spending Christmas alone. She wished she could have asked him for dinner but it didn't seem right with her husband away and his mother here.

Alice lifted the chicken and roast potatoes from the oven and drained the vegetables in a colander over the sink, saving some water for the gravy, which she made in the roasting tin with the chicken juices.

She dished up the food on plates that had been warming in the bottom of the oven and called for everyone to take a seat.

They all tucked in, wearing newspaper crowns from inside the crackers. Brian had cut the crowns out and Cathy had crayoned patterns along the brims. She smiled proudly as her crown slipped down over one eye and they all laughed.

'Better than no paper hats at all,' Brian said, adjusting Cathy's back into place. 'Maybe next year we'll actually be able to buy proper crackers in the shops.'

'Let's hope so, eh, Brian,' Granny Lomax said. 'And maybe there'll be one more of us around the table for dinner.'

❀

'Brian, go and ask Bessie if she and Bert would like to pop in for a sherry while we listen to the King's speech,' Alice called from the kitchen, where she was finishing the washing up.

'Okay,' Brian called back and dashed outside. He was back in minutes with Bessie on his heels. 'Bert's asleep with the cats but Bessie said she'd love a sherry,' he announced.

'Thanks for the invite, chuck,' Bessie said. 'It'll be a pleasure to listen to this year's speech without Bert's snoring drowning the King out.'

'Sit yourself down in the front room and I'll bring you a sherry through,' Alice said, drying her hands on a tea towel. She reached a small glass down from the cupboard and filled it with sherry.

Granny Lomax greeted Bessie and moved up the sofa to make room, indicating the space beside her with her hand.

'Thank you,' Bessie said, patting her hair in place.

Alice handed Bessie the glass and topped up her mother-in-law's. She smiled at Bessie, who looked smart in a nice red dress. It wasn't often Alice had seen her neighbour without curlers in, covered by a turban, and her old worn-down slippers on her feet. She was surprised by how much younger Bessie looked dressed up a bit.

'Cheers, ladies,' Alice said, clinking her own glass to theirs. 'Here's to the end of the war next year and getting our lives back to normal.'

'Hear, hear,' Bessie and Granny Lomax said.

'Hear, hear,' said Cathy with a giggle.

'Right, here we go,' Granny Lomax announced as the King began his speech; his sixth since the beginning of the war. Alice's thoughts went back to the first Christmas dinner she and Mam had shared with Terry's mother back in 1940, when Brian was evacuated and she didn't even know that Cathy was on the way. Both mams had fallen asleep shortly after the speech began, stuffed full of good food, in the warm and cosy sitting room at the bungalow. She felt her eyes fill as she thought about her mam and how much she missed her. The speech was a long one, as always, and Cathy fell asleep on the rug in front of the fire. Brian listened intently as the speech neared its end, and sat forward as the ladies struggled to stay awake.

> The successes of my armed forces would not have been achieved but for the devoted labours of those throughout the Commonwealth and Empire who have striven ceaselessly to arm and equip them. It is over five years now since my peoples first took up the struggle to free the world from aggression and the contribution of the civil population is beyond all praise. The United Nations await with sober confidence the unrolling of future events. Joined in an unbreakable alliance and fortified by constant collaboration between the governments concerned and by frequent personal meetings between their leaders, they look forward to that day on which the aggressor is finally defeated and the whole world can turn to the rebuilding of prosperity and the maintenance of an unassailable peace.

Brian smiled. 'I don't think it will be too long now before "the aggressor is finally defeated",' he said. 'The King sounds quite confident to me.'

'Do you think so?' Alice chewed her lip worriedly.

'I do,' Brian replied. 'This time next year we'll be rejoicing and getting back to normal.'

244   PAM HOWES

'Well, you understand all them long words better than I do,' Bessie said. 'Let's hope you're right, chuck.'

❀

Brian accompanied Bessie back next door and walked Granny Lomax home while Alice prepared the buffet tea party. Cathy was still sleeping on the rug in front of the fire – not something Alice would normally allow in the afternoon, but she would be in a good mood for their visitors instead of complaining that she was tired. A late night once in a while wouldn't hurt and they'd all have a lie-in tomorrow. They were having tea at the bungalow with Granny, so it would be a nice relaxing day.

Alice had wrapped a few little gifts for her visitors and she went to put them under the tree. They weren't much as she'd struggled this year with the cost of entertaining as well, but her tips from the Legion had all been saved in an old jam jar in her wardrobe since they'd moved in. She'd done quite well at Paddy's Market and managed to buy everything she'd planned to and titivated things up so they looked as nice as she could make them.

She buttered some thinly sliced bread and finely pared the left-over chicken from the bone, like she'd seen Winnie do at the Legion, mixing it with left-over stuffing to make it spreadable and go a bit further. The sarnies would be nice and tasty and she had a few sausage rolls that she'd managed to make with a tiny portion of sausage meat and hard-boiled egg that she'd mixed with it. Everyone had said they would bring a bit of something for the buffet to help out. They'd have already eaten a big enough dinner, but it was nice to enjoy a few sarnies with a glass of sherry.

Brian arrived back after popping in to see his old school friend on the way home and Alice woke Cathy up just before five and took her upstairs to wash her hands and face to perk her up a bit.

'Now don't touch those things under the tree,' Alice warned. 'You've had your presents off Father Christmas. Those are for our guests. They've already given us ours. Go downstairs now while I have a quick freshen-up. Sit in the front room with Brian and be good. I won't be long.'

Alice heard the doorknocker and Brian letting people in as she was getting changed into a clean navy floral-patterned dress that buttoned up the front. She looked at herself in the full-length mirror and smiled. Her cheeks were flushed, giving her a bit of colour. She slicked her lips with her Tangee lippy and smacked them together, then ran her hands through her wavy hair, which had grown longer and now fell into soft waves on her shoulders. She took a deep breath and went downstairs, prepared for another houseful.

Winnie had lent Jack her gramophone and several records to bring round and as Alice walked into the front room he was setting it up on the coffee table,which he'd moved to the side of the room. He turned as she came in and gave a low wolf-whistle and winked at her.

'Looking very nice.'

Alice laughed. 'Thank you and Merry Christmas to you, Jack.'

'And the same to you, gel. Hope you don't mind me bringing this. Winnie thought it might help the party go with a swing.'

'Not at all. It's very kind of her.'

'It's mainly Bing and Glenn Miller, mind!' Jack handed her a carrier bag. 'She's put a few bits in there for the buffet too. Arnold came and got me this morning before they went out. I had a smashing surprise cooked breakfast with them and I told them I was coming to you for my tea. There are two bars of chocolate for certain young people in there as well.'

Alice shook her head. 'Winnie is so kind. She really is. Thank her for me tomorrow, Jack.'

'She's a smasher; she's the mam I wish I'd had.'

Alice rubbed his arm as her eyes filled. She blinked rapidly. Winnie mothered them both.

'Brian, can you do coat duty, love. Just put them all on my bed. Ah, there's the door. Hang on to save you going twice in two minutes.'

Alice let in Sadie and Gianni, along with Millie, and showed them into the front room. Brian took their coats and Alice hurried into the kitchen with the bag of food from Winnie and smiled as she spotted mince pies and more sausage rolls that were twice the size of her own. There was also a slab of fruit cake, no doubt acquired from the Yanks; her guests would be dining like royalty tonight. As she laid everything out on the table Jack appeared at her side, carrying two bottles.

'Just rescued these from my pockets before Brian took my coat up. Beer for me and Freddie, and sherry for you ladies.'

'Oh my goodness, Jack, thank you so much.' Alice felt overwhelmed by all this generosity.

'No, thank *you*, for inviting me. I appreciate it very much. Ah, there's the door. Shall I get it? Oh, Brian is acting mine host, he's beat me to it.'

'You can see to the drinks, if you will,' Alice said. 'The glasses are over there on the sideboard.'

'Consider it done.'

Alice smiled as Jack poured the drinks and asked for a tray.

'I haven't got one. This isn't the Legion, you know. You'll have to carry them through two at a time or let them help themselves.'

When everyone else had arrived and Brian had finished his coat duties, Alice announced that the buffet was ready. Freddie's wife had baked some cheese straws, Marlene had brought a box of chocolates and Millie's mam had sent some tomatoes, savoury biscuits and a small piece of Cheddar cheese.

'By heck, you've done us proud here, Alice,' Freddie said, his eyes widening as he took in the spread. 'There's enough for an army.'

'Get stuck in, everybody,' Alice said. 'What doesn't get eaten tonight will do us tomorrow. Side plates are there next to the sarnies and Jack's doing the drinks so just help yourselves. Winnie's kindly sent her gramophone over with Jack, so I'll go and put a record on.'

Everybody tucked in to the sound of Glenn Miller's 'In the Mood'.

'Such an awful shame about him,' Millie said. 'Going to France in that plane and then it just vanishing over the Channel like that. I wonder if the Germans shot him down.'

'Well they said on the news it was bad weather,' Freddie said. 'I don't suppose we'll ever find out the truth. He's yet another casualty of this bloody war. Poor fella. He brought a lot of pleasure to so many with his smashing tunes.' Freddie got to his feet. 'Raise your glasses to Glenn Miller. May he rest in peace.'

They all drank a toast, remembering the lovely tunes they'd enjoyed and danced to throughout the war.

'Aye, there'll never be another Glenn Miller,' Jack said, shaking his head sadly.

'Well, let's remember the good times when we danced to 'im. Glenn got us through some awful moments,' Marlene said.

Jack got up and put another record on the gramophone.

'Oh, Gianni, you love this one, don't you,' Sadie said. Her little boy's face had lit up when the dulcet tones of Bing Crosby filled the room with 'Swinging on a Star'.

He nodded and he and Cathy laughed at each other and got up to dance around.

'This is lovely,' Freddie said. 'Surrounded by my favourite people, great food and music, and peace and quiet outside at the moment. Hard to believe there's still a war on right now.'

'Well, the King sounded hopeful earlier,' Brian said.

'Did 'e?' Marlene said. ''E speaks them long words an' I don't know what they mean 'alf the time.'

'Me neither,' Alice admitted.

'And I fell asleep,' Jack confessed with a grin. 'I heard some of it, but slept through most. Let's hope Brian is right.'

Alice cleared away the empty plates and Jack helped her and then refilled the glasses. She smiled as she watched him chatting away to Freddie. He needed a family and in spite of him saying he didn't like kids he seemed reasonably unperturbed by the three in the front room. Alice decided she'd make it her mission to find him a suitable girlfriend next year some time. There must be someone out there that he could get along with, surely.

After stoking up the fire and putting on another record, Alice handed around the gifts she'd put under the tree. Freddie and his wife seemed happy with the cream lace arm caps for their sofa. Gianni loved his toy plane and Sadie her green silk scarf. It had been a bargain and, carefully washed and pressed, looked brand new. Millie's little present had been made from two old beaded necklaces that Alice had unthreaded. She'd reused the beads, alternating them to make a pretty patterned bracelet. She'd found a little white flat box that she'd painted green leaves and holly berries on using Cathy's watercolour paints, and she'd lined the inside with a scrap of red velvet. The finished effect looked like an expensive bracelet in a posh box.

'This is beautiful, Alice,' Millie said, slipping the bracelet onto her wrist.

'Thank you. All my own work.'

'Wow! When Rootes closes you should go in for making your own jewellery. I bet you'd do really well.'

Alice laughed. 'We'll see. Jack, I got this for you.' She handed him a small parcel and watched his face light up as he unwrapped a stick of Old Spice shaving soap. 'I asked Arnold what it was that you usually smell of.'

Jack laughed. 'Well at least he didn't say stale fags. Thank you, gel, this is what I always use every day and I'm almost out, so spot on with the timing.'

As her guests admired their gifts Alice reflected on what a lovely day they'd had. There was a bit more hope in the air than last year.

Maybe this was it, the final Christmas without Terry. Hopefully, next year and for their fifth wedding anniversary, he would be home with his family, where he belonged.

Chapter Twenty-Eight

April 1945

Alice looked up as Freddie dashed onto the factory floor and shouted above the racket for them all to down tools and gather around him. It was late Monday morning and the last day of April.

'*Now* what's up?' Marlene muttered and put down her riveting gun. 'An' let's hope he don't take too long. It's nearly dinnertime; me belly thinks me throat's bin cut an' *you're* due to go 'ome, Alice.'

Alice smiled as Freddie cleared his throat and puffed out his chest with importance.

'News has just reached us that Hitler is dead. Details are sketchy at the moment but the word coming in from Berlin is that it appears he's committed suicide and shot himself.'

Silence followed Freddie's announcement, and then as realisation dawned clapping and a loud cheer came from the assembled workers.

'Bloody 'ell!' Marlene exclaimed. 'I don't believe it. So does this mean the war is definitely over?'

Freddie shrugged. 'Let's hope so, eh? I'll put the wireless on now and we can keep abreast of the news as it comes through. It's on in the canteen, so you might as well go down for dinner a few minutes early.'

The canteen was buzzing as Alice joined the others after getting changed ready to go home. She got herself a mug of tea from the counter.

'I'll have a brew with you before I go for the tram. I'm a few minutes early so I may as well as wait in here,' she said to Marlene, who was getting stuck into a bowl of scouse. Alice sat down and took a sip of her tea. People were straining to hear what the news reporter on the wireless was saying. She didn't let herself get too excited in case it was all a hoax and Hitler wasn't really dead after all. But if the news was true, Terry could be home in the not-too-distant future.

Alice finished her tea and got to her feet. 'I'll see you tomorrow,' she said to Marlene. 'I'll go and pick Madam up and catch up with the news at Terry's mam's.'

'Bye Alice,' people called as she left the canteen and hurried to get on the tram.

❀

Cathy was playing in the garden with her dolly's pram as Alice arrived at the bungalow. Cathy waved to her mother and carried on trundling the pram up the path, talking to her babies. Alice went indoors to where her mother-in-law was in the sitting room, an anxious expression on her face and the wireless on full blast.

'Have you heard?' Granny Lomax began.

Alice nodded. 'It is true then?'

'Well, according to the news, yes. He's committed suicide along with that woman he married only yesterday, that Eva Braun one. Good riddance to the pair of them, I say.'

'Do you think this is it then? The war is nearly over?'

Granny Lomax puffed out her cheeks. 'I blooming well hope so. The government needs to get its act together now and bring our boys home. We're all waiting for Mr Churchill to make a statement later today.'

✾

A few weeks after the official announcement of Hitler's death, Alice looked up as Brian spoke. He'd had his head buried in the newspaper since he'd rushed out to the newsagent's for it earlier. She felt a rush of love for him; his serious expression reminded her of their late dad when he'd been engrossed in the *Echo* – except Brian had come back with *The Times*. There were no *Echo*s left, he'd told her. Hardly surprising – everyone would want to know what was going on now the war was supposed to be definitely over.

'What did you say?' she asked, folding the sheets she'd brought indoors from the washing line.

Brian puffed out his cheeks and shook his head. 'Just reading in here that there were more than eighty-five million fatalities in total with the war. That's including the Holocaust and the massacres. How awful to think that one evil mind and a handful of his cronies were behind all those deaths. What sort of a monster was he? Such a pity he committed suicide: the coward. They should have captured him and thrown him to our soldiers, they'd have soon made mincemeat of him. Anyway, Alice, they were saying in the newsagent's shop that people are gathering in Sefton Park to celebrate later. VE Day, they say today is called. Can we all go? It sounds like fun and I think we are all due some of that right now. When do you think they'll let our Terry home? I'm dying for a go on his motorbike.'

Alice grimaced. 'I'm not sure I like the sound of that, Brian. You know I hate motorbikes. Terry's last letter didn't give me a firm date as to when to expect him. But it can't be much longer; they said on the news it will be any time after June. At least I know he's safe now. I was hoping he'd be back in time for Cathy's fourth birthday in August, but we'll have to wait and see. And yes, of course we can go to the park. It's a lovely day so I'll pack us up a picnic. Run round to Millie's for me and see if she's home yet. She wrote to let me know the band's not playing this week or next due to everything being up in the air with the troops and demobilisation taking place, so she's coming back to Liverpool for a while. Ask her if she'll join us if she's in. And nip to Sadie's to see if she and Gianni want to come as well. Might as well make a party of it, if everyone else is doing that.'

'What about Granny Lomax?'

'Er, okay, if you want to.' Alice sighed and turned back to her sheet-folding. Although her mother-in-law continued to look after Cathy for her while she worked, and she came round a bit more often than she had done at first, things weren't quite the same as they used to be. Alice did her best to include her as much as she could, but invitations were turned down as often as they were accepted.

Brian reached for his blazer and dashed away. Alice called Cathy in from the garden and told her what they were planning to do. Her daughter was growing up fast and her dark hair hung down her back in fat plaits.

She smiled and clapped her hands. 'Gianni coming too?'

'Yes, I think he is.' They hadn't seen as much of the little boy since he'd started school last year and Alice knew her daughter was missing her best pal. But she'd be starting school herself next January, so they'd be seeing even less of him. Hopefully she'd soon make other little friends, though. 'Go upstairs and put your best dress on so that you look pretty for the party,' she told her.

Cathy beamed at the thought of Gianni coming along to play and ran off to get changed. Alice wondered how she would take to Terry when he arrived back. Cathy didn't have much experience with men, apart from Freddie, who she loved like a grandpa figure; she'd shied away from Jack when he'd popped his head around the door and said 'Boo!' to her recently. Mind you, Jack wasn't very good with kids anyway so that wasn't anything to go by. Hopefully blood would be thicker than water and she'd take to her father quite naturally.

❀

Sefton Park was crowded with people greeting each other. Children were running around happily, shrieking with delight as they discovered old pals they'd been separated from, their parents having brought many of their evacuated offspring home now things were settling down a bit. It was lovely to be outside on a warm sunny day with no fear of an air raid to threaten their pleasure.

Millie held on to Cathy's hand on one side and Gianni's on the other. They were both peeping shyly at each other and having little fits of the giggles. Alice carried the picnic basket and Brian carried a couple of old blankets to put down on the grass to sit on. Granny Lomax had declined his invitation, telling him that she was just leaving Aigburth to visit a friend in Chester for a day or two. The friend was news to Alice as Granny had never mentioned anyone in Chester in all the time she'd known her, but maybe it was an old friend and she'd got reacquainted with them recently. Alice felt sad that she was pulling away from them all, apart from Cathy who she doted on still. But once Terry arrived home it might bridge the gap a bit.

Cathy squealed and let go of Millie's hand and shot across the grass towards the bandstand. Freddie heard his name being called and spun around. He caught his little god-daughter and swung her up into the air, spinning her around until she wriggled to be put down.

'Is your dad playing this afternoon, Millie?' Alice asked as a brass band tuned up in readiness for a session.

'Yes he is. Mam should be here with him. Ah, there she is, under that straw hat with the pink bow! Flamboyant as always.' Millie laughed and waved as her mam caught her eye and waved back.

Alice sighed. 'My mam would have loved this. Everybody coming together to celebrate the end of the war. If only we'd known there was something wrong with her brain function instead of just thinking it was her nerves, we might have been able to help her earlier, but even our doctor didn't recognise it as early senility. I just hope and pray it's not hereditary.'

'Oh, don't even go there,' Millie said with a shudder. 'Let's just remember her in happier times and enjoy this day of freedom from that tyrant who nearly finished us all off.'

They stood in front of the bandstand and listened to Millie's dad's brass band playing some jolly tunes. The little ones in the crowd began to dance and people were singing, spirits rising by the minute. Alice was swaying her hips from side to side and tapping her foot in time to the music when an arm snaked around her waist, squeezing her tight and making her jump. She spun around in shock to find Jack smiling lopsidedly at her.

'Oh, Jack. You frightened the life out of me,' she said as he grinned. She could smell whisky on his breath, as usual. 'Been drowning your sorrows – again?' It was out before she could stop herself, and she was taken aback by his sudden dark scowl.

'I've had a couple, yeah, but hasn't half the country today?' he slurred. 'You need to loosen up a bit, Alice love. Get a drink down you. Bet your Terry's had more than *his* fair share to celebrate these last few days.'

'I'm sorry,' Alice apologised. 'I didn't mean anything by it.'

'I'm sure you didn't,' he said, still scowling slightly. 'Supposed to be a happy day today. Isn't that what this is all about?'

'Yes, yes of course it is. Listen, why don't you join us? We've brought a picnic and Millie's home for a few days; it'll be nice for her to catch up with you as well.'

'Thank you,' Jack said, his expression softening a little. 'I'd like that. After all, I don't have anyone else to celebrate freedom with, do I?'

Alice sighed. He didn't and she'd had no luck in finding him a girlfriend either. He didn't seem to have any friends other than her and Millie. Once the troops were home he may well reacquaint with his old pals, she thought.

❀

On a mid-June afternoon Alice, Granny Lomax and Cathy stood anxiously on Lime Street station with what seemed like hundreds of other women and children, some carrying small paper Union Jack flags to wave, all waiting to greet husbands, boyfriends, brothers, sons, fathers and uncles. Brian was at school and would join them later at the bungalow, where Granny had insisted they all congregate for tea. Alice would have preferred to go to their own home, but this time she allowed Granny to indulge herself by hosting her son's demob party. The troops were all being sent home, several thousand at a time on trains, boats and planes. Terry had written to say he would be on a train to Lime Street today, although the exact time he was due to arrive wasn't known; just some time mid-afternoon.

Granny Lomax had brought a flask of tea with her, two cups and some orange juice for Cathy. They sat down quickly on a bench as a family party vacated it and she dished out the drinks.

'Glad I thought to do this. I guessed correctly that the café would be packed to the rafters.' She handed a Marie biscuit to Cathy, who was swinging her legs to and fro under the bench, oblivious to all the excitement buzzing around them, and then offered one to Alice, who declined.

'I'm too churned up to eat anything,' Alice said.

'I'm sure. Are you looking forward to seeing your daddy, Cathy? It's a very exciting day for you and him. Meeting each other for the first time.'

Cathy shrugged and nibbled on her biscuit.

'I'm not sure that she grasps what's going on,' Alice said. 'I keep talking to her about her daddy and she's been shown the photos with him in and she can point him out when asked, but finally meeting the real person is a huge thing for her – as it will be for all the children born while their fathers have been away.'

'It will take time, but I'm sure she'll be just fine.' There was a surge of people on the platform and excited shouts and squeals. Granny Lomax jumped to her feet with excitement and then sat down again, looking dejected. 'Wrong platoon,' she said. 'Maybe the next train, eh?'

'It's not quite mid-afternoon yet,' Alice said, looking at the station clock. The crowds were thinning out slightly as the recently arrived soldiers and their families left the station. The butterflies in her stomach were creating havoc. What if she didn't recognise him, or he her, for that matter? She'd had a couple of group photos of him sent to her a year or so ago but it was hard to make out who was who among the tiny figures, although Terry had written on the back where he was positioned. She turned as someone called her name, and saw Millie rushing towards them.

'I haven't missed them, then?' Millie gasped. 'Mam did my hair for me and the flipping dryer stopped working. I couldn't come down here with sopping wet hair. Had to wait for Dad to sort it out. It was a fuse that had gone and he couldn't find the fuse wire he usually keeps in a kitchen drawer. Anyway, I'm here now. Jimmy is travelling with Terry, so I didn't want to let him down.'

Alice gave her a hug. 'Glad you're here. I thought you'd forgotten.'

Millie laughed. 'Not a chance. I've had a couple of letters one after the other begging me to meet him. There's no way I would let him down.'

After another anxious hour of waiting and making small talk, a large black engine steamed into the station, belching smoke and hooting loudly.

'This might be the one,' Granny Lomax said, beaming from ear to ear. 'My boy is almost home where he belongs.'

Alice picked up Cathy and held her breath as the crowd on the platform surged forwards but were held back by station staff.

'Let them get off the train, Madam,' one red-faced guard said to a large woman who poked him in the chest with her umbrella when he put out a hand to bar her way. 'If he's on it, he'll be out in a few minutes. They'll all have their bags to bring through so give them some space, for goodness sake.'

As they waited and scanned the faces of the men, Alice spotted Terry, striding along with Jimmy, kit bags on their backs. They stopped and dropped their bags onto the floor and held out their arms. Millie ran forwards at the same time as a tall man with hair the same colour as Jimmy's and a small blonde-haired woman did. Jimmy called Millie forwards to meet his mum and dad.

'This is the girl I'm going to marry, if she'll have me,' he announced, covering a speechless Millie's face with kisses as his parents cheered.

'Well, will you, marry me, I mean?' Jimmy said, looking into her eyes.

'Yes,' Millie said, nodding, tears of joy coursing down her cheeks. 'Of course I will, Jimmy.'

As Jimmy swept Millie into his arms again, Alice was still standing frozen to the spot, watching as Terry's mother dashed towards her son and he enveloped her in an embrace. He looked over the top of her head at Alice and raised a questioning eyebrow. With a choking sob she ran towards him, Cathy in her arms, and he enfolded them in a hug that was so tight Cathy squealed to be put down. Alice handed her to Granny and moved back into Terry's arms to be kissed and hugged once more. Terry held her at arm's length and gazed into her eyes. Looking into his, all the doubts she'd ever had while he'd been away vanished in an instant. He was home and he was safe. Her tall, handsome, dark-haired, brown-eyed soldier-boy was home, he was hers, and as he whispered that he loved her and would never let her go, she knew he meant every single word.

A Letter from Pam

I want to say a huge thank you for choosing to read *The Factory Girls of Lark Lane*. If you did enjoy it, and want to keep up to date with all my latest releases, just sign up at the following link. Your email address will never be shared and you can unsubscribe at any time.

www.bookouture.com/pam-howes

To my loyal band of regular readers who bought and reviewed The Mersey Trilogy, thank you for waiting patiently for the new series to begin. I hope you'll enjoy meeting Alice and Millie and co as much as you enjoyed Dora and Joe's stories. Your support is most welcome and very much appreciated. As always, a big thank you to Beverley Ann Hopper and the members of her FB group Book Lovers, and Deryl Easton and the members of her FB group The NotRights. Love you all for the support you show me.

A huge thank you to team Bookouture, especially my lovely editor Abi for your support and guidance and always being there, you're the best, and thanks also to the rest of the fabulous editorial team.

And last, but most definitely not least, thank you to our wonderful media girls, Kim Nash and Noelle Holten, for everything you do for us. And thanks also to the gang in the Bookouture Authors' Lounge for always being there. I'm so proud to be one of you.

I hope you loved *The Factory Girls of Lark Lane* and if you did I would be very grateful if you could write a review. I'd love to hear what you think, and it makes such a difference helping new readers to discover one of my books for the first time.

I love hearing from my readers – you can get in touch on my Facebook page, through Twitter or through Goodreads.

Thanks,
Pam Howes

Pam-Howes-Author

@PamHowes1

Acknowledgements

As always, my man, daughters, son-in-law and grandchildren. Thank you for your support. I love you all very much. Xxx

Thanks once again to my lovely 60's Chicks friends for their friendship and support. And a big thanks to my friends and Beta readers, Brenda Thomasson and Julie Simpson, whose feedback I welcome always.

Thank you to the band of awesome bloggers and reviewers who have given me such wonderful support for my Mersey Trilogy and again with the first in the new Lark Lane series. It's truly appreciated and without you all an author's life would be a difficult one.

12974007R10160

Made in the USA
Lexington, KY
27 October 2018